Floodgates

Books by Mary Anna Evans

Artifacts
Relics
Effigies
Findings
Floodgates
Strangers

Floodgates

Mary Anna Evans

Poisoned Pen Press

Poisoned Pen Press
6962 E. First Ave., Ste. 103
Scottsdale, AZ 85251
www.poisonedpenpress.com
info@poisonedpenpress.com

Printed in the United States of America

This book is dedicated to the people of New Orleans. No one else lives life with quite the same artistic flair. Over three centuries, they have built a worthy gateway to the heart of our continent that still serves us well. I have every confidence that they will rebuild it better than ever and that they will do it with style. We could all use a *soupçon* of their *joie de vivre.*

L'aissez les bons temps roulez...

Acknowledgments

I'd like to thank everyone who reviewed *Floodgates* in manuscript form: Michael Garmon, Erin Hinnant, Rachel Garmon, Amanda Evans, Cheryl Landry, Marguerite Strong, Rachel Stodard, and Lillian Sellers.

I'd also like to these folks for their expertise on archaeology, New Orleans history, and disaster response: Dr. Robert Connolly of Chucalissa Archaeological Museum, Dr. Jill-Karen Sobalik of Earth-Search, Inc., and Dr. Gordon Wells, of the Center for Space Research at The University of Texas at Austin. They helped immeasurably in making *Floodgates* as accurate as possible, but all errors are completely mine.

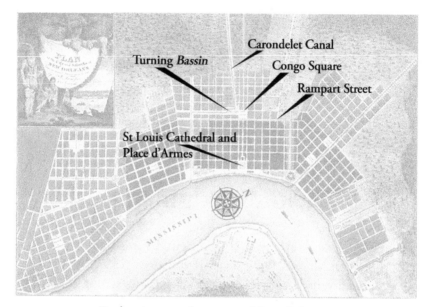

Early nineteenth-century New Orleans
Rollinson, 1827

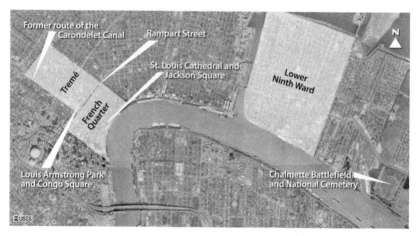

Modern New Orleans and Chalmette
US Geological Survey

The Mississippi River will always have its own way;
no engineering skill can persuade it to do otherwise...
—Mark Twain

Prologue

Excerpt from *The Floodgates of Hell*
by Louie Godtschalk

Many people died when New Orleans went under.
I knew it intellectually. While the rain slashed
down and the ravenous wind tried to peel back every
last shingle on my roof, I knew that people were
dying out there. The eventual toll beggared even my
prodigious imagination, but I spent the storm knowing that Death was passing me by. And I knew that
others wouldn't be so lucky.

In the days afterward, the streets filled and they
stayed full. I saw photos of the dead in newspapers
and on television, but my brain protected my soul by
refusing to make those people real. Katrina was eight
days gone before I saw her first drowning victim. It
was dark, and the stinking water was darker, but there
was no mistaking the fetal form of the body floating
in the knee-deep water.

I'm a writer. It's all I know how to do, so I'm lucky
to have readers who want me to do it. I knew that I
needed to say something about the things I'd seen,
but what would it be?

One day, I realized that my hometown owed its
life to the people who pushed back the water. My

city was midwifed by engineers, but I knew absolutely nothing about them. And neither did anybody else. On that day, my topic found me and you hold the results in your hands.

I have put more than my usual blood, sweat, and tears into the writing of this book. As I finish a story that meanders through nearly three centuries of mortal conflict between man and nature, I still find myself daunted by the prospect of introducing it to you. How can I possibly explain why I was moved—no, compelled—to tell the story of the men and women who held back the tide so that my hometown...my New Orleans...could remain delicately afloat in a spot where God never intended humans to live?

Or maybe God did intend that very thing. There is something uniquely human about doing things that no one with good sense would ever attempt. I think the fact that our improbable follies are so often achingly beautiful is proof that we carry the spark of divinity. New Orleans, Stonehenge, the pyramids, Venice, the Eiffel Tower...they have all had their useful purposes, but that's not why we love them. We love them because they are lovely.

Unfortunately, lovely things can be easy to break.

Chapter One

Faye Longchamp was surprised at herself. She was working on a dream project, excavating a plantation site to find the subtle traces left by its slaves as they lived their lives. Perhaps today she would find a worn tool, mended many times, or a handmade toy or a chipped bowl. Those things spoke to her of life and the passage of time, and they appealed to the romantic soul that she pretended she didn't have.

So why couldn't she stop thinking about the battlefield behind her? Faye hated battlefields.

As a rule, Faye's worklife revolved around the day-to-day routine of ordinary human beings. She wanted to know how people lived in the past. She wasn't much interested in the details of how they killed each other. History teachers who forced students to memorize the dates of every last battle in every single war made Faye nuts. Not to mention the fact that she fell into the political camp that considered war to be a waste of perfectly serviceable human beings.

She understood that wars could be fought with noble motivations. For example, she agreed with most of the world that Hitler and slavery had both been blights upon humanity. But that didn't mean she wanted to spend her career digging up cannonballs that had killed a few teenaged soldiers before crashing to the ground.

"Faye." The sound of her name brought Faye back from the long-ago battle. When Nina spoke, Faye listened, because Nina only talked when she had something to say.

Nina Thibodeaux, her assistant for this job, was capable of working as single-mindedly and silently as Faye did. And that was saying something.

When there weren't any tourists around, chatting with each other and gabbing on cell phones and wandering too close to the tape cordoning off Faye's excavation, it was quiet here at this grassy park where the Battle of New Orleans was fought. In fact, it was strikingly quiet, considering its location between a busy highway and a river thick with cargo ships. On the rare occasion that either woman spoke, the sound was as out-of-place as a marching band in a graveyard...and since the battlefield grounds butted up to a military cemetery, that image wasn't far off the mark.

Nina stood up and brushed her dirty hands on her jeans. "I'm going to take a break."

Faye was almost as startled as she would have been if Nina had sauntered away, snarling, "I'm cutting out for the rest of the day. Maybe I'll be back tomorrow. Dock my salary. See if I care."

Nina never ever took a break that Faye didn't suggest. Once, Faye had been so engrossed in her work that she'd forgotten about lunch until nearly two. Nina had never said a word.

Faye met few people whose work ethic matched hers. Most people thought her laser-like focus was strange. Maybe even a little scary. Nina could match Faye, minute by minute, in her single-minded scrutiny of every grain of sand and every dried-up twig that her odd blunt-nosed trowel brought out of the unit she was excavating.

Faye, like most archaeologists, liked a sharp point on her trowel for detail work and a razor-sharp edge for maintaining clean vertical walls. Nina, who was not one to follow the crowd, used an oversized margin trowel without a point. It looked something like a steel spatula with a cushy red handle. This meant that her co-workers started ragging her about how stupid it looked whenever boredom threatened to set in. This happened every day, along about ten-thirty.

The jokes weren't all that creative, and they always came from the same source, Faye's field tech Dauphine. Most days she warmed up with the same tired line. "Gonna flip some scrambled eggs with that thing?"

This line wasn't just tired; it was a bit geeky. "Scrambled eggs" was slang for the garbled soils in an excavation where the sides have caved in. It was well-nigh impossible to interpret soils that had been reduced to "scrambled eggs," and it was well-nigh impossible for Nina and her spatula-like tool to avoid hearing that question every damn day.

Nina didn't mind. She seemed to enjoy the camaraderie implicit in being the butt of insider jokes, so Faye figured she wasn't derelict in her supervisor's duties when she let the laughter happen.

Heck. Blunt-nosed trowels weren't even all that bizarre—Faye had a good handful of friends who used them at least some of the time—so the teasing was fairly pointless. It just gave Faye's tiny three-person team a reason to laugh together, and she couldn't see anything wrong with that.

It was obvious that Nina didn't have the slightest interest in being cool, since she somehow managed to find clothes that were even less flattering than Faye's army surplus finery. Nina was the last person Faye would expect to follow the crowd, yet the crowd seemed to like her anyway.

Faye didn't care one whit that Nina didn't have much to say, and that neither her clothes nor her trowel looked the least bit hip. She understood the woman. And she liked her, too.

Nina's quick glance over one shoulder gave Faye an inkling of why her assistant had suddenly needed to recharge her batteries. A 1960s-era American car, probably some variety of Ford, was parked by the visitor's center. Its chromium yellow paint job shone mirror-bright. It had the muscled look of a car that was supported by a ton of steel and powered by a gasoline-sucking engine with more cylinders than it strictly needed.

A man stood beside the car. Wind blew across the open battlefield through dark blond hair that was just long enough to move in the breeze. He wasn't tall and, though he wasn't ugly, he wasn't particularly handsome. Still, he had a wide grin visible from twenty paces, and he leaned against his car's solid fender with a relaxed insouciance. New Orleans was overrun with men like him—men whose appeal to women rested solely on charm and swagger and manners so courtly as to be anachronistic.

He waved to Nina, and she went pink with pleasure. Faye was tickled to see it. Even she wasn't as relentlessly serious as Nina.

"Go! And leave your stupid-looking trowel here." Faye flapped her hands as if to push Nina away from her work. "Take your time. Take a long lunch, if you want to. Who is he?"

"Charles? Oh, I dated him a while ago. I have no idea why he's back, but…well, I don't much care."

Nina fluffed her shoulder-length hair, then she walked toward Charles a little too quickly for a woman hoping to look nonchalant. Faye had never thought of Nina as the hair-fluffing type.

Nina was the kind of person who would rank third in her class, but never first. Nothing about her called attention to itself—not her mid-brown hair, nor her freckled skin, nor her small hazel eyes squinting behind her rimless glasses. When she graduated, top employers would probably pass her over in favor of blunt-spoken students with lower grades but better self-promotion skills, and it would never even occur to Nina to ask why. Maybe a glowing letter of recommendation from Faye would make a difference when the time came. The glow that Charles brought to Nina's face might make a difference, too.

Charles greeted her by putting a hand on her waist. Then he leaned in close to whisper in her ear. Faye was too far away to really see the woman's skin tone, but body language told her that Nina went even pinker with Charles' touch.

The hand stayed right where it was until Charles had finished steering Nina toward the Ford's passenger door and opening it for her. Faye's fiancé, Joe Wolf Mantooth, had a country boy's old-fashioned manners, but this guy was smooth. Maybe a little scary-smooth, but that was Nina's business.

Dauphine, a field tech whose skills made Faye's life a world easier, pretended she hadn't noticed her seasoned colleague suddenly revert to being a girl. Faye listened to the subtle roar of the aging car's well-maintained engine as Charles steered it around the loop road and out of the park.

"Well, Dauphine," Faye said, picking up her own trowel with its properly pointed tip. "Something tells me that we're on our own for a while."

Chalmette, the site of Andrew Jackson's 1815 victory, wasn't like other battlefields. At least, Faye didn't think so. She avoided battlefield parks when at all possible, but she'd suffered through classes under history professors who took their students to every battleground within reach. The more ardent among them spent class time showing videos of their vacations to faraway scenes of war. Faye didn't have much patience for touring an open expanse that looked more or less like a pasture, just because some shooting happened there once.

Chalmette was different because she could *see* why it was more important than your average cow pasture. She could stand on the earthen wall that the Park Service had constructed to show tourists what a "rampart" looked like and look downriver at the wide plain where the British had massed themselves, waiting to strike. To her right flowed the unruly Mississippi, barely contained by its levee. Upriver stood the modern city of New Orleans, where it had guarded the Mississippi and its wealth for nearly three hundred years. And to her left, commercial development along St. Bernard Highway brought the 21st century right to the 19th-century battlefield's back door.

But behind her...behind her was the ground where the outnumbered Americans stood against an invasion that could have killed their fledgling country—and that long-ago army had been sadly short on trained soldiers.

Northern volunteers had floated downriver for this fight. Storied "Kaintuck" marksmen and Choctaws had gathered here, too. Slaves had fought beside their masters. And the pirates...

Faye smiled to think how Jean Lafitte's notorious privateers had proven themselves as artillerymen and patriotic Americans, when they might have sold Jackson's army to its enemies. They'd certainly had the opportunity when the British army offered Lafitte the Pirate a fortune to turn traitor.

Instead, he'd provided the Americans with gunpowder by the shipload, as well as the all-important flints. Flint-lock rifles could hardly be expected to fire without them.

This was fascinating stuff, but the battlefield hadn't brought her here, and it was the park employees' business to explain its significance to the tourists traipsing through. The antebellum plantation sites just behind the American line had been the lure.

Faye knew her professional attention span could be short, because she was interested in pretty much everything. If she kept frittering away her energy on romantic musings about long-ago wars, she'd never finish this job, she'd never pick a dissertation topic, and she'd never get out of school.

Still, the sense of history that pervaded this place stirred her. She'd never worked at a site where history-book-level events took place. It was hard to wrap her brain around the notion that the larger-than-life personalities of Andrew Jackson and Jean Lafitte had walked this very ground, but she was having a lot of fun trying.

Joe was going to love it here.

She hadn't seen her fiancé in a month, and it felt like a whole lot longer, but he was on his way. He'd arrive by sundown, six or seven hours, tops. It wasn't such a long time, really, but it was.

"Dr. Longchamp…"

She turned as the young park ranger, Matt Guidry, approached. "It's just Faye. I'm still a year or two away from that Ph.D." And insisting that everyone call her "Doctor" when she did finally graduate would feel unbelievably stuffy. "I'm sorry, Matt. I interrupted you. Did you need me?"

His wide gray-blue eyes made her want to reach out and mother him. "Did you still want to go with me during your lunch break? To look at my neighborhood?"

She'd been so distracted by a long-ago war that she'd forgotten something she was actually looking forward to doing. Well, "looking forward" wasn't the right way to describe a visit to the scene of such destruction. But she did want to do this.

Matt's mostly Cajun family came from a storytelling culture. This gave an unmistakable flair to his stories, like the one about the wind-torn night when his parents were plucked off a suburban rooftop that barely poked through Katrina's floodwaters. Matt had described his ruined neighborhood—and the people trying to rebuild it—so vividly that Faye had wanted to see it all for herself.

"Yes, Matt. I do want to go with you. Very much."

Chapter Two

There were no waterlines. The gutted-out houses stretched as far as Faye could see in all directions. If there had been trees before the storm, the water or the wind had taken them. There was nothing to obscure her view of one brick shell after another, each dead home centered neatly on its rectangular plot of ground.

She wanted to get a mental picture of the kind of cataclysm that could do this, but she couldn't tell how high the floodwaters rose until she found a waterline.

"When the storm breached the Lake Borgne levees," Matt said, "The Wall of Water hit, and the whole town of Chalmette went under."

That was the way people around here said it—The Wall of Water—as if every word were capitalized. They didn't use the word Katrina often, either, preferring the simplicity of "the storm" or the outrage communicated by "The Levee Failures." More often than not, people added editorial commentary like "The Goddamn Levee Failures." Sometimes, the colorful modifiers were in French. At the very first opportunity, Faye intended to find out what those cool-sounding words meant.

"The levees in that direction didn't do a damn bit of good. The waves washed them away like they weren't there. Then they just went over the top of the next batch of levees, which is a recipe for a bad breach," he said, with a careless wave not directed toward the river.

It wasn't the Mississippi that had nearly killed Chalmette. It was the loss of the Lake Borgne levees, said to have been constructed from soil dug out of the Mississippi River Gulf Outlet, a shipping channel made personal by its familiar name, "Mr. Go." Faye was no engineer, but she thought she'd want more than sandy dredge spoil between her and a hurricane. For whatever reason, those levees breached, and Chalmette went under.

Matt was still talking. "The Wall of Water was fifteen feet high here. 'Course, you didn't have to be anywhere close to the levee for things to get real bad, real quick. All of St. Bernard Parish was underwater."

Fifteen feet. That explained the lack of waterlines. The water had washed right over the tops of these houses. Without even a roof to perch on, people caught in the maelstrom would have simply had to ride where the water took them, hoping they weren't sucked under or crushed by floating debris.

"I know you wanna see the Lower Nine," Matt said.

Faye, who had been too overwhelmed by the scene to be thinking about much else, said, "What?"

"You know. The Lower Ninth War. It was all over the TV after the levees broke. Everybody that comes to town always wants to go there and see the houses Brad and Angelina are putting up for folks. You want to go. I'll take you."

Faye wasn't so sure she did want to go. The destruction of Chalmette seemed quite enough to take in one day, but Matt was her tour guide, so she got in the car.

The Lower Ninth Ward was a work-in-progress. There were houses that still sagged and sported blue tarps over their shingles. There were whole blocks shorn of houses that had left no trace but their bare foundations. And, here and there, a few new houses offered hope for renewal.

Some of the abandoned houses were adorned with yellow signs, each marked with a big red "X," marking them as slated for demolition. Faye looked around, puzzled. "Um, Matt. I don't see much difference between the houses that are condemned and the ones that aren't. They all look pretty bad."

"The parish condemned any building messed up by the flood that wasn't gutted out and secured. That makes it tough on people waiting for insurance money or government money, but it's gotta be done. A building just sitting open is gonna attract kids or vagrants, and that's dangerous. And a houseful of stuff that's been rotting this long is a health hazard, for true."

Faye looked up and down the residential street. Only some of the driveways sported the FEMA trailers that had been the roof over the heads of thousands of people for years now. The other homeowners must be living somewhere else, and that somewhere else could be anywhere. Baton Rouge. Houston. Phoenix. Boston. Any place they could find a job and a place to stay.

"What about the people who haven't been able to come home yet? How do those people get their houses up to snuff, so they won't be condemned and torn down?"

"There's different ways to get the work done." He pointed to a house that was buzzing with exuberant teenagers wearing face masks and protective clothing. "That's one way. Church groups are still coming from all over to help out. God bless 'em."

Some of the kids waved as they walked past. Others were too absorbed in clowning around in front of a friend wielding a camera phone. Faye smiled. Even amid tragedy and destruction, a fifteen-year-old was still a fifteen-year-old.

"A few streets over, there's a house where a shrimp boat sat in the driveway for months. The tour buses drove by every day so people could point and gawk. And over there," he gestured in the direction away from the levee breach, "there's a house that's still got an airplane in the back yard, leaning over on its nose. It's a little bitty plane, but it's still kinda cool. Wanna go take a look at it?"

There was no constructive reason for Faye to go look at a plane that had floated from God-knows-where until it came to rest on somebody's patio. But she was human enough to want to see it, anyway.

"Yeah. Let's go see the plane."

Matt grinned. When he did that, he looked as young as the kids behind them, light-heartedly gutting out somebody's drowned home. For some reason, Matt made Faye think of the soldiers who fought with Andrew Jackson. He was out of college, so he had to be 22 or 23, at least. Some of Jackson's soldiers— most of them, maybe—had been even younger than he was right now. Probably even as young as the ebullient church kids.

Faye and Matt had hardly gone five steps when a shriek behind them turned into a chorus of screams. Turning quickly, Faye saw seven people bolt out of the house where they were working, running like the very devil was on their tails, and they weren't all teenagers. This was no stampede of silly children scared by a ghost story. Whatever had caused that shriek, it was something that had scared the group's adult leaders as badly as it had scared the kids.

It was the real thing.

Faye's work boots weren't made for running, but she got there quickly, even faster than young Matt. The panicked crowd clustered around the two of them, even the adults. This happened to Faye a lot, and she couldn't say why.

Women who were five feet tall and scrawny certainly didn't command respect from a physical standpoint. Still, something in Faye's demeanor made people who hardly noticed her in good times turn to her for help when things went south. Having a man in uniform at her side didn't hurt, either, even if a park ranger who didn't look old enough to shave wasn't quite the same thing as an armed and experienced officer of the law.

"What is it?" Faye barked. "What has happened here?"

"Somebody's dead in there," wailed a girl wearing braces on her teeth.

"Bones…" A curly-haired boy paused, and the sun gleamed on his dark, beardless cheeks. "I saw some bones."

One of the group's leaders had recovered herself. She spoke in the calm, motherly tones of an elementary school teacher.

"Now we don't know that it's a person dead in there. It could be an animal."

A young man whose insolent face was belied by his trembling hands said, "Marissa said she saw a leg bone. Marissa's an idiot, mostly, but I reckon she knows how long the bones in her legs are. What else around here is big enough to have bones that big? Deer? What would a deer be doing in a house, buried under garbage?"

"I saw stranger things after the storm." The young people grew quiet when Matt spoke. Every head turned his way. Sorrow lent gravity to his voice. "I saw…"

He turned and walked quietly away from the nervous crowd of teenagers, and Faye couldn't blame him. How could he possibly describe what he'd witnessed to these children?

Faye, who had persisted in thinking of Matt as a boy when he wasn't, was impressed by his composure. A nervous quiet settled in the aftermath of his words, and the silence gave Faye a chance to think.

"Did anybody call 911 yet?"

A tall graying man wearing a clerical collar nodded and pointed to the cell phone he was holding to his ear.

Matt turned and spoke to the group, though he was still backing away as he did. "Nothing to do now but sit and wait. They'll be here soon enough. I've seen this happen before."

Faye was reminded that, though this situation was unsettling and bizarre for her and the church group, finding dead bodies had been a way of life in parts of New Orleans during the first weeks and months after Hurricane Katrina.

As if he'd read her mind, Matt said, while still backing away, "I really thought we were done with this."

Faye could see him retreat into himself right in front of her. He turned and walked quickly down the sidewalk, hands clasped behind his back and eyes focused on a spot of sky just above a distant rooftop. She knew what it was like to need to be alone, so she let him go.

Chapter Three

Faye, being who she was, was drawn to the pile of garbage that the kids had pulled out of the house. History was history, even if it was only a couple of years old. When she and her crew began excavating at the battlefield park, one of the first strata they encountered was the layer of silt and debris deposited by Katrina's floodwaters. Gutting this house was archaeology, in its way, as surely as her own day-to-day work was. Looking over this pile of rotting artifacts was as good a way as any to spend her time until the police showed up.

The garbage pile stank. There was no other word for the stench. Everything in it was covered in mildew and filth, even things that would themselves never rot. The plastic parts of the electric iron atop the pile, for example, could be buried and forgotten for many years, yet still be recognizable if a future archaeologist uncovered them. The heavy wooden beam lying next to the iron probably wouldn't be, although those future archaeologists could probably see where it had been by the dark prints it left behind in the soil that eventually accumulated here.

Faye squinted at the electric iron for a minute, wondering when she last did something so drastic as to iron any clothes. Then three words popped into her head.

Irons don't float.

Since the kids were still working, she assumed that they hadn't reached the bottom of the garbage, where she would expect an iron to be. And there were a lot of other things in this garbage pile that were too heavy to float. Not the broad wooden beam, though it was plenty heavy. The storm had washed away whole houses made of wood. But that sewing machine? And that dumbbell next to the iron—it had to weigh twenty pounds. Yet if they were the last things removed before finding the bones, the odds were good that they had been on top of the corpse.

The water had done weird things, including leaving an airplane in somebody's back yard. It could have washed away a whole house with a sewing machine in it. She could picture that. But once the house was just splintered wood, the sewing machine would have dropped to the bottom. It beggared imagination to picture any other scenario. So how had it gotten on top of a body that was probably pretty buoyant itself?

It was possible. She could think of a number of ways such a thing could happen, but something about this pile of junk didn't smell right to Faye. Actually, it smelled really wrong, but its stench was not the point. She just didn't think this situation looked natural and Katrina, though she embodied forces completely outside normal human experience, was at rock bottom a natural phenomenon.

Faye turned to the insolent-faced boy because, beneath the attitude, she sensed another rational soul. "Where was all this stuff before you hauled it out here? Right on top of the body? In the same room? Or somewhere else in the house entirely?"

"We've only been working on the sun porch today. It's a little room, really." He was still slouching, but he was also sizing Faye up through his dark, slitted eyes. "Sort of like a patio somebody closed in. If you laid down on the floor in that room, you'd stretch nearly wall to wall, and you're pretty short. Anything that was in there before we started working was on top of the corpse, or close to it."

He said "corpse" with a bit of relish. Faye remembered being a teenager. A certain morbid air came with the territory.

"Walk around to the back of the house with me," he said, nodding in that direction. "I'll show you."

Faye found that the boy had described the room accurately. It was small—maybe eight by eight, possibly even less—and it protruded awkwardly from the back of the house. There had been a group of three narrow windows on each of the three exterior walls. Now, there were just empty openings.

Standing outside one of those windows and looking in, Faye could see the interior of the small room almost as well as if she'd actually been inside. Part of a long white bone, a femur, could be clearly seen, its femoral head poking out of the top layer of debris. It sure looked human to Faye. If it was, then another dumbbell rested right where the person's pelvis should be, completely entangled in the festering pile of garbage. The dumbbell looked like it had sat in that spot for years. But how could it possibly have gotten there?

Her morbid young friend was right about one thing. No deer could have stepped through one of these little windows to die, nor floated in with the floodwaters. These bones had been part of a person, not a wild beast, and everybody in the vicinity knew it.

The sun porch seemed to have served as a hobby room, where the owners of the house exercised and sewed and did other things that would have cluttered up the main living areas. Thinking of the regular, everyday life this person had lived brought the reality of death home. She turned away from the window.

Faye had a very strong feeling that this was no ordinary victim of the storm that was slowly receding into the past, but she was afraid the police would come in and whisk the skeleton away. Retrieving the remains of drowning victims had been depressingly routine not so very long ago. Why would they waste time and money determining the circumstances of this person's death when those reasons were so very obvious?

Except they weren't. Faye could think of a handful of ways for that dumbbell to come to rest on top of a dead person's pelvis, but one of those ways bothered her. It bothered her an awful lot.

What if that dumbbell was resting on top of a corpse because somebody put it there?

Chapter Four

Faye had steeled herself against being dismissed. Ignored. Brushed off. Why would the police spend even a minute listening to her far-fetched suspicions? She was completely unprepared for Detective Jodi Bienvenu.

"I'm glad you shared your concerns with the responding officer—" Jodi had begun.

Faye had recognized this sentence as the opening salvo of a brush-off. She'd expected this, but it still stung.

But Jodi had kept talking, saying in her thick south Louisiana brogue, "—and I'm glad I was close enough by that I could come out before you got away." She'd put a foot on the yellow tape cordoning off the ruined sun porch, so Faye could step over it. "Come on in here, you. Come and show me what you're talking 'bout."

Faye did what she was told, but she stood well back from the bones, trying not to touch anything. The technicians had only begun to unpack their gear. It was way too soon to risk letting an untrained civilian like Faye mess things up.

"Um…Detective Bienvenu, isn't there some kind of rule against me being in here before your forensics team has a chance to…you know…do whatever it is they do?"

"It's 'Jodi,' not 'Detective Bienvenu.' Anyway, why'd you have to go and talk about rules? This is New Orleans. We don't have anything around here you could actually call a rule." Jodi used her hands to encompass the entire room. "Besides, would you look at this pile of stinking garbage? Let's say you're right. Let's say this poor soul had help in turning up dead. Even so, this crime scene was worthless yesterday. Today? After a dozen teenagers have tromped through it for hours? It's worse than useless."

Faye realized that the detective had a point. "Then why are you bothering to listen to me? Why not just call this an accidental drowning and be done with it?"

"Because you make sense when you talk. And because I pray at the shrine of Saint Anthony."

Faye managed to avoid saying, "Huh?", but she must have been doing a poor job of hiding her befuddlement, because Jodi explained herself. "You didn't go to Catholic school, did you? Saint Anthony's the patron saint of lost things and missing persons. He suits me a lot better than Saint Jude."

Again, Faye cleverly avoided saying "Huh?", and Jodi cooperated by explaining herself.

"Saint Jude is the patron saint of lost causes. I don't like my cases to get to the point where I have to run crying to Saint Jude, no. Lots of times, fighting a lost cause is unavoidable, but it's never a good thing. Me, myself, I like to start with Saint Anthony."

Detective Jodi Bienvenu felt a healthy disdain for civilians who thought they'd be a lot of help with a criminal investigation, simply because they'd watched several seasons of CSI. But she also had a healthy disdain for police officers who dismissed valuable insight merely because it came from a non-professional. Criminal investigations were about facts and rational detective work. They were about logic. She knew that. But Jodi Bienvenu knew they were also about intuition and feelings and ideas that just didn't let go.

Perhaps her respect for things that were unprovable but still true was something she'd breathed in for her entire life. Such things permeated the air here in this illogical city. It was not unusual to meet people who held equally firm beliefs in the protective powers of Catholic saints and voodoo charms and benevolent ghosts. New Orleans was full to overflowing with ghosts these days. Jodi prayed that at least some of them were benevolent.

She was fortunate enough to work for people who shared her respect for the indirect path to truth. So she was unlikely to catch much heat for tackling this investigation in an unusual way.

This woman standing beside her, Faye Longchamp, had just spent ten minutes presenting a quietly passionate argument that this sad little affair was a murder, not a storm-induced drowning. She had marshaled her facts, presented them logically, and made a good case.

Jodi knew detectives who would dismiss Faye's ideas because they came from a civilian. She knew others who weren't capable of taking Faye seriously because she was a little tiny woman. And some Neanderthals at the department would ignore her because she wasn't white.

There were fewer of those every day, as retirements and funerals cut heavily into their aging ranks, but Faye had a wariness that Jodi recognized. When your gender and your race had worked against you all your life, you knew deep-down that there was a heavy cost to being wrong. People like Faye made sure they were right before they opened their mouths, which made them very useful to have around.

The logical part of Jodi's brain heard Faye speak and appreciated her cool intellect. But the illogical part of her brain, the part that took fragments of the truth and assembled them without conscious thought—that important part of her liked Faye intensely. Because as much as Faye might insist that she answered every one of life's questions with a reasoned evaluation of the facts, Jodi didn't believe her.

This was a woman whose intuition was so engrained into her being that she didn't even know it was there. This was also a woman of an uncommonly brilliant mind, and Jodi knew that she, by comparison, was simply smart. Smart and cagey.

Intuition and maybe a little touch of voodoo were telling Jodi that she should keep Faye around. If anybody could help her make sense of this case, it was Faye Longchamp.

While the crime scene technicians began the delicate work of photographing the bones *in-situ,* Faye stood aside with Jodi, talking possibilities.

"Maybe someone drowned in this room during the storm or just afterward, then the floodwater left a pile of junk on top of the body as it receded…" Faye stopped talking and shook her head, because she still thought that scenario was so very unlikely.

She thrashed about for some better suggestions. "But that would mean that irons and sewing machines have learned to float. So maybe the person was already dead and the body got here later, on its own, by floating or something, and…um…the same thing happened—you know…floodwaters washing heavy stuff on top of it. Except I just keep coming back to the fact that dumbbells sink pretty fast. This scenario *could* have happened naturally, but it just doesn't feel right."

Jodi's arms were crossed, and she was motionless, except for her right index finger tapping a steady rhythm on her left bicep. "I don't know how all that stuff got there, but if there was enough of it piled on the corpse early on, I guess the weight would've held it down later, when it started to bloat up."

Jodi was a dainty woman not much taller than five-foot-nothing Faye, but her brash, gregarious nature seemed bigger than she was. With honey-colored skin, and eyes and hair that were an only slightly darker shade of brown, she seemed too… well…too *pretty* to be talking about bloated corpses.

Faye squinted at the bone protruding from the heap of refuse. "I'd say an iron and a sewing machine and a couple of dumbbells would have been enough to keep a body underwater."

"Probably, but you never know. After awhile, a dead person gets an awful lot of buoyancy on 'em." Jodi grimaced. "You know, I wish I didn't know so much about that."

"I bet." Faye considered the positions of the bone and the dumbbell. "Maybe somebody found this dead body in the water and…um…didn't want it to float away. So he piled a bunch of stuff on it, planning to come back later."

"Maybe. But then what? He got busy and forgot he left a corpse behind?"

"Maybe he died, too."

Jodi pursed her lips and nodded her head a little. "Could be. Lotta people died that week, and not all of them during the storm. But that's not what you really think happened. That's not why you took my sad little routine body retrieval and turned it into an investigative nightmare. I know what you're thinking. But I want you to say it out loud."

Faye thought of her training in analyzing stratigraphy. If one thing is on top of another thing, then the thing that's on top came later…unless the archaeologist doing the work can think of a damn fine reason why that isn't true. She sifted through the explanations for the stratigraphy of this site. Her mind wouldn't let go of the most disturbing option.

"Okay. I'll say it." Faye took a deep breath. "Maybe this person had human help in getting dead, getting here, and getting covered up. Maybe somebody needed to dispose of a corpse in late August 2005. What better solution than to take that body to a flooded-out house and sink it to the floor? It would be weeks before anybody found it and, when they did, nobody would look at it and think, *Murder victim.* Nope. The long list of lives taken by Hurricane Katrina would simply be inflated by one… and a murderer would walk away free."

Faye hated it when people got away with murder. Judging by the look on Jodi's face, she did, too.

Chapter Five

Faye should have realized that Nina would come.

Calling Nina to tell her that she would be away from the dig for hours had been the considerate thing for Faye to do. She hadn't burdened her assistant with troubling details like her suspicion that this was no accidental death. And she certainly hadn't burdened her with the unsettling feelings she'd had since she first saw a denuded human bone protruding from a pile of flood debris. Still, Faye wasn't one to gloss over unpleasant truths, so she'd given Nina a brief description of what she'd seen.

If she'd had her wits about her, she'd have known that Nina would come running. The woman had grown up near here, just like Matt. When she got word that someone had been found dead here, nothing was going to stop her from running home.

Not many minutes passed after Faye thumbed her cell phone off until she saw Nina bounding out of a still-rolling Ford. Charles hit the parking brake and caught up to her in seconds, running with an athlete's easy grace.

Nina rushed to Faye, loping awkwardly like someone who hadn't run a step since high school P.E. class. She looked uncertainly at the detective at Faye's side, as if unsure which of the two women could answer her question. Finally, she blurted out, "Can one of you tell me who it is? Who's dead?"

Jodi's voice slipped from the conversational tone she'd been using with Faye, all the way down into the range that said *I'm-an-*

officer-of-the-law-and-I've-got-everything-under-control. "We've got our people working on that identification."

Nina turned her eyes back to Faye, and they showed a naked need for reassurance. Charles still stood beside her, with his arm cupped around her elbow. Faye wondered why Nina didn't look to him for comfort. He slipped an arm around her waist, but she never took her stricken eyes off Faye.

Because the situation apparently wasn't painful enough, a television van pulled up to the curb and disgorged a cameraman who couldn't have been over twenty-five, a graying man who hadn't seen twenty-five in a long time, and a crisply dressed young woman. Faye could tell that the woman was the newscaster because she was carrying a microphone.

The oldest member of the party carried a notepad, which he was rapidly filling with notes. He stooped over the pad, squinting like a man who rarely worked in unfiltered sunlight, but his obvious discomfort didn't slow his frenetic scribbling.

Jodi walked toward the TV crew, maneuvering their position so that the exposed human bones remained out of view of the camera. Faye heard her talking to them, but she didn't say much.

Yes, a body had been uncovered.

Yes, it was buried under debris that seemed to have been undisturbed since shortly after Hurricane Katrina.

No, there had been no identification of the victim.

"Can we talk to the person who discovered the remains?"

"That person is fifteen years old. I'd suggest that you talk to her minister."

Adroitly maintaining control of what the camera did and did not see, Jodi beckoned to the minister, then backed away in Faye's direction while he was interviewed.

"It's been a long time since we found a hurricane victim," Jodi said. "This could be the last one, I guess. I hope. I imagine the TV station will give this some serious air time, with a very serious title like *Closing the Door on Katrina.*"

The reporter finished with the minister, then beckoned to the gray-haired man, who was still scribbling on his pad.

Faye edged closer, because the man's scholarly air seemed out-of-place in this setting. She wondered why he was riding around with a TV crew.

The reporter pointed her microphone at him, saying, "This is Louie Godtschalk, author of an upcoming book on the Katrina levee failures. He's here today to do research on the book, and we've asked him to tell us about—"

Godtschalk held up a pale hand. "No. The levee failures prompted this book, but that's not my topic. I'm writing a history of New Orleans, told in terms of water. The city is here because of the river—our country desperately needed it to be here—but many, many people have had to work for their entire lives to keep it dry. New Orleans is an engineering marvel, really, and I don't think that story has ever been told—not the mechanical side and certainly not the human side."

He cleared his throat nervously and cocked his head to the left, as if his collar were too tight. He clearly didn't like being on the air. Faye wondered if he was prepared for the wave of media attention that could accompany a successful book on the flooding of New Orleans.

"After Katrina…when the flood came…I began to wonder whether the lives of those brilliant innovators might make an interesting story. When people started asking questions like, 'Should we rebuild New Orleans, now that we've seen what can happen here? Do we want to fight a losing battle, again and again?', that's when I knew that I had a story that was important enough to—"

As the author spoke, Faye was shocked to see Nina rush at him like an avenging mouse.

"A losing battle? Don't you say that! Don't you ever say that! If you say that on television, then people will believe it's true."

Nina kept moving until she was nose-to-nose with the man. "This was no losing battle. And it was no natural disaster. This was a travesty that didn't have to happen."

The author didn't even try to finish his sentence. He just stood gaping, on-camera, at a woman who seemed to have simply taken all she could stand.

"They told us that our levees were solid, and we believed them. They told us that they would hold up under a hurricane that was plenty worse than Katrina. Hell, Katrina didn't even give us a direct hit. God help us, if she had."

She raised a trembling fist. Faye couldn't imagine that Nina had raised a fist to anybody in her life, ever. "Have you read the independent report on the levee failures? Have you read it?"

Faye could tell that the author was trying to say that, yes, he'd read it, but Nina's frustration had been bottled up too long for anything or anybody to stop it from spewing out.

"Did you know that the design engineers used the same safety factor for our levees that they use for protecting cow pastures? Wouldn't you build a little bigger safety factor into something that protected a million people and billions of dollars of their stuff? I would, but I'm not an engineer, am I?"

Nina shook the still-upraised fist. "Did you know that there were *trees* growing on some levees? How could that be allowed to happen? Levees are made of dirt. How can a pile of dirt hold up under that much water pressure when it's full of tree roots? But I'm not trained to look after levees. What the hell do I know?"

Faye was thinking that Nina seemed to know a lot. Charles was still standing where Nina had left him, with his hand sticking awkwardly into the air where her elbow had been just seconds before. He was looking at her as if he'd never seen her before.

Faye hoped he'd appreciate her friend Nina a little better from here on out. Some men were so busy charming women that it never occurred to them to wonder what was going on in their heads. Well, now he knew what was going on inside Nina's head. He knew that she was strong and passionate and interesting. And, after that evening's newscast, so would the rest of New Orleans. Maybe Charles would find that he had competition.

The newscaster looked like she wanted to ask a question. It didn't look good for her to lose control of the moment so completely, but a little deft editing could probably fix that. Nina clearly had no intention of giving up her audience. Faye had the definite sense that she was now talking to the viewing public, though her eyes were still boring into the hapless author.

"Did you know that there was a two-hundred-foot hole in the Orleans Canal levee, because nobody could agree on who was supposed to finish that levee? Don't you tell me we shouldn't rebuild our homes! Not when our money—everybody's money—was being poured down a rat hole. You can build a levee that's a million miles long, but if there's a 200-foot hole in it, then you just spent that money on exactly nothing. Doesn't it make you angry that your money was wasted that way?"

Godtschalk smoothed his thinning hair off his forehead, and nodded. He tried to speak, but Nina was having none of it.

"Not rebuild New Orleans? Will we rebuild San Francisco and Los Angeles when the next big earthquake takes one of them out? Let me answer that one. We will. And neither of those cities will look like this, years after the fact." She spread her arms wide and spun slowly in place, gesturing at the ruined houses spreading out around her, one desolate block after another.

Slowly, she let her arms drop to her sides and, tears on her face, turned to gaze mutely at the camera for a moment. Then she raised a hand and pointed at a spot somewhere behind the camera. "My home was three blocks in that direction. If the levees that my tax dollars…and yours, Mister Book Author…if the levees that our money built had held, then I'd be living there, instead of sleeping on my cousin's couch. Don't you be telling these people that my home's not worth rebuilding."

Nina started slowly backing away from the camera. The newscaster slashed her hand across her throat, and the cameraman quit filming after Nina's first few steps. Faye could see her friend shrinking back into herself, and she missed the new, fiery Nina.

Within three steps, Nina had stumbled over a curb and dropped to one knee, but the news audience wouldn't see that. They wouldn't see a clumsy, dowdy woman willing to make herself look stupid, if that's what it took to be heard. No. They would see a prophet weeping for a lost city.

Jodi sighed like a woman who'd lived through too many surprises for one day. She asked the reporter, "Was that live?"

The newscaster didn't have to say yes. Her I'm-going-to-get-a-Pulitzer smirk said it all. Faye reflected that the woman had done exactly nothing. The Pulitzer people might very well respond to what she just saw, but Nina was the one who had done her research and gotten her point across to the masses. *She* was the one who deserved a Pulitzer.

◇◇◇

Louie Godtschalk tucked his notepad under his arm, and decided to forget the academics and politicians that he was scheduled to interview. Well, perhaps he wouldn't forget them. He'd just set them aside for the day or two it would take him to draw this passionate woman's story out of her. Because she unquestionably had a story. No writer worth his salt could possibly look at her face and fail to see that.

The detective, too, looked like a woman with things to say, and he'd wager that those things were worth hearing. And the biracial woman standing next to her, the tiny thing wearing army-green pants and heavy boots—she looked like someone worth knowing. She also looked like someone who didn't suffer fools gladly.

Louie Godtschalk came from Louisiana Creole stock, and the men in his family were routinely coaxed and bullied into their best selves by the women in their lives—women with guts and heart. The frothy little girl who had thrust her microphone in his face was not one of those women, but these three were.

Louie knew that he was pushing the tolerance of American readers with his esoteric little book on the making of New Orleans. How many pages about drainage and levees and (God help him) sewage could he expect people to read, when they had access to all the mindless drivel in the world? Not many. But these women might be his answer. If he followed them around for awhile, they might lead him to stories that would hold the attention of even the flightiest American.

Chapter Six

Jodi's forensics team had made progress. There was no longer any need to refer to the victim as "it."

Beneath the dumbbell, and wrapped around the pelvis that Faye had known would be there, were a half-rotted pair of size two jeans. The forensics lab would carefully remove the jeans and use scientific methods to determine the sex of the pelvis, but the jeans already told the tale.

Faye supposed there were men in the world who would have worn jeans with multicolored beads stitched across the butt, but she didn't think many of them weighed a hundred and ten pounds. She decided not to spend much time meditating on the fact that this woman's jeans had survived water and heat and mildew and rot so much better than their wearer.

Jodi cleared her throat to get Faye's attention. "We've had us a nice little chat about this crime scene. A few hours of it, to tell the truth. To hear you talk, Ms. Longchamp, I'd think you'd spent a lot of time with cops."

Jodi didn't make eye contact. Somebody should tell her to watch her body language. When a cop is interrogating a witness, it's a poor idea to let that witness know that she's saying one thing and thinking another. Faye decided to let someone else give her that advice.

"Call me Faye. As for me spending time with cops, well, there are a couple of good reasons for that. I've had enough bad luck to lose some friends to homicide. And one of my other friends—"

"You're telling me that some of them survived?"

It felt weird to laugh in the presence of a victim of drowning or worse, but Faye went ahead and did it anyway.

"Yeah. I have lots and lots of surviving friends. And one of them is a county sheriff. He talks to me about his work sometimes. Once, he even hired me as a consultant. Law enforcement sure pays better than archaeology."

"No kidding? I didn't think they made paychecks smaller than mine. What kind of consulting did you do?"

"He was questioning some suspects who were caught digging up artifacts in a National Wildlife Refuge."

"So that's a federal crime." It was a statement, not a question.

"Right. I'm pretty sure he thought the Feds didn't know jack about archaeology, and that they were going to mess this thing up bad. The people they were questioning were also suspects in the murder of a pretty high-profile local resident, but the pothunting charge was all he had on them. He hired me as a consultant to look at the artifacts they were carrying when they were picked up. Also, he wanted me there when the Feds interrogated the guy who was paying them to dig up public property and cart it away."

Jodi scratched her arm, and Faye was reminded that standing in this fetid place made her want a hot shower. No, two hot showers. And a lot of soap.

"Were they the killers your friend was looking for?"

"No. But the pothunting charge stuck."

"Then I'd say you did damn fine work."

Jodi glanced at the technicians gently extricating the bones from the garbage and filth cradling them. Faye saw the detective take in a little breath and square her shoulders, and she liked Jodi even more. She worried about people who got accustomed to dead and decaying human bodies.

"If you're so determined to make this a murder case," Jodi said, turning an appraising look on Faye, "tell me why you think this woman's lying here dead."

"I guess I'd start with the run-of-the-mill reasons people get killed. Maybe a robbery went bad?"

"Possible. Everybody spent the week of the storm running around with their pockets full. When you leave home and you don't know when you're coming back, it's only natural to gather up as much cash as you can."

That made sense. Faye always felt like she was on solid ground when a conversation was making sense. "Since the dead person was a woman..." She paused, thinking she might let that phrase speak for itself, but decided not to be a coward. "The newscasts made it look like the city fell into complete anarchy after the levees failed. I wouldn't have wanted to be a woman alone when that happened. Do you think this was a rape that ended in murder?"

"Could have been. Her clothes are in decent shape. They're not torn. All the buttons are where they're supposed to be. That doesn't mean she wasn't raped, though."

Faye was thinking of valuable things that *weren't* money. "During that week, I imagine you could have been killed for a working cell phone."

"Yeah. Or a boat, more likely." Memories clouded Jodi's face. "A boat equaled escape. A boat equaled life. If someone you loved was trapped on a roof somewhere, you would have given anything for a boat. If you were the right kind of person—make that the wrong kind of person—you might have killed for a boat."

"How will you track down this woman's identity? I have no idea how that's done."

"I've talked to the missing person's division—" Jodi began.

"St. Anthony's people?" Faye remembered after it was too late that it really wasn't cool to make light of someone else's religion, but Jodi was laughing.

"Yeah, but I had to talk to the saint's assistant, because the head honcho saint of missing persons isn't taking my calls until I catch up on my acts of contrition."

"You've been that bad?"

"Yeah." The sparkle in Jodi's eye didn't look all that contrite. "Anyway, they say there's nobody left unaccounted for in this neighborhood. So this isn't where our dead lady lived. We're still working on getting hold of the owner of this house."

"Nina might know something. Or Matt. He seems to know the area."

Nina and Charles were long-gone.

Faye looked around for the young park ranger and realized that she hadn't seen him since right after the bones were found. Checking her watch, she saw that it was past quitting time and wondered whether Matt had driven away and left her without transportation. It was obvious that he'd been upset, but Matt was a southern boy. He wouldn't have done that to a lady, not even when that lady was wearing dusty clothes and filthy boots.

She walked out to the curb and looked down the street. Sure enough, the car was right where they'd left it, and she'd bet money that Matt had left the keys in it for her.

"Poor kid. I bet he just didn't want to be here. I mean, this could've been somebody he knew."

"I prefer my witnesses to stick around." Jodi filled out the form on her clipboard and using her pen with a little more force than necessary. Substituting a paper-ripping penpoint stab for the period at the end of a sentence, she said, "When people remove themselves from sight before law enforcement arrives, I always wonder why."

Chapter Seven

Joe was waiting for Faye at the battlefield, standing on the levee and watching the Mississippi flow past his feet. Faye paused in the parking lot, leaning against her open car door, just to look at him.

His head was turned away from the city, as it always was from any city, and this put his face in shadow. But looking away from New Orleans wasn't going to give Joe the wild land he craved. Not here. This was a land of oil refineries and shipyards, of smokestacks and distillation towers and filled-in wetlands.

Andrew Jackson had stood near here with his field telescope, tracking the motion of the British army far down the river. If he could stand here now, he would recognize nothing—not the riverfront, not the drained wetlands, not anything, really…well, maybe the reconstructed replica of the earthworks that saved his army. Probably not even that.

Joe's hair, glossy and almost as black as Faye's short straight locks, blew in the evening wind, and she knew he didn't like it to do that. Joe was a man of extraordinarily acute senses, a born hunter, and hair blowing in his face bugged the devil out of him. He usually kept it tightly bound in a ponytail that reached almost to his waist. Faye knew that he'd taken it down for her, because she liked it when he wore his hair loose.

She'd only paused a moment before she slammed the car door shut and started running. Joe's ears were keen enough to hear the slamming door from a distance, even over the rushing river waters. He could probably hear her feet strike the soft, grassy ground.

He turned and waited for Faye to throw herself into his arms. He said nothing beyond, "I missed you so much." That was really all she wanted him to say. He didn't even seem surprised when she burst into tears instead of kissing him hello after all this time apart.

Joe never seemed surprised. He had a talent for taking life as it came. He missed nothing, because he was always paying attention. This, too, was a hunter's gift.

He let Faye cry, and he listened to her tell about the stinking piles of refuse where bugs and rats had lived undisturbed for years. He listened to her describe the ruined houses where plywood took the place of windows and nobody would ever be home again. And he listened to her—he really heard her—when she spoke of the naked white bone protruding from all the ugliness.

Faye loved Joe for all the ordinary reasons women loved men. He had an extraordinarily handsome face and wise green eyes. His long limbs and broad shoulders and lean muscles were the very image of what she thought a man should look like. But she loved him more because he listened to her.

Joe was following in his car as Faye drove home. She hoped he didn't mind the quirky, shabby apartment she'd been able to afford on the project's paltry per-diem housing budget. She'd never have found even this dump, if she hadn't hired Dauphine as a project technician.

Every once in a while, one of Faye's shovel bums wasn't the typical hungry grad student, and Dauphine wasn't a typical anything. She seemed to eke out a living by milking a half-dozen unreliable income streams, including Faye's favorite intermittent job of all time—part-time voodoo mambo.

As best as Faye could tell, a mambo was a voodoo priestess of the highest level. Mambos were considered healers, tellers of dreams, and brewers of spells, potions, and hexes. They mingled with spirits. They preserved rituals and songs, passing them along by initiating the next generation. Dauphine's *gris-gris* bags, sewed from fabrics as raucously colored as the bright gauze clothing she wore, were sold in every gift shop in town.

Dauphine was a woman of status in her community, but even mambos had to pay the bills. She had wielded a trowel at local archaeological excavations for years. Fortunately for Faye, Dauphine was also a landlady with a cheap garage apartment behind her house, and it was for rent.

The apartment was in the Tremé neighborhood, which was fairly convenient to work. Truthfully, though, it was more convenient to the French Quarter and its charms, both historical and hedonistic. Faye didn't have a hedonistic bone in her body, but she sometimes wished she did.

As things stood, she got her hedonism second-hand, by enjoying the people-watching opportunities in the French Quarter and its environs. What must it be like to throw caution so completely to the wind?

The last time Faye'd had a free afternoon, she'd spent it wandering down Bourbon Street, nursing an overpriced beer. A part of her had envied the carefree college students stumbling from bar to bar, though not the young lady leaning over to vomit on the old brick-paved street. And no wonder. Faye knew that she'd be losing her dinner, too, if she'd drunk something that particular shade of blue.

She'd resisted the urge to lay a motherly hand on the girl's shoulder and say, "Have a beer, sweetheart. It'll settle your stomach."

And she'd also resisted the urge to spend an afternoon's wages on a platter of oysters at a Bourbon Street tourist trap, when she knew full-well that the waiter at Felix's, just a few steps away, would settle a platter of raw, ice-cold bivalves in front of her for a lot less cash. And there would be a thirteenth oyster nestled among the dozen that she'd paid for, because the old establishments believed in the customer-pleasing local tradition of *lagniappe*—a little something extra.

Faye had eaten well and cheaply on her jaunts to the Quarter, once she'd learned that a cup of gumbo and a po-boy could be had for less than the price of the unfortunate girl's blue drink, if she was willing to buy it at a grocery store's walk-up counter and eat it somewhere else. A picnic at a park bench in front of America's oldest cathedral—and with the *lagniappe* of being within earshot of gypsy fortune tellers and jazz bands—suited Faye just fine.

Walking home through streets that shifted rapidly from a tourist's paradise to quaint old residential neighborhoods, Faye had looked for the crime-torn war zone that post-Katrina news coverage had led her to expect. She'd seen…not much.

There were a couple of overdressed ladies loitering on street corners who glanced up to see who was walking past, then looked away in disinterest. She also noticed some expensively dressed young men who looked like they'd just love to sell her some drugs. The poor guys had no idea that they were making eye contact with a woman far too miserly to waste her money on an expensive thrill. Not when there was beer in the world.

And living in Tremé had a special cultural spark: stores that carried everything a voodoo priestess could possibly need. Faye liked to browse through them and let her imagination run free.

She was sure Joe was going to love this place. Pretty sure. His Native American spirituality, deeply rooted in solitude and introspection, had pretty much nothing in common with the flamboyant magic of voodoo.

Gravel crackled under her tires as she drove past Dauphine's gently aging brick house and parked out back. Joe hopped out of his car quickly enough to open her car door for her, and he held her hand as they crossed the driveway.

Her apartment perched precariously over its garage, with window frames painted the exact shade of blue that repelled evil spirits, according to Dauphine. The ancient live oaks outside her window gave it the feel of a tree house. They were stupendous enough to rate a brief glance from Joe who, for all Faye knew, could talk to the spirits of trees. She was glad to see that his eyes flicked quickly back her way, and they stayed there.

Joe didn't talk much but, right this minute, there was only one thing she really wanted him to say.

"I missed you, Faye. I missed you every minute."

That was what she'd needed to hear.

Joe could never have described it in words, but when he was apart from Faye, something wasn't right. It was the same feeling he got when the birds hushed and the lizards stopped rustling in the grass. A disturbance floated in the air. It might be a hurricane. It might be the intrusion of someone who shouldn't be there. Or it might be simple loneliness. He knew she had her own work and her own life and he understood when she had to go away. But that didn't mean he slept well when she was gone.

He was glad to have gotten here when he did, because he could see that she needed him. Well, he hoped she always needed him, but no one should be alone after the things Faye had seen today. When he saw tough, practical, get-the-job-done Faye dissolve into wordless tears, there was no doubt that things were bad.

She'd wept when she greeted him, and she'd kept weeping while the story burst out of her. He'd have been worried if she hadn't. The sight of violent death leaves a mark that's hard to wash away. This pain would pass for Faye, but it would take time, and time was on Joe's mind a lot, these days. He'd been thinking about time all day, in fact. Before she told him about the lonely corpse, dead in a pile of trash, it had been on his lips to ask her the question, the one and only question that ruffled his habitual contentment.

"When, Faye? You said you'd marry me. When?"

Chapter Eight

There was an element of convenience to an apartment so small. If Joe leaned over and reached out one of his long arms, he could fetch a couple of slices of pizza out of Faye's little refrigerator without getting off the bed. And if he reached up, he could slide them into the microwave that sat atop that refrigerator.

The ancient television was within reach of Faye's side of the bed, which was nice, since the remote was long-gone, if it had ever had one at all. Needless to say, the apartment wasn't wired to accept cable transmissions, even if Dauphine had been the type of landlady to provide that level of decadence. No matter. Faye was looking for the local news.

It didn't take long to surf four channels. Faye quickly recognized the newscaster who'd been the lucky recipient of Nina's telegenic outburst.

Since the live broadcast earlier, someone had taken the interviews and edited them well. The story began with a short moment devoted to Jodi, as she calmly communicated something official and vague about the skeleton that had been uncovered in the Lower Ninth Ward.

Louie Godtschalk, the author, rated a few more seconds as he talked about his upcoming book chronicling the underpinnings of New Orleans history. The reporter had then inserted footage of herself giving the details of his book, smoothly compensating for the fact that Nina had interrupted the man in mid-sentence.

"Louie Godtschalk has a daunting task ahead of him. He's planning to make engineers interesting." She paused for an ironic grin. "As a lifelong resident of Orleans Parish, it has never occurred to me that I have pocket-protector-wearing science guys to thank for the ground beneath my feet. But the construction of a city in a strategic but inhospitable spot like this one was a job for brilliant innovators, and Mr. Godtschalk wants to tell us their stories."

Then the scene cut to Godtschalk as he continued explaining his work. After that, the editor had made no more cuts, choosing instead to run Nina's entire tirade. Faye was chagrined to see herself in the background, filthy field clothes and all. There she stood, looking out of the TV at all of New Orleans, wearing a blank deer-in-the-headlights face.

Joe smiled and squeezed her hand, as if he thought she looked just beautiful. Love was truly blind.

The reporter wrapped up her story with a sound bite proving that she might well have gone to journalism school. "The impassioned speech you just heard is not Nina Thibodeaux's first attempt to air her views on post-Katrina politics. She is the founder of an advocacy group for residents with grievances against their insurance companies or FEMA, and she blogs regularly on issues related to the levee failures and the politics of our city's recovery. Whether her efforts will change governmental policy remains to be seen. I, for one, admire her guts."

So did Faye.

Where was Joe?

The worn cotton bedsheets were cool, so he'd left her a while ago, and he'd done it quietly. Joe did everything quietly.

His moccasins were still tucked underneath the bed. One of them was resting sole-up, and she could see dirt ground into the places where the ball of his foot and his heel and each of his toes dug into the ground for support. The supple skin had stretched to the shape of his long narrow feet.

If she held the shoes to her face, she would smell leather and soil and salt water and Joe. She knew this because she had done it before. When he went home, her sheets would smell like Joe until she washed them and hung them on Dauphine's clothesline to dry. Then she would be truly alone. Maybe Joe had brought an extra pair of moccasins that he wouldn't mind leaving behind to keep her company. She could sniff them now and then, when she got lonely.

She raised up on one elbow, looking for him. Moonlight and night air streamed through open windows. The bedroom was empty. The bathroom door was open, revealing no one. When she noticed that a battered pot was missing from its usual spot atop her hot plate's single burner, she was pretty sure she knew where Joe was.

Checking the open shelving above the hot plate, she saw that a large pottery bowl was also missing. Dauphine had made it, so it was glazed in a half-dozen saturated colors. She'd painted a woman in the bottom of the bowl, with warm brown hair and opaque green eyes. Faye had presumed it was a self-portrait, until she complimented Dauphine on her work.

"Me? Oh, the lady's not me, no. The lady is *La Sirene*. She rules the sea. And she rules me, too." She'd cocked her head and looked closely at Faye before saying, "I have served the lady since she stole me from my *maman* at the seaside. It was my doing. I put my whole head in the water. *Maman* told me not to do it, but I was hard to tame even then. I heard the lady calling and dove in to find her. She wrapped me in seaweed, like *l'Enfant Jésus*, and sang to me. We sat in a great whirlpool while her fishes swam like jewels around us, and she just sang."

Faye lived on an island. No warm day passed without a plunge into the Gulf of Mexico. Her whole head had been in the water countless times, and no water goddess had ever carted her away. It wasn't that Faye didn't believe in magic. Magic had just never happened to her.

"What did *La Sirene* sing to you?"

"I hear the melody when I sleep, but the words slip through my mind like the lady's shimmery fish. One time she stopped singing and spoke to me. Her voice was like music even when she wasn't singing. It rumbled and moved the water. I do remember what she said then. Four words. Just four words that held my life and death."

Faye waited for the words, until she realized that Dauphine wanted her to ask for them.

"Please tell me what she said."

"She said, 'Do you eat fish?'"

"Do you?"

"I did, oh, yes, I did. But after resting in a clear sea that was working alive with fishes, I knew that I never could eat them again, so I said, 'No.' When I got home, *Maman* said that the lady would have eaten me if I had said, 'Yes.'"

"How did you get away, if you were all wrapped up in seaweed?"

"Oh, the lady let me go. There would have been no other way. After she had taught me all there was to know about healing and water magic, she let me go. She opened her arms and the seaweed dropped to the bottom of the ocean. I swam home and learned what my magic had cost me."

"What?"

"Seven years. I came home to find *Maman* and *Papa* gray-headed, and my *grandmère* in the grave. Still, I long to go back to that place where the water carries away all pain. I will go there when I die, if the lady wills it."

Rational Faye had chosen a strict and meticulous science for her life's work. She could not imagine that Dauphine's story was literally true. But even though she thrust her head under the ocean every chance she got and nothing bad had ever happened, she had no trouble believing that the sea was wise and old and deadly.

"You know I am a mambo, don't you, *ma chère*? I have gone to Haiti for training, so that I can use the magic given me by *La Sirene*. You have a young man, yes?"

Faye had nodded, reminding herself not to be too impressed with such lackluster psychic abilities. Knowing that she had a "young man" didn't require any voodoo at all. Faye was pretty sure Dauphine had overheard her at least once when she was on the phone with Joe.

"I can tell you how to hold him to you."

Faye had waited for a sales pitch, followed by a request for a small monetary donation. Neither of these things had come. Dauphine was feeling generous.

"Here's what you do. On a Monday morning, take your first urine and put it in a jar. Put it under your bed for nine days, and your man will never stray."

There had to be a sensible response to this suggestion, but Faye couldn't honestly think of one. Dauphine didn't seem to care, because she was bubbling with yet more woman-to-woman advice.

"I can also give you what every woman's body tells her she wants. You want it more than most, I think. You want it in your body and in your head and in your heart and in your soul. You want a child."

This, too, was not an awe-inspiring feat of psychic prowess, though the words "You want it more than most," echoed a bit for Faye. She thought she probably did want a child more than most, though you sure couldn't tell it, based on her life choices so far.

Dauphine seemed to have intuited that this was not the best time for calling up a baby, so she just handed her the bowl, saying, "Keep this in the room where you sleep. When you are ready, we will do what is needed to bring the child. Until then, *La Sirene* will care for you."

Right this minute, though, the *La Sirene* bowl was missing, and so was Joe. He had taken it for his own rituals. The lady would be staring out of the water at him tonight, when he poured steaming water over purifying herbs and dipped his hands for cleansing. Her bowl would sit on the ground in front of Joe's crossed legs while he sat beside his ceremonial fire and communed with the dead girl's soul.

Faye wondered how she could have forgotten that Joe would do this lovely thing. She'd seen his ceremony for the dead before, and she should have known that she'd see it again tonight.

Joe's parents had never taught him Creek ways, so he'd cobbled together his own spirituality, learning what he could from an assortment of Native American tribes, then putting his own stamp on their religious practices. If a soul could be ushered into peace after all this time alone, then Joe could do it.

Faye crept to the window. She could see Joe, lit by the flickering firelight. He was motionless, alone with his thoughts and with a spirit that had waited with its drowned body until someone like Joe found her and set her free.

It hadn't occurred to Faye that Joe wouldn't be alone. Dauphine moved in and out of the shadows around him, dancing with a loose-limbed and aggressive freedom. Perhaps this was a voodoo mambo's version of his ceremony for the dead.

She leapt and crouched and swung her hips to imaginary music. Her shoulders undulated as she shimmied past Joe, leaning forward as if to brush her large breasts against his back, then pulling away. If he noticed any of this, Faye couldn't tell.

Dauphine's quavering voice soared high. It was rough with passion, so rough that it didn't sound like Dauphine at all. The lyrics of her song made Faye cold in the marrow of her bones.

Seven stabs of the knife, of the dagger
Seven stabs of the knife, of the dagger
Lend me the basin, I must vomit my blood
Lend me the basin, I must vomit my blood
My blood pours down
Come, Lady…

Dauphine's right hand reached high above her head then, in rhythm, swung down toward the ground. She was clutching something in that hand—gazing at it, singing to it, caressing it—but it was a dark blur until she moved nearer to the fire. She raised it up again into the moonlight, and Faye got a better look at this thing that had passed so close to Joe's head, time and again.

It was a knife.

Excerpt from *The Floodgates of Hell*
by Louie Godtschalk

I want to tell you the story of a city that has thrived in a spot where no city should ever be. How do you start a story like this one?

Fortunately, when you've studied history as long as I have, you realize that someone has already said the very thing that you want to say, and they've said it better than you possibly could. So I will reach back a century or two or three and let some grand old gentlemen explain their life's work: helping an irreplaceable city stay alive.

I have become rather attached to the men—and engineering in those days *was* the purview of men—who were gracious enough to write down their stories. When I pick up a memoir or diary, it is as though the writer still lives. He has merely been waiting, asleep, for the hundred or more years it has taken me to seek his companionship. Even his friendship.

Of all those gentlemen, my favorite is Colonel James McGonohan. We are such kindred souls in this timeless friendship that I have used...stolen... borrowed...okay, we'll say that I appropriated the title of his memoirs. He and I are telling two facets of one tale—the parting of endless waters to make way for a magical city. What better title could either of us choose?

Here is the opening chapter of the reminiscences of a man who was a friend to both Andrew Jackson and Jean Lafitte. I hope you enjoy his friendship as well as they did. I know I have.

Excerpt from *The Floodgates of Hell,*
The Reminiscences of Colonel James McGonohan
1876

I had served more than two years in the Army of the
United States prior to January 8, 1815, yet I mark that
day as my first as a true soldier. My entire military
career, before that day, was a series of mere skirmishes
by comparison. On the plains of Chalmette, a pleasant
walk downriver from the romance of New Orleans, I
saw the unfathomable desolation that war can wreak
for the first time.

Thunder cannot compare to the din of constant
cannon fire. The sound of a mortar discharging death
swamps everything. The roar of artillery on that day
drowned the crack of our Dirty Shirts' rifles, but it
couldn't stop those shots from finding their targets.
Dirty Shirts...I haven't thought of those words in so
very many years. By the time the battle began, the
red coats of our British foes were well-nigh as dirty
as those of our most raggedy Kaintuck, yet still they
called our brave boys Dirty Shirts.

At the Battle of New Orleans, the culminating
conflict of the War of 1812, the British learned that
brass buttons do not fend off grape shot, and intricate
marching maneuvers do not outrun death. When the
cannons fell silent, 2,000 dead and wounded—but
very well-dressed— British soldiers lay on the battlefield. Nay, 2,000 dead and wounded British soldiers
covered the battlefield.

Their red coats gave the impression of a vast field
of blood, even when viewed from so great a distance
that their spilled blood could not possibly be visible.
Yet behind the American rampart, a stout wall of earth
more than a mile long and as much as eight feet high,
lay less than a hundred casualties.

New Orleans erupted in effusive gratitude after that great victory. Her citizens thanked General Jackson for their city's salvation with parties and balls and pageants and fêtes, all presented with an oddly French flair, considering that the celebrations honored the victory of an American army in defense of an American city. Yet when I returned to the battlefield, I walked down the mighty bulwark that had protected our men from the army of the most powerful nation in existence, and I gave credit in my own mind to the less storied soldiers—the ones who built that wall.

I was one of those military engineers. I served under General Jackson in the Indian Wars and the War of 1812. When the battle was done and the remnant British army had withdrawn through the hellish Louisiana swamps and sailed home, I returned to the Chalmette battlefield. I stood atop the wall of earth that had protected thousands of Americans—some of them my friends. Without that wall, they would have suffered the same end as that great bloody sea of British soldiers. The Redcoats' bodies were long gone by then, but I could still see them. I can see them now.

When I realized that my skills with life's practical inventions—bridges, roads, dikes, and berms—could save so many of my countrymen's lives, I at first thought to devote my own life to serving the army as a military engineer, doing just that. In my twilight years, I realize that the soldiers on the other side of that rampart had fathers and mothers and wives and sweethearts, just as our soldiers did, but even the most brilliant human alive lacks perspective at age eighteen.

I have built roads to move an army through a trackless wilderness. I have built bridges to bring that army across that wilderness without getting their feet wet.

At Chalmette, I even held power over floodwaters, if only for a time. I helped breach a levee wall, splashing a little piece of the great Mississippi River onto the Redcoats' path, forcing them to wade for miles in a Louisiana winter that was as bitter cold as many a December day at my Ohio home.

The Battle of New Orleans taught me that sometimes a military engineer's job is simply to make the enemy's life just a little more miserable than it already is. But I also learned at Chalmette, on the banks of the fickle and roaring Mississippi, that we frail human beings can guide water, but we can never control it.

I have not left New Orleans for any significant period of time since General Jackson saved the city and the river and all the land that the river drains—half a continent!—for the United States of America. When I have visitors from more ordinary climates, they marvel at our fair city's talent for housing extreme beauty, unmatched graciousness, and unrivaled debauchery in a single compact and low-lying spot. I think their admiration would be better placed if they were to marvel at the work of my engineering brethren.

New Orleans must be where it is. Geography dictates it, and I watched many soldiers die for no reason other than that geographical imperative.

But it can't be where it is. Water rolls past the city's face in the form of a river. Lakes cradle the city's sides and back. Water falls from the sky in torrents. Water lurks so close below that the ground is merely a floating crust.

Any port city is defined by water, but New Orleans is bathed in it. How could we expect anything else here, where the Mississippi washes the whole continent's wealth to sea?

If we are to maintain a city in such a place, then an army of men vain enough to think that they can hold back a river—men like me—will be required to keep its buildings and the people in them above water. I turned my back on my career as a military engineer, because I would rather help a city live than help my enemies die.

Now it is time to pass the responsibility to a new generation. For those who would take on this challenge, an old soldier offers a few words of advice gleaned from seventy-nine years of hard experience:

Never underestimate your enemy.

Never play the odds. You will eventually lose, because your enemy can be lucky just as easily as you can.

Always seek to make your enemy want to do the things you need him to do.

And, most of all, remember that, in these wet climes, water is your enemy. You can guide water, but you can't control it. Keep it in the river and out of the streets.

Chapter Nine

It was inconvenient that Joe had arrived for a visit on a Monday, when Faye had two more workdays looming in front of her. But only two days of his visit would go to waste. The all-or-nothing schedule of this kind of fieldwork—ten days on and four days off—gave her a long weekend to anticipate, and she and Joe had planned his visit to make the most of it. He'd just have to sight-see or hang around the battlefield while she worked for a couple of days, then they'd be free to play.

Faye was a homebody. She ordinarily preferred her constantly-under-renovation plantation house over any vacation spot, but she was pretty sure that New Orleans was the most romantic city on earth. Okay, Venice and Rio were contenders, too, but New Orleans was the most romantic city she'd ever *seen*. And it was hers. Or so she pretended.

Faye's family braided together as many cultures as New Orleans. She didn't know squat about her Longchamp ancestors, but their name hinted that they must have been French at some point in history. From the last photo of her father, taken just before he left for Vietnam, it was clear that Africans figured into the Longchamp family tree as well. From his looks, she'd say that more branches on that tree extended back to Africa than to France, but appearances only provide clues to the truth. They are not the truth. Faye was scientist enough to understand that.

One day, in her copious spare time, she was going to delve into the Longchamp family's genealogy.

On her mother's side, she had ancestors that *were* undoubtedly French. Others were English and Creek and African. In other words, Faye's cultural heritage paralleled that of New Orleans itself. This was undoubtedly why she liked it here.

When walking down a New Orleans street, she was rarely the only person of uncertain racial heritage within eyeshot. There weren't all that many places in America outside the biggest metropolises where that was true. She'd seen so many people here who looked like her that she was tempted to fake being a native, until she realized how quickly her lack of the distinctive local accent would expose that lie. New Orleans natives sounded like they were born in Brooklyn then transplanted to—where? France? Mars?—before settling down here in the Crescent City.

It didn't matter. She loved the cadence of their speech, and she loved the town.

The prospect of spending four days walking around the French Quarter—the storied *Vieux Carré*—with Joe had made the last ten days of this job's unrelenting physical labor worth every minute. She wished that she could have hired Joe as her assistant, and not just because she liked the way he smelled. He would have been a lot of help to her, but he had his own education to pursue. It wouldn't be right to slow him down.

Fortunately, Nina had proven herself in the role of Faye's assistant. Faye was glad to have her on the team.

Like Faye, Nina was a returning student with more experience in archaeology than her college transcript suggested. Faye had earned her decidedly non-academic experience by digging up the artifacts her ancestors left behind on the land she'd inherited—Joyeuse Island. Before entering graduate school, Nina had earned hers in the usual way, by volunteering for any dig that would take a willing worker who was only available on weekends.

Nina was a New Orleans native, so all her volunteer work had been done nearby, and some of it had been done right here at the Chalmette battlefield. If Faye'd been asked to design the perfect assistant, Nina would have been pretty close to her ideal. Well, except for Joe. Joe *was* the ideal assistant, particularly when you factored in the fringe benefits that a man of his singular beauty could provide.

At the moment, though, she and Joe were both hardworking students without much time for romance, not unless you counted the sheer romance of archaeology. And there was more than a bit of romance to the work she had come to Chalmette to do, even though the stimulus for it was predictably prosaic: somebody wanted to build something.

When Katrina blasted through south Louisiana, she took the battlefield park's visitor's center with her. The park service wanted to rebuild it in another spot and, frankly, you couldn't put a shovel in the ground anywhere in the area without the risk of obliterating history.

A review of the possible sites for the new visitor's center had determined that the least objectionable place for the new building was near the buried remnants of the Rodriguez plantation house. In laymen's terms, something historical would be disturbed wherever they built the thing, but the powers-that-be had judged that there was a fighting chance of avoiding utter catastrophe in this spot.

The Rodriguez house had taken cannonfire during Andrew Jackson's battle, but survived. Just to make things interesting, there had been another plantation house known as the Beluche house nearby—right under the park's public restrooms, in fact— that had stood even before the Rodriguez house.

Faye and her crew would be doing an archaeological survey, working in advance of the construction team to make sure that nothing old and irreplaceable was destroyed. If things went really well, Faye hoped to locate outbuildings that had stood behind each house. And if God was really good to her, she'd be able to discern which outbuilding went with which house.

She was toying with the notion of a dissertation exploring the ways masters and slaves used space. European settlers tended toward orderly arrangements of outbuildings, arranged around an open area for outdoor work like soapmaking or blacksmithing. Their African slaves had brought with them different notions of how life should be organized. This site could possibly enable her to look at two plantation complexes from two different periods in the same field trip, which could be quite a time-saver. Faye didn't know any graduate students who weren't all about getting their work done and getting the hell out of school.

She and Nina had spent January poring over earlier archaeological reports and histories of the site. They'd spent February digging test pits and developing a plan for a more detailed investigation. The Feds had liked their proposal for follow-up work, so Dauphine had joined them in March, and they'd all been hard at work for two months. Faye was proud of the things they'd gotten done this semester. The summer should be even better, except for the distinct risk of sunstroke.

As if to make up for Nina's easygoing nature, Dauphine existed only to embrace life's oddities. She eschewed practical field clothes in favor of flowing, wide-legged pants and colorful cotton blouses. Fuchsia, lime, scarlet, lavender—if Faye found herself craving an afternoon nap, she could just look at Dauphine for a caffeine-free pick-me-up.

No matter what neon color Dauphine was wearing, her braids were always wrapped neatly in a sky-blue scarf. The happy color flattered her praline-colored skin and framed an extraordinary pair of eyes. They were green, like Joe's, but they looked nothing like Joe's eyes. His eyes were a clear emerald, while Dauphine's were a milky green, the color of slow-moving swamp water. They were wide and calm, yes, but not placid.

Faye didn't think that Dauphine's eyes missed much. They gave the impression that she was cataloging everything she saw, because it was all useful. In Faye's limited understanding, a voodoo mambo was a scholar of nature and a minister to humans in all their frailty. She suspected that Dauphine was very good at whatever it was a mambo did.

She was a damn fine shovel bum, as well. Faye knew her team was top-notch, but the project timetable, like all project timetables, required the team to do the impossible. Faye thought that this team could actually pull it off.

The pre-Civil War foundations they were hoping to find had eluded them, so far, but some interesting things had turned up nonetheless. These finds hardly filled Faye's cupped hands—two hundred years is a long time—but they hinted at something more surviving beneath the park's neatly manicured grass. Among the fragments of pottery had been a bit of transfer-printed British pearlware, chipped and polished into a neat disk. Faye thought it might have been used as a counter for the African game mancala. They'd also found two pink marbles nearby, both made out of...well...marble, as well as a silver coin with a hole drilled through it.

She knew that wearing a silver coin tied around the neck was thought to ward off evil in African-American culture. Mancala was also rooted in African culture, though it had spread into general use. The marbles, like the mancala counter, could have been used by adult or child, as a mere entertainment or as part of a gambling game.

In a time when material goods were hard to come by, any of these objects would have been special possessions. The possibility that she was looking at someone's cache of treasured items, scattered through the soil by the blade of a plow, made Faye eager to get to work every day.

Faye hoped there was something fascinating waiting for her, buried, and not just because she was a history nut. This was her first actual job as a professional archaeologist who wasn't associated with the university. When the job announcement popped up in her e-mail, the salary had been big enough to make Faye gasp for breath. It might not be a lot of money to some people but, by an archaeologist's standards, the federal government paid very well.

Dr. Magda Stockard-McKenzie, Faye's graduate advisor, had listened carefully to Faye's arguments for taking a couple of semesters off from school. The job paid well. The work could strengthen her dissertation considerably. It paid well. A job as principal investigator would look just beautiful on her résumé. It paid well. Good performance on a federal job could open doors that would affect her entire career. And it paid well.

Magda agreed that it made sense for Faye to take the spring and summer semesters to manage this job, then re-enroll in the fall. Actually, she had said, "Shit, Faye. I don't see a down side to this idea. Why are you asking me? If you were stupid enough to pass this up, you wouldn't want *me* on your dissertation committee. I'd vote you down in a heartbeat."

So Faye was on her own, without Magda or the university to back her up, and she was giddy with the power of it…when she wasn't queasy over the idea of screwing up a project this important to her career.

Monday's work hadn't been nearly as efficient as she'd hoped. The morning had gone well, but she'd lost the afternoon to tragedy. Well, not the whole afternoon. Dauphine had gotten a lot done, while her boss Faye was busy talking about possible murder with Detective Jodi. Nina, too, had been busy doing other things, like exercising her First Amendment right to rally the populace with incendiary words.

Faye glanced around a park that would be deserted until midmorning when the first steamboat disgorged a load of sightseers at the levee. There was a real possibility that her team might get some work done today.

Matt, whose ranger job didn't seem to give him a lot to do when he wasn't conducting tours of the battlefield, ambled over to watch them work. Faye was gratified to see that having a spectator didn't affect her workers' pace a bit.

"Got any idea what y'all are looking for?"

Faye tried to answer without slowing her own pace, hoping to set a good example for the others. It didn't work, so she set her trowel aside and gave Matt her full attention. The events of the day before had been hard on him, and they clearly still weighed on his mind.

"You know where they found the foundations of the Rodriguez house, back in the eighties?" She pointed to an open piece of ground nearby, set in an L-shaped grove of ancient live oaks. "We have some drawings of the house from the time of the battle or just after it—"

Matt was nodding his head as if he wanted her to get to the point.

"I'm sorry, you already know that. You've got copies of the drawings in the visitor's center. You know Latour's and Laclotte's drawings? They've been really useful. Those two guys headed up Jackson's field engineers and, in those days, there wasn't much difference between an engineer and an architect. When they drew a picture of a house, they got the details right. If only they weren't such good draftsmen…"

Faye was still crouched in her unit, because she figured that standing up to talk would be too comfortable, and she wanted to finish quickly and get back to work. Also, she was hoping the park ranger would take the hint and go away.

Matt, ever-anxious to learn more about this spot of ground where he spent his days, didn't seem to have an endless amount of work like Faye's. Or if he did, it wasn't calling him.

He squatted down to hear her better. "How can being a good draftsman be a bad thing? There's no other way to get the kind of detail those guys could draw, not when you're talking about a time before photography."

"Yeah, but I wish they hadn't been so persnickety about perspective. Both of them drew the Rodriguez house from a spot between the house and the river, because these houses always faced the river. That means that the house itself obscures most of the area behind it. We have eyewitness accounts and some other documents that may not be real accurate, but we don't really know whether any outbuildings stood here. There could've been a smokehouse or a privy or slave quarters in this very spot. Or there could've been nothing. We won't know until we look."

A police car pulled into the parking lot, and Jodi got out. Matt rose to his feet, mumbling, "Thanks for explaining things, Faye."

He seemed to expect the detective to be looking for him, and he was right. Jodi slammed the car door, looked around, and started walking toward Matt without even stopping to talk to the rangers in the visitor's center. The woman was clearly on a mission. She beckoned to Matt, and they found a private spot under a shade tree on the far side of the reconstructed rampart.

Faye couldn't hear them, and there was no reason for her to want to know what they were discussing, other than sheer nosiness. She stretched her legs for a minute, preparing to crouch down and got back to work, when Nina popped up out of her unit like a bespectacled prairie dog.

"Know what I heard about Matt?"

Was workaholic Nina actually offering to spread some gossip? Within the past twenty-four hours, Nina had sprouted an over-charming ex-boyfriend, passionate political views, and now an unsuspected appetite for dishing the dirt. And Faye had thought the woman was only interested in dirt from an archaeological standpoint.

Faye was human, and there is a reason that people have been gossiping since somebody told Hera that Zeus was running around on her with a heifer. Other people's frailties were endlessly fascinating.

"What did you hear? Look at that man's baby face. He hasn't lived long enough to have a sordid past."

"Exactly. He hasn't had time to build a career, either, but look what he does for a living."

"Um…he's a park ranger. Am I missing something here?"

"Park ranger jobs are hard to get. The pay's good, and government benefits are amazing."

Faye knew what she paid for the shoddy coverage offered by her student health insurance policy. "Now I'm jealous."

"Yeah, me too. It's not just the perks, either. Lots of people want to work in New Orleans. Rookies usually have to start at a park that's three hundred miles from nowhere. And this job's especially nice, because it's not like Matt's out hiking in the Rockies, hauling injured hikers off a mountainside. He gives short tours to lazy tourists who don't want to walk far. There aren't any hills to climb or wild animals to worry about. In between tours, he sits in the air conditioned visitor's center."

"So you're saying that people Matt's age have to wait in line for a job like his."

"Yep."

"What do you think he did? Bribe somebody?"

"Heck, no. He grew up in the same kind of middle-class neighborhood I did…well, it *was* middle-class before Katrina made it a flooded-out hellhole. You saw it. The same middle-class people are living there now, except they're living in trailers instead of nice houses. Anyway, Matt's people didn't have enough money for a bribe, but it didn't take money to get him this job."

Now Nina was messing with her. She was spinning this story for all it was worth, egging Faye on to ask for more rumors and innuendo. But like anybody else, Faye knew how to play the gossip game. To get the good dirt, you had to make the person who held it feel important. You had to make her *want* to give it to you.

"So what did Matt and his people do? Did somebody sleep with a government official?"

There. Faye figured *that* question ought to get Nina's gossip-spreading juices flowing. And it did.

"Yeah. Sort of. Married people sleep together, don't they?"

"Usually."

"Well, Matt's father is related somehow to a woman whose step-daughter is married to Matt's boss' boss. Also, I think their ancestors served in the same Confederate regiment."

Only in some parts of the American South would this statement have made any sense whatsoever. The upshot was, though, that Matt enjoyed a cushy position because of who he was and who his family knew. Family connections were important, no matter where you went, but only in New Orleans was a man likely to be acquainted with his fifth cousin, once removed.

"No wonder Matt has the face of a choir boy," Faye observed as she lowered herself into the excavation. "He's led a sheltered life. His family has always taken care of him."

"Maybe a little too much." Nina stepped into her own unit. "But they couldn't shield him from the turmoil of the past three years. Matt lost loved ones in the storm. He almost lost his parents. He would have, if the rescuers had been any slower in coming."

Twenty minutes later, Faye watched Matt walk back to the visitor's center by a circuitous path that came nowhere near her work site. More than once, he rubbed the heel of his hand across his face, the way men do when they don't want anybody to know they're crying.

Faye had watched Jodi spend the past twenty minutes reading all the educational placards in the vicinity of the excavation where she and Nina and Dauphine were piling up the backdirt. It was now straight-up noon, and Faye had a sneaking suspicion that the detective wanted to talk to her and that she was just killing time until Faye sent her crew off to find some lunch.

Faye's hunch was right. Immediately after Nina and Dauphine went to fetch their sack lunches from the project trailer, Jodi approached Faye with an invitation. "There's a greasy spoon a couple of miles down St. Bernard Highway that has a cheap lunch plate. How do you feel about po-boys?"

"Since I got here, I've tried just about every variety, and I've loved them all. How do the bakeries around here get that crisp crust and still leave the bread soft on the inside?"

Faye was using a hose, some foamy soap, and a fingernail brush to get the worst of the dirt off her hands. It wasn't working.

"Beats me. Something in the water, maybe? So…you wanna do lunch?"

"Police business?"

"Heck, no. Working all the time makes a girl old fast. Oh, maybe I know something about yesterday's bones that might get an archaeologist's attention…"

She grinned at Faye's obvious interest, and kept talking. "Besides, I can always use a good woman friend. I've got me a lot of friends but most of them are dumb as a post, which you're not. I love 'em and all, but I can only spend so much of my life talking about nothing but liquor and pretty men. I mean, they're two of my favorite subjects, but—"

Joe had been standing nearby, slowly pouring water out of the paper cup in his hand and watching where it flowed. Faye had no idea why he was doing that, but Joe had a reason for everything he did. Dauphine was standing a few feet away, too far to be standing *with* Joe but too close to pretend that she was looking at anything beyond a dark and handsome man who had a strange obsession with wet dirt. Faye wasn't sure what she thought about that.

When Joe noticed Jodi, he turned his attention away from the mud he was making and walked over to greet her. Wiping a hand on the rag hanging out of his back pocket, he shook her hand, then turned his head to ask, "Ready for lunch, Faye?"

Jodi's mouth was saying, "Oh, if you already have plans…", but her eyes were fastened on Joe. He elicited that response from most women, even those who claimed they didn't want to talk about pretty men quite all the time.

Faye had been looking forward to a few minutes alone with her fiancé, but Jodi knew exactly how to pique her interest. Faye really, really wanted to know what the police had learned about the dead woman.

She and Joe were going to spend the rest of their lives together. What was one hour more or less? Of course, that was how married couples woke up after decades together and realized they didn't know each other any more. Her pre-wedding nerves jangled a bit, but she ignored them.

"Oh, no, you're welcome to join us, Jodi. Let me introduce you to my fiancé, Joe Wolf Mantooth."

Joe wiped his hand again before offering it to Jodi in greeting. "Nice to meet you. Faye told me…well, I heard you both had a tough afternoon yesterday." He jerked his head in the direction of the parking lot. "Let me meet you two at the car. I need to wash some more of this dirt off my hands." He moved quickly toward the park's public rest rooms with his long, deliberate strides.

Faye needed to go wash another layer of grime off her own hands, too, but she waited to do that just long to whisper, "Yes, he's pretty. And he's not dumb as a post, either. But he *is* mine."

Chapter Ten

Joe hadn't said much during lunch. He was naturally quiet. He also liked people, and he liked hearing what they had to say more than he liked to talk. But mostly, a large portion of his attention was being devoted to ciphering out how their food was prepared.

Joe was an artist in the kitchen and, throughout lunch, Faye had enjoyed watching him tear off one piece of bread at a time, just so he could watch the crust shatter. He had put each piece in his mouth and sat there for a time without chewing, Faye figured that had been enough time for him to figure out the ingredients and their proportions. She was pretty sure that Joe had the equivalent of a gas chromatograph in his mouth.

Tearing each piece slowly gave him a good look at the texture. With Joe's kitchen expertise, that texture probably told him how long the dough was kneaded, and how long it was left to rise. Faye was confident that, when she got home, she'd be able to have New Orleans-style French bread any time she wanted it, because Joe would have figured out the bakers' secrets. And she expected to want some of this bread pretty darn often, because it was delicious.

Jodi had frittered away most of their lunch talking about good liquor and pretty men, without sharing whatever it was she'd learned that she thought would be so fascinating to an archaeologist. Faye hadn't minded. Jodi wasn't the only one who didn't have enough good women friends in her life. Faye could use some more of those, too—the kind who could talk about science as easily as they could talk about the opposite sex, intriguing though that opposite sex might be. And Jodi could certainly steer a frivolous conversation around a hairpin turn and onto serious topics with lightning speed, when it suited her.

"I only came out to the park this morning because I wanted to talk to that cute little ranger, Matt. Well, I also had something to show you, but I'll get to that."

Somehow, Faye had begun to doubt it.

"I came to see Matt," Jodi chattered on with a vivacity that shook her golden-brown curls, "because I don't like my witnesses wandering away when I'm about ready to ask them some questions. I wanted to tell him so, face-to-face."

Jodi always talked with her hands, but this seemed to be a point she wanted to *really* emphasize, because she put down her sandwich to free up her right hand for gestures. "Also, I wanted to ask the man those questions he cheated me out of yesterday by sneaking away. Tell you what, though—I got more than I came for. For sure. Turns out that he's related to the dead woman we found. If I'd known that, I'd have been a little more delicate about telling him the victim's name."

Poor Matt. That explained the tears.

"Who was she?"

"Her name was Michele Broussard, but he told me that people called her Shelly. They were third cousins, and she was apparently several years older, but they'd spent some time together when they were growing up. Families around here sort of… sprawl. You don't see all your kinfolk all the time, because you just can't. Not when there's two hundred and fifty of them. But still, you know who they are and you have a shared history. Matt took her death hard."

Faye remembered how Matt had drifted away from the crime scene. "Do you think maybe he suspected it was her, all along?"

"No real reason for him to think so. Not that I know of, anyway. Her home address is in Lakeview. I have no idea how she—or her body—came to be in the Lower Nine. Neither did

Matt. So how could he possibly have expected that skeleton to be his cousin?"

Jodi took a big bite out of her po-boy. "Still, imagine you had a family member who was still missing. How would it feel to know that there'd been a body in that house all the time that you were living in your crummy FEMA trailer, somewhere down St. Bernard Highway? You'd have to wonder if that nameless pile of bones had been your cousin Shelly. Or whether Shelly's bones were lying in another pile of garbage, somewhere else in the city."

"Have you found out anything else?"

"Only that you probably know more of Shelly's friends. Besides Matt, I mean."

Joe laid down a French fry and leaned forward, asking the first direct question he'd delivered since they sat down to eat. He didn't like it when trouble came anywhere near Faye.

"Why do you think Faye might know the dead woman's friends? Faye's only been here a couple of months."

"Because Shelly was an archaeologist, like Faye. She worked in this area—even helped out on one project at the battlefield—and New Orleans is a tight-knit place for a town this size. If Faye has ever met any local archaeologists—on this trip, at professional meetings, in school, whenever—then the odds are decent that they knew Shelly."

"For example…" Jodi picked up her purse and poked around, looking for her wallet. "…Matt tells me that Shelly and Nina once worked together on a dig in the Quarter. They may have been undergrads together. Shelly was, oh, maybe two or three years behind Nina."

Thinking of what it would be like for Nina when she found out, Faye had a queasy moment. She always felt like that when she was smacked up against the head by the fact that death really happened, and that it happened to people like her.

Jodi laid some money on the table, next to the bill, and Faye moved to do the same, but there was way too much money already there.

"Oh, you don't need to cover our lunch…" Faye began, as Joe started to push Jodi's money back in her direction. It had taken quite some talking on Faye's part before Joe could be convinced to let Faye pay her own way. Ever. He was not going to take well to the notion of Jodi treating both of them.

The waitress walked by the table and Jodi handed her the money, saying, "I'll need a receipt."

Then she turned to Faye and Joe and waved a hand at both of them. "Settle down. It's on the department. This was a job interview."

Faye looked at Joe as if she expected him to express some kind of desire to be a policeman, because Jodi couldn't possibly be talking about her.

Pocketing the receipt, Jodi said, "I remembered what you said about working for your sheriff friend as a consultant. Well, I don't have any work for either of you at the moment, but it occurs to me that I might. I've got a dead archaeologist, who worked at the same place as you, Faye, and who knew some of the people working there with you. I don't know diddly-squat about archaeology. My gut tells me that I'd better start filling out some consultant-hiring paperwork."

Faye settled back in her chair. She wasn't often completely surprised, but she sure hadn't seen this one coming.

Jodi kept making her recruitment speech. "I don't know quite how just yet, but I'm pretty sure I'm going to need the expertise of an archaeologist. Maybe two." She aimed a nod in Joe's general direction. "You are studying archaeology, aren't you?"

Joe nodded.

"Okay, then. You're both smart, and you've got experience in this kind of thing. The department don't pay much, but it's something. I've never known anybody that had so much money that they couldn't use a few more dollars. Keep a spot on your schedules open for me."

Faye remembered the size of the consultant's fee that Sheriff Mike had paid her. It might not seem like much to Jodi, but there had certainly been enough dollars in that paycheck to get the attention of a poor and hungry graduate student. Faye liked getting paid for doing something interesting.

Jodi was scratching around in her purse again, even though she'd already paid the bill and tipped the waitress. It was time to get back to work, but Faye remembered that the detective had said that she wanted to show something to Faye, and she didn't want Jodi to forget. Curiosity had kept Faye awake on many a night, so she'd learned the hard way to follow up on things like dangling loose ends.

She touched Jodi on the arm to get her attention. "Didn't you have something you wanted to show me?"

"Several things, actually. I was saving them for last. Now I've lost 'em. They're somewhere in this bottomless pit I call a purse." Jodi's arm disappeared into the handbag up to her elbow. "Oh, yeah. I stuck them all in my wallet…so I could find 'em." She sighed and rolled her eyes. "I am all the time hiding things from myself."

Jodi retrieved several pieces of paper and handed them over without a word, one at a time, with an expectant face that said she wanted to see what Faye made of them. They were all photocopies of papers that looked ragged and creased. The letters and images on them had been blurred by dampness, but they were mostly still legible.

"Did you find these with the body?"

"Yep. Damn, my people are good. Look at what they salvaged." Jodi tucked the toothpick she'd been chewing on even further back in her mouth. She leaned forward to admire her technicians' work a little more.

"How is that possible after all this time?"

"We found the originals in the pocket of her size two jeans, folded up and zipped into a plastic coin purse that turned out to be pretty darn waterproof. I'm thinking that Shelly was trying to protect them. Most everything in this town is always at least a little damp, and you can multiply that about a million times for the week of the storm."

She pointed to blurry, discolored spots on each piece of paper. "See? A teeny bit of water oozed in around the coin purse's zipper, and it did its damage for certain sure. My lab had a devil of a time making these things semi-legible, but they managed. If Shelly had stuck this stuff, unprotected, in her pocket, my techs would've been stuck working with nothing but woodpulp."

She kept doling out the papers to Faye, one at a time. Joe leaned over Faye's shoulder to get a better look.

The first paper was a photocopy of a list of names—apparently surnames—that had been written on lined paper. They were still decipherable, despite some serious blurring, because the handwriting had been large, round, and clearly inscribed. The first and third names on the list, Landry and Guidry, caught her eye, as did the last one, Broussard. The intervening names—Bergeron, McCaffrey, Johnson, Martin, Dupuit, and Prejean—meant nothing.

"Shelly's name was Broussard, right? Matt's is Guidry?" Faye searched for something familiar in the other names. "And Charles' is Landry?"

"Yep. You've gotta remember that those names are all a little bit like Smith and Jones in these parts. So are some of the others. But it sure does seem like a coincidence that one of those names belongs to Shelly, and another belongs to Charles, who worked with her, and another belongs to Matt, whose girlfriend works with them both. This is a teeny-tiny town, in a lot of ways."

"Do the other names mean anything?" Joe asked.

"Not that we can tell."

Jodi handed over another page, very similar to the first. The original had been a piece of lined paper, just like the one Faye held. Again, there was nothing on the paper but a list of names.

Faye squinted at the list. "They're the same names. Just in a different order."

"Exactly. And…?"

"The handwriting is different…" Joe offered.

It wasn't just different. It was markedly different. If Faye hadn't just read through the same list of names, she might never have deciphered some of them, written as they were in a cramped and angular hand. She looked over the list to see whether there was an obvious reason that the names' order had been scrambled.

Had they been alphabetized?

Johnson, Guidry, Broussard, McCaffrey, Dupuit, Bergeron, Prejean, Martin, and Landry.

Nope.

"Any ideas? Why are they different? And why did Shelly need both of them badly enough to zip them up in that little bag?" Jodi asked.

Faye shrugged. "I've got nothing."

"Well, I have," Jodi said as she triumphantly held out another photocopy, this time of a newspaper clipping. The original had been tattered and dirty. Its paper had been torn in several places and pieced back together, and one corner couldn't be salvaged. Most of the print on the copy was badly blurred, but a photograph was featured with the article, and its bold geometry was unmistakable.

Faye scrutinized the clipping. When it was first published, this photo had cast a tragic pall on the front pages of newspapers all over the country—probably all over the world. There was no mistaking the broad curve and high contrast coloration of the Superdome. There was also no mistaking the floodwaters that surrounded it. And there was no doubt about why this bleak picture put an incongruous smile on Jodi's face.

"She survived the storm."

Jodi responded with a quick nod, but she didn't say anything. She was waiting for more. What was it? Faye understood what the photo showed. But what did it mean? Then the answer hit her.

"This shows us that Shelly survived for a good while—long enough for a photographer to get on a helicopter and take this picture, and long enough for a newspaper to print and distribute it. That was a matter of several days, I'd say, and we'll know for sure as soon as we find the newspaper where this article appeared. And she didn't spend those days trapped in a flooded house, waiting to die. She went somewhere and bought a newspaper. Or somebody did."

Faye drummed her fingers on the table's wooden top. "That means that it was probably several days after the storm before she went to the flooded-out house where we found her. Then she...what? Drowned? It's possible, if she didn't swim well, or if she hit her head and fell in. But by that time, she wasn't dealing with waves and wind and a deadly current. Just oily, filthy, stinking water that wasn't moving a bit. You can drown in that, but not as easily. And if she didn't drown, then my notion that somebody brought her dead body to that house and hid it there doesn't seem so nutty after all."

"Oh, she didn't drown. I forgot to tell you that part. The medical examiner said that he could tell from the condition of the bones of Shelly's neck that she'd been strangled to the point that her neck was broken. So you were right. That's one reason I wanted you for a consultant—because people with your analytical skills and attention to detail are right a whole lot of the time. But what else does this clipping tell us? And don't forget that this is still a job interview. Dazzle me with your deductive powers. No, wait. Let Joe do it."

Joe didn't even hesitate. While Faye was talking, he'd been thinking. As usual.

"Well, somebody prob'ly saw her after the storm. She had to get the newspaper from somewhere, and there's not many places it could have come from. Wasn't any place to buy it in the city. So either she bought it from a self-serve rack somewhere out of town, or somebody from out-of-town sold it to her, or else somebody around here gave her the paper or the clipping."

Faye knew it was typical that her observation had to do with logistics and timing, while Joe's had to do with people and how they related to the world.

She also knew she should have let Joe finish his thought, since he didn't talk all that much, but she couldn't help herself. She asked Jodi, "Do you know which newspaper it came from?"

Jodi shook her head and said "No, but it won't be hard to find that out." She kept looking expectantly at Joe. "Go on."

"That's about all I can think of," he said, "except that maybe other people saw her, too. We might could even find some of those people and they could maybe tell us something about how she died."

"Or why," Faye interjected again, ruefully realizing that, once again, Joe was thinking of people and she was thinking of reasons. She then reflected that if Joe intended to talk at any time, for the rest of his life, then his wife-to-be would be smart to buy herself a muzzle—before he bought one and strapped it on her.

"Yep. Joe only got one thing wrong." Jodi's voice was decisive, maybe even smug.

Faye raised an eyebrow. Joe's logic had sounded pretty good to her, and logic was Faye's life.

"You know the part where you said '*we*' could find one of the people who saw Shelly, and they might tell '*us*' something about what happened to her?"

They nodded.

"Well, there shouldn't be any 'we' or 'us' in that sentence. Leave us law enforcement types to do that kind of work. You two just sit tight in case I have some questions that I need an archaeologist to answer."

She handed over the last two pieces of paper. They were copies of aerial photographs. Faye recognized Lake Pontchartrain and the distinctive arrow of the 17th Street Canal piercing its way into the city. "Lakeview?"

Jodi nodded.

"Look at all that water," Joe said in a hushed voice.

He was right. The dark and tragic stain of a massive flood covered most of the photo. The other photo of Lakeview showed regular, everyday, dry city streets full of cars, signifying that day-to-day life was proceeding as usual. There were no tarps on roofs, nor any swaths of empty land, where the houses that should have been there had been washed away. Faye was pretty sure that this photo had been taken before the storm.

"Why was Shelly carrying before-and-after photos of Lakeview?" Joe wanted to know. "You found her in the Lower Nine."

"But you said her home address was in Lakeview. Didn't you?" Faye pointed out.

Jodi nodded. "These photos may be an indication that she intended to go to Lakeview. They might show us that a mugger or rapist or killer brought her to the Lower Nine against her will. Or they might just mean that she was carrying a depressing souvenir showing what had happened to her neighborhood."

"Of course, she came to the Lower Nine against her will," Faye said, surprised by her certainty when she really had no facts to go on.

Jodi looked surprised, too. "How can you be so sure?"

"Did she have family in Lakeview?"

A shadow fell on Jodi's face. "Yes. Her parents. They both drowned."

"Then by the time Shelly laid her hands on this photo, it had been days since the storm and she hadn't seen her parents. She was found deep in the middle of a huge area of destruction. A woman doesn't set out to enter a disaster zone alone for just any old reason. I think Shelly was out there violating the curfew because she was looking for her mom and dad. I think she was going home." Faye still felt certain of her utterly unprovable premise. "Wouldn't you be?"

Faye studied the photo, wishing for her magnifier. She'd spent a lot of time poring over aerial photography, because it was incredibly useful in archaeology. Old structures, even entire ancient cities, that were invisible at ground level could be detected with the naked eye on an aerial photograph. Satellite photography gave the same information at a scale that had revealed entire trade networks around some of those vanished cities, in the form of long-gone roads.

God doesn't draw in straight lines, but people do. Human scars on the land take a very long time to heal.

Did this photo show something else? Would something hidden in this scene help Jodi find out what happened to Shelly? She hoped so. The scars Shelly's death had left on the hearts of her friends and family would also be slow to heal.

Chapter Eleven

The afternoon hadn't been pretty. Jodi had wanted to talk to Faye's workers. At the very least, she'd wanted to find out how well either of them might have known Shelly. If, while they were chatting, one of them mentioned something that might shed some light on her death, so much the better. As it turned out, Jodi got lucky on both counts, but Faye had been left to pick up the emotional pieces.

Dauphine had been a woman on a mission when she returned from her interview with Jodi, packing up her threadbare knapsack and talking all the while. "That poor child. She worked beside me for weeks, right here at this battlefield. Such a sweet spirit she had, and she's been wandering all this time. Not even a candle burned for her dear soul. Well, I'll burn one every night for a year. If God wills it, I'll burn 'em."

Dauphine was out of sight before Faye even realized that the woman hadn't asked permission to leave work early. Or maybe Dauphine wasn't leaving work, from her point of view. Maybe she was just shifting gears from field technician to voodoo mambo a few hours earlier than usual.

Nina's interview with Jodi left the archaeologist ashen-faced. In fact, Jodi had walked her back to the excavation and handed her over to Faye personally, because she'd felt Nina was too upset to be alone.

Faye's experience in dealing with employee crises was limited. She had no doubt that she was born to be a scientist, not a manager, but this was clearly no time to be cold and business-like. She'd spent the past months becoming friends with Nina, which probably broke every rule in the boss' handbook, but when your friend has suffered a painful loss, you take her someplace private and listen to her.

"Come on, Nina. Let's go for a walk."

The park's loop road was such a good place to take a walk that the locals seemed to use the place for a private track. Its broad sweeping curve was dotted with joggers every day, in the cool of the mornings and evenings. Faye figured their tax money kept the park service going, so it was nice for them to get that little bonus. Walking its mile-and-a-half length should give Nina enough time to pull herself together.

Nina had looked at her feet as she walked, hiding eyes that were pink and watery with grief. "Shelly was a sophomore when I was a senior. We were roommates that year in one of those 'dorms-for-geeks.' You know…the ones where they have quiet hours so that people who want to study can hear themselves think? But Shelly wasn't a geek. She was plenty smart, sure, but she was fun, too, the way Detective Bienvenu is fun."

Nina tried to smile, but couldn't pull it off. "We'd be studying together and Shelly would lift her head up from her book and tell me one of her silly stories. Those stories made my study time a lot more pleasant. I always wished I could think of something funny to say back, but I never could. I don't know why I thought I needed to do that. Maybe to balance things out so that I wasn't always on the receiving end of her friendship. But I'm just not fun that way."

Nina waved a hand at Faye, so she wouldn't feel compelled to argue over whether or not Nina was fun.

"Shelly introduced me to her friends," she continued, "and they liked me because she liked me. I dated one of them for a couple of years, in fact. Charles. You met him yesterday."

Faye nodded and tried to think of something to say other than, "Nice guy." She couldn't. It was hard to know what to say to someone who was hurting so much.

"I've spent plenty of time in school learning about archaeology, but that year with Shelly was an education in getting along with people. I watched her, and I learned how to make conversation just for the pleasure of talking to someone. I learned that you don't have to be all that gorgeous or elegant for people to like you. Shelly wasn't pretty, and she wasn't ugly. She was just a plain-faced girl who was beautiful when she smiled."

"Did you two keep in touch after you graduated?"

"Yeah. Well, at first, Shelly was the one who did all the keeping in touch. It was that social skills thing again. I missed her, but I was busy with work and my new apartment and other stuff that I thought was important, and I always let way too much time go by before I called her. Shelly could've been mad about it, and that would have been the end of our friendship. But she kept calling until I got it into my thick head that friendship is important stuff, too. It took some doing but, after that, we managed to grab lunch or a drink every month or so. Just to catch up."

Faye felt that way about her friendship with Magda. They were both chasing their own tails all the time, trying to squeeze their bottomless-pit jobs and their adorable but time-consuming men into days that only came in twenty-four-hour sizes. Adding friendship to that mix sometimes seemed like an impossible feat, but Faye knew that friends were necessary for happiness. Sanity, even.

She and Magda saw each other at work regularly, but as for having lunch or a drink…that happened about as often as Nina's visits with Shelly. Once a month, if they were lucky.

"Since…since the storm," Nina went on, "I've missed her so much. When they don't find a body, you always hope…or you wonder. I don't know what you call that sense of waiting. But the sense of death…the sense of something ending…I just learned today that you don't really get that until you know, without a doubt, that a person's really gone."

"You didn't hear from her after Katrina hit? After the storm?" Faye asked, then she stopped herself. This would have been an inane question if she hadn't just learned from Nina that Shelly survived the storm for a matter of days. Nina didn't seem to find it inane at all.

"No. The cell towers were down. The phone lines were out. The water and the curfew made it impossible to get around the city. It was weeks before I knew for sure where all the people I cared about had gone, and they were flung all over the damn country. So it was a long time before I gave up hope that Shelly would show up one day and tell me that she'd—oh, I don't know—been staying with an aunt in Baton Rouge. Or working in Shreveport. Anything but this. She's been lying dead all this time, and not so very far from here."

Faye found the image supremely unsettling, and she didn't even know the dead woman. She changed the subject. "Was Shelly still in graduate school?"

"No. She ran out of money and didn't want to take out any more loans. It's not easy to make a living in archaeology without a Ph.D.—"

"I'm not even sure you can make a living *with* a Ph.D."

Nina flashed her first real smile since she'd heard the news about Shelly. "I'm not listening to you. I'm entertaining fantasies of eventually driving a car that's not old enough to start first grade."

"Mine's old enough to drive. No. It's worse than that. My car's old enough to drink."

Faye looked out over the battlefield, which was a bad idea. This was not an easy place to quash eerie thoughts of vivacious Shelly lying dead until she was nothing but bones. The road under her feet circled a killing ground where 2,000 British soldiers had once lain dead or wounded. Somewhere near here was the mass grave where they'd been dumped. How long would it have taken to dig 2,000 graves? How much land would have been consumed? And what in hell had been so important that it was worth the loss of so many lives?

"What kind of work did Shelly do after she left school?"

"She got a job at an engineering firm—the one where Charles works, actually. He's already made manager there, over the entire engineering department. That was just three years ago, and they're already talking about promoting him again."

Faye thought she detected more than a trace of pride on Nina's face. Charles didn't look much older than Nina—mid- to late-thirties, maybe—so he *was* rather young for such a high-level job, but Faye had gotten the impression he was capable of serious ambition.

"Anyway, after Shelly started working with Charles, she introduced us. The firm doesn't keep many archaeologists on staff, but they have a few to help with environmental impact statements and other projects that require an assessment of the cultural environment. She was even thinking about going back to school in civil engineering."

"Lord knows it would have paid better."

"No kidding. It would have only taken a couple of years, and the company would have paid for it. Shelly said that the two disciplines overlapped a lot. Civil engineers and archaeologists both need to know chemistry and physics and soil science. Shelly had learned a lot about aerial photography as an archaeologist, and she was a wizard at using GIS to put mapping information in order. All that work was a perfect fit with her engineering job. I'll never get to talk to her about it now, but I know it meant a lot to her to use those skills to save lives after Katrina."

Faye had been still staring at the quiet battlefield, but Nina's words made her whip her head around toward her distraught assistant. "After Katrina? You knew for sure that she was alive after the storm before Jodi told you? And you know where she was and what she was doing?"

"For a few days, yes. She was doing relief work at Zephyr Field. That's what I heard. I just told Detective Bienvenu about it. She said there wasn't anything in the missing persons file about any witnesses seeing Shelly alive during the first days after the storm. That may be. But I know some folks who saw her. They say she worked like a dog during those first days, helping save hundreds of people."

"How? Was she in a boat? Or one of the helicopters?"

"Nope. She was telling the boats and helicopters where to find people, so they could scoop 'em up before they drowned. She knew how to take the GPS information from an emergency cell phone call to figure out where the person was calling from. Then she could use a satellite image to show rescuers just where to go, so they could pluck the caller off a roof or out of the water. Those satellite photos were incredibly important. Street signs aren't much good when they're underwater. Or gone. Shelly worked day and night to get that information out to the rescuers."

Faye remembered how deep the water got in Chalmette. So much water had rushed through there, and it had done it so fast. She doubted a single street sign had been left standing.

Talking about Shelly seemed to be helping Nina's feelings. "She saved a lot of people. That's what makes the whole thing so damned sad. Her parents...their names were Dan and Aimee and they were such good-hearted people..." Nina swallowed hard. "Her parents drowned in their own attic, because nobody knew for sure where they were. Don't you know what Shelly asked every rescuer she saw? Everyone she talked to?"

Of course, Faye knew what Shelly had wanted so desperately to know.

Did you see my parents out there? Dan and Aimee Broussard? Did any of you see my parents?

"After the first days, even the hearsay petered out. Charles saw Shelly early on, but he lost track of her. The whole city was hell on earth, and I don't imagine it was any different for the rescuers. Later, when Shelly was listed as missing, I talked to everybody I knew who might have seen her there. Everybody."

Nina lifted her head and shoved her glasses back up her nose. Faye had seen Nina do archaeological research. She was a flippin' bulldog. If Nina were looking for a missing friend, Faye sure wouldn't want to get in her way. If Faye were ever missing, herself, she hoped Nina would be on her trail.

"I talked to some people who did rescue work with her— mostly engineers she knew from the office. Charles was one of them. They'd gathered someplace in Metairie that didn't flood, until they heard that rescuers were working at Zephyr Field, needing help they knew how to give. Once they heard that, they hustled their butts out there and got down to business right fast. You don't mess with an engineer who's on a mission. One of them had a company satellite phone. You know it was worth more than a pound of gold to rescuers working that week."

"What happened to Shelly after that?"

"I couldn't ever find anybody who knew. To hear people talk, she was there for days, then she just...wasn't. If I'd had to guess, I would have said that she went looking for her parents, but they lived in Lakeview. So why in heck has her body been lying in the Lower Ninth Ward all the time?"

Faye couldn't begin to answer her.

"Did Jodi show you the things found in Shelly's pocket? Photographs and a newspaper clipping and some lists of names?"

Nina nodded her head. "Detective Bienvenu wants me to tell her if I remember anything that'll tell her what it all meant, but I've got nothing."

Faye could tell that Nina was nearly talked out. As they rounded the final curve of the park's loop road, the temporary visitor's center came into view. Matt was walking out the door toward the levee, preparing to give yet another guided tour to yet another boatload of tourists.

Faye decided that Nina might be willing to answer one more nosy question. She nodded in Matt's direction. "Did you know that Matt and Shelly were cousins?"

"I did."

Nina's short answer and terse tone caught Faye's attention.

"Don't you like Matt?" The young man was so soft-spoken and inoffensive that Faye couldn't imagine why Nina's voice was so tight when she spoke of him.

"I don't know Matt well. He spent a good bit of time with Shelly, especially near the end, because he was dating someone she worked with. So was I, actually, but Charles didn't like to hang out with co-workers in his spare time, so I didn't know their crowd. Shelly, on the other hand, would hang out with anybody. When Matt started coming around her office, she made sure that he was part of her group of friends. She said it was nice to spend time with family, especially a cousin you knew when you were both kids."

Nina's tone was too careful. Why didn't she want to say whether Shelly liked Matt or not? Was she just being polite?

Good manners trumped just about anything in this part of the world. Faye knew people who would like an ax-murderer if he was polite. She decided she wanted to see what it would take to get Nina to say something about Matt as a person.

"So Shelly liked him."

"Shelly liked everybody."

Interesting. Nina had dodged the question a second time. Faye decided to let a little silence happen. Sometimes, a person would say whatever popped into her mind to make the silence go away. Nina's stiff body language and guarded voice told Faye that the woman had something to say. Soon enough, she said it.

"Shelly liked everybody," Nina repeated. "Matt was family, so I guess she loved him. But she did say he was weird."

Chapter Twelve

Faye had managed to salvage the rest of the workday by propping Nina up and telling her not to think, just to screen soil. Faye had always found repetitive, slow work quieted her mind. She considered it a form of meditation. This was a good thing, because a lot of archaeological work could be described in just that way. Repetitive and slow.

Much of Faye's life had been spent cleaning dirty little pieces of junk. No, make that dirty little pieces of *fragile* junk. Even in the field, where it was sometimes necessary to move dirt by the cubic yard, encountering an important find changed everything. When her excavating work called for precision, she was sometimes reduced to moving dirt with a sable-haired paintbrush, to avoid destroying something irreplaceable. Archaeologists who were capable of turning off a nattering brain and letting the work take its own pace were happy archaeologists.

Nina already looked less sad and stricken, as she ran soil through a screen designed to catch tiny artifacts that might otherwise be overlooked. Nina had shown a lot of talent for doing detailed work with her hands. Screening soil often made impatient Faye want to scream, but Nina seemed to be content enough, settling in for some quiet time with a pile of soil.

As Nina concentrated, she hummed quietly. Faye paused when she heard a familiar melody. Yes, the young woman was humming jazz standards. Nowhere but in New Orleans would Faye expect a 37-year-old to know "Basin Street Blues."

◇◇◇

The big excitement of the afternoon came when Dauphine uncovered several good-sized shards of pottery with an especially pretty Blue Willow design. The work team's voices carried across the flat, silent battlefield, drawing Joe from his explorations of Rodriguez Canal, which had traversed this ground for so long that it was already old when the War of 1812 roared through.

Even this find left Faye feeling distracted and depressed. All over town, Hurricane Katrina and the ensuing floods had left deposits of broken china and glass and…well, pretty much everything… that were slowly being covered over and forgotten. One day, archaeologists were going to treat that layer of soil as casually as, say, the people who had excavated blackened rocks at the ruins of Troy.

"Look!" the archaeologists had said as they peeled back another layer of Troy's history. "The city was destroyed by fire in thus-and-such a year."

Each scrap of new information on the fire had been published, proving one scholar's theory while obliterating another's. Much effort had been spent and many journal pages printed, arguing over the historical significance of the charred city, but the personal significance of the fire to the people who survived it had been almost completely overlooked by the scholars filling those pages.

The survivors had lost family members. They had lost friends. They had lost homes and possessions.

They had lost everything.

Faye was glad she wouldn't be around when scholars in another age started debating the question of what had really happened during the deluge that consumed New Orleans.

Faye's workers had left, but she was still lingering in the work trailer, straightening her office and putting her thoughts away for the day. She wasn't a bit surprised to see Jodi at the door.

Hardly raising her head from the odious clerical task of the moment—filing—Faye said, "I bet you are madder than a wet hen."

"Yes. Are you going to tell me why, so I don't have to make myself madder by saying it?"

"No problem. Glad to be of help. You're peeved because Shelly has been missing for years. There's a file on her at Missing Persons. We now know that people—we don't know how many people, but some—saw her alive during the rescue effort after the storm. Yet nothing in that file shows that Shelly survived Katrina, and you didn't have a clue until you found that raggedy newspaper clipping in her pocket."

"That pretty much says it all." Jodi sank into the low chair across from Faye's desk. "Now, does it necessarily mean that the investigators didn't do their jobs? Nope. Communications were wrecked for months. People were scattered all over the country. It's completely possible that the people who saw Shelly were never questioned. It's even possible some of them died that week, too. Nevertheless, now I've gotta try to track 'em down, years after the fact. Crap."

"Nina probably knows some people—"

"You trying to tell me how to do my job? Nina already gave me a list of folks who might know folks who saw Shelly before she died. One of them is a guy named Charles Landry."

Faye shrugged. "Is this the Charles that's Nina's ex-boyfriend?"

"Maybe you *should* try to tell me how to do my job. You got that information mighty fast."

Faye shrugged again.

Jodi shook her bangs out of her eyes. "Never mind. I can tell that you ask the right questions, because you think like an investigator."

She gestured around Faye's office at the clean trowel resting atop the bookshelf, the labeled boxes of finds, the reference books on the shelf, and the laboratory requisition forms stacked on the corner of her desk.

"You *are* an investigator. You just pack a shovel and a Ph.D., instead of a gun and a badge."

"No Ph.D. yet—" Faye started.

Jodi dismissed that detail with a waved hand.

"I couldn't possibly care less about whether you have a Ph.D. or not. What do you know about geographical techniques— GPS, aerial photograph analysis, stuff like that?"

"I've got a GPS that I use every day that I'm in the field. It makes my life a heckuva lot easier than it was just a few years ago. Before GPS, I had to use surveying equipment to keep records of my sampling sites. GPS is *so* much easier. As for aerial photos, I've taken two graduate classes on aerial photograph analysis. I'm trying to figure out a way to shoehorn that into my dissertation topic, somehow. It's not all that pertinent, but I really enjoy the work."

"Perfect. You're my new consultant. Expect me back here tomorrow, paperwork in hand."

Faye noticed that Jodi didn't ask her whether she wanted the job, nor whether she even had time to take it on.

Jodi kept talking, answering Faye's questions before she asked them.

"I just want to pick your brain right now. That's what a consultant's for. I won't mess with your work schedule, unless I just can't help it. We can talk after you quit work for the day or at lunchtime or whenever. I'm not so sure I have much need for your friend Joe, as much as I'd like more chances to get a look at him, but—"

Joe showed impeccable timing by sticking his head in the door. "Faye? You know how the drainage around here's been bothering me? The way the water flows *away* from the river?"

"Is that why you've been pouring water on the ground and watching it run? I thought that was strange."

Jodi's chair was more or less behind the open door. Joe clearly hadn't noticed her there, because Faye had never seen him talk this much in front of anybody but her.

"It *is* pretty weird," Joe said, not realizing that she'd been calling *him* strange, not the poor helpless water. It was probably better for domestic harmony to let him think so.

He brandished a text on the Battle of New Orleans.

"This book says that surface water around here has always drained away from the river, toward a swamp that used to be back there." He waved at the park boundary that paralleled the river. "You'd think water would have run right into that big old river over there, but it never did. I don't know why it didn't. That's just the way it is."

"I wondered where you went this morning. You've been to the bookstore?"

"Library. I drove by a couple of pumping stations while I was out there, too, and I drove right past a levee that some engineers were fixing up. You should see it, Faye. Big ol' machines driving big ol' slabs of sheet metal into the top of a big ol' levee, so they could make it even taller. And it was pretty darn high to begin with."

Two years before, Joe would have preferred an hour with a bear to an hour with a book that had the heft of the one in his hand. Now he'd just finished his second semester of college coursework. It was amazing what a few tutors could do for a man blessed with plenty of brains, but cursed with learning disabilities the size of boulders. A little healthy curiosity didn't hurt, either.

Faye had wondered why Joe was so worked up over the way water worked in New Orleans, until she gave the question a minute's thought. Joe was accustomed to intuitively understanding the way the natural world worked, but there was nothing intuitive about New Orleans' relationship with water. The city seemed to be founded on the proposition that water could be made to flow uphill.

He stood in the open door and waved at the reconstructed earthworks behind him.

"They built the rampart right next to that canal, because the water just made it that much harder for the British soldiers to get to the top of the big pile of dirt. Slowed 'em down. So it was that much easier to shoot them. Before that, the canal was a mill run. That has to mean the mill was turned with water coming *out* of the river, 'stead of into it. Musta been a sluicegate in the levee, or something. Then the water headed out there, toward that swamp that ain't there no more."

He pointed again at the stand of trees between them and St. Bernard Highway, but he never stopped talking.

"The canal and the earthworks went way into the swamp, back when Andrew Jackson was alive, but that end of the canal has been gone for years. Still, you know, I think I see something back there on this satellite picture. Earthworks, maybe. I think you and me should take a walk back there this evening and see what we can find."

He handed the photo to Faye, then he noticed Jodi. Within seconds, Joe had greeted her with a polite nod, excused himself, and left. Just because Joe had gained some confidence in his abilities didn't mean that he'd ever be comfortable talking shop in front of strangers.

"Okay," Jodi said. "So the pretty man thinks like an investigator, too."

She peered over Faye's shoulder with an expression that said she clearly saw nothing intelligible on Joe's small-scale photo. "It also seems that he's very, very good with aerial photograph interpretation. That's the last thing we know Shelly did. Also, the people who knew she was alive after the storm were all sitting side-by-side with her, using that self-same expertise. I think I can use Joe. Early tomorrow, I'll bring paperwork for both of you to sign."

She stood to leave, then turned back to Faye with a wolfish grin. "How do you think you two will blow those consultant's checks?"

Faye made a mental inventory of her to-be-bought list. It was long.

"My property taxes are due. I need to replumb my cisterns sometime. Those pipes are only, oh… 200 years old. They were built to last forever, but forever may have come. Oh, and I'd like to buy some more solar panels."

"Cisterns, taxes, solar panels…you know, none of that stuff sounds like any fun. Necessary, but not fun."

It had been so long since Faye wasted money on something fun, that it took her fifteen seconds to understand Jodi's point.

"I suppose you have some idea of how I should spend my ill-gotten gains?"

"If I had a boyfriend that looked like yours, I'd have a few ideas. Unexpected money should be spent on something fun, darlin'. Those checks that the department will be cutting you and Joe would pay for a long weekend in a very nice room in the Monteleone. Maybe not the bridal suite, but close."

Faye found herself entertaining some interesting ideas, in spite of herself. She told her miserly conscience to shut up so she could hear the woman talk.

"I'd eat at a different restaurant every night…if I were you… and I'd stick to the ones so old that they're haunted by the ghosts of dead chefs. Galatoire's. Antoine's. Arnaud's. Places like that. And I'd save one night to eat room service in that big old bed with that big young man."

Faye's attention was officially distracted from the threadbare condition of her pocketbook.

Jodi gave a quick nod, as if she were finished dangling temptation in front of her new employee, before delivering the *coup de grâce* almost as an afterthought.

"And I'd make damn certain sure I didn't drink any champagne that hadn't spent some time in a cave in France."

Faye found herself deeply committed to doing something financially rash.

◇◇◇

After Jodi closed the door behind her, Faye slumped back in her chair and thought of the unfinished work represented by every item in the office. She had an excavation to manage, data to interpret, a report to write…how was she going to do all that, while being at Jodi's beck and call? But how could she say no to this consulting job if it might uncover information that would bring Shelly's family peace? Or if it promised to bring her a weekend in paradise with Joe?

Faye could see that she'd be losing some sleep over the coming days—and nights—but she didn't mind. She loved her work. She also felt a real need to find out what happened to Shelly Broussard. And, come hell or high water—a terrible metaphor, given the situation—Faye intended to enjoy her time with Joe during his short visit.

Excerpt from *The Floodgates of Hell,*
The Reminiscences of Colonel James McGonohan
1876

It is a peculiarity of the human mind that we envision people from the past as quaint. It is difficult for me to imagine that men of my grandfather's time, in their powdered wigs and kneepants, carried the same senti-ments in their hearts that I have carried in mine over this long life. And someday, far into the twentieth cen-tury, my little grandson will be wearing his whiskers and waistcoat in a fashion that I cannot imagine, and I will seem no more real to him than a painted portrait.

A man cannot hold a mental image of his parents in a romantic embrace without wincing. The idea that his grandparents might once have burned with passion...why, that idea is incomprehensible.

As an engineer, I have an engrained need to under-stand how things work. Some of my colleagues limit their thirst for understanding to gears and pulleys and machines. I am a bit unusual in that I am drawn to the human machine and to history. (My dear wife would say that I am a bit unusual on the whole, but I have not invited her to contribute to this memoir.)

I am happiest when I stumble upon something that increases my understanding of people and things and of the ways they relate to one another. I truly want to understand my grandparents as human beings, rather than think of them as feeble folk who were never once young.

As an engineer in the exceedingly damp city of New Orleans, I find that my desire to understand the people of the past extends to the ways our fair city was raised out of the muck. I have done much read-ing on the schemes our forebears concocted to keep their feet dry. Our city was designed back in 1718 with ditches cut around every city block, in hopes that these small canals would keep the land drained. Alas, they merely served as stagnant receptacles for refuse—and worse—and the unpaved streets remained mud wallows.

While a young man, I listened to stories of life in our fair city during those long-ago, damp days. The citizens of New Orleans have always been intent on the enjoyment of pleasant society. Mere mud could not keep our convivial citizens from their balls and galas.

Before each such fête, I am told, the ladies donned their petticoats and ballgowns and delicate slippers. They displayed their finery in their own ballrooms for the gentlemen of their family to admire...then they doffed those delicate slippers and handed them to their servants. Next, they reached down and hiked their petticoats and ballgowns up above their knees, preparing to wade through streets that were often too muddy to admit a horse and buggy.

Trailing their servants and their escorts, these bare-legged ladies paraded in public in a condition that, at any other time, would have rendered them unfit for polite society. Even worse, it would have rendered them unmarriageable.

Upon achieving their destination, they were greeted with basins of water in which their grimy lower limbs were bathed snowy-white again. After a quick moment spent tidying themselves in a bedchamber, the belles re-emerged, resplendent, to be duly admired as if mud had never been invented.

Ah, if only yellow fever were never invented. If mud and swamp miasmas and insects and putrefaction did not bring disease, then I could have made myself content to send my daughters into the night with mud caking their unshod feet. Alas, I have seen too many friends bury their daughters to reconcile myself to that state of affairs.

If the desire for cleanliness and comfort had not been enough to interest me in the science of keeping my city dry, yellow fever alone would have been sufficient. No man could ever forget walking, time and again, through the deserted streets of a city emptied by people fleeing pestilence. And no human being could ever forget the bright-hot glow of fever in the eyes of a cherished friend in his last hours of life.

I am near eighty years of age. During my long career, I have designed canals and levees and drainage machines, and I have watched them take shape. I have seen my machines hold back floodwaters, and I have also seen them fail. But if I could have accomplished one goal, it is this one: to rid my city of pestilence. The day will come when women will not grow pale at the sound of the words "yellow fever." The day will come when children do not know the meaning of those words.

I would give anything to see that day.

Chapter Thirteen

Faye liked to watch Joe sleep. When he was asleep, he looked even younger. This probably should have bothered her more than it did. After all, whether he was awake or asleep, Joe was nine years younger than she was, but her concern over their age difference had ebbed in the months since they got engaged.

She'd been incredibly self-conscious at first, wearing more makeup than she liked and constantly searching her reflection for wrinkles and grays. To her relief, there weren't many of either yet, which she could attribute to good genes. She was cruising toward forty faster than she wanted to admit, but she was routinely presumed to be the same age as her fellow graduate students who hadn't taken a thirteen-year educational hiatus.

Her grandmother had entered her eighties with more pepper than salt in her hair. And her mother's olive skin had still been smooth and taut when lupus took her at sixty. Maybe she was fooling herself, but Faye thought it was possible that she herself didn't look all that crone-like standing next to her gorgeous fiancé.

Joe was pushing thirty. Surely he would soon have one or two strands of silver in that almost-black mane. They would stand out so dramatically that even oblivious Joe wouldn't be able to miss them. He simply wouldn't care.

And that was why she didn't get that lump in her throat so much any more, the one that said this was too good to last. It had been a while since her breath caught in her chest at the sight of a pretty young thing checking out Joe's lean hips and clean profile. For nearly a year, she'd watched Joe stride through a world of women who wanted him, waiting for him to decide he didn't want to be tied to the old broad by his side. It hadn't happened yet.

Maybe it wasn't going to happen. She saw no sign that Joe looked at these women, then looked at her and made a decision. He didn't seem to see them at all.

She had relived the moments before he asked her to marry him, and it was obvious that Joe didn't care how old she was. When he proposed, he'd listed all the reasons he'd been hesitant to tell her how he felt, and age didn't even figure into his reasoning. He'd thought she was too smart for him and, God help her, he'd been under the misapprehension that she was too pretty to want him. The woman in her would treasure that last statement till the end of her days.

He'd told her that he'd thought through the reasons she might not want to be with him, and he had come up with this: "I know that I love you. I've loved you ever since you caught me camping on your island, but you were too tender-hearted to make me go away. And I know that I would be good to you. I think maybe that's enough. If I can give you those two things, then maybe I'm good enough for you, after all. I want to be."

When he put it that way, how could she possibly have said no?

Then why hadn't she been able to make herself set a wedding date?

Joe was stirring. While he slept, Faye had been straightening the apartment. A space so small felt crowded easily, even when cluttered by nothing more than a discarded pair of moccasins, a scattered pile of books, and an empty pizza box.

She picked up the fallen tower of books and started stacking them up again. Faye didn't expect to ever live any place that wasn't cluttered by books. She'd spent a lot of her life making room for herself among stacks of books she was reading or had read or intended to read someday. She was nearly finished cleaning before she noticed that some of those books weren't hers.

Joe raised an eyelid and peered at her. "I borrowed some of those from the rangers at the battlefield park. Some came from the library. Had to buy a couple of the others."

Faye was used to being the bookish one. And she wasn't accustomed yet to the fact that Joe sometimes had a little spare pocket money to spend on things like books. He had a job working for an archaeology professor who paid him rather well for an undergrad, because there just wasn't anybody else around who knew so much about how stone tools had been made throughout history. If somebody handed Joe a pile of rocks, he could outfit a fearsome army in short order. His unusual skills had become highly salable.

She recognized the top book. It was the one Joe had been waving under her nose while she was trying to talk to Jodi—an old memoir called *The Floodgates of Hell*. It was an interesting name, considering recent New Orleans history. He'd also acquired a history of the Army Corps of Engineers, a textbook on hydraulic engineering, and a couple of popular history books about the history of the Mississippi River. Faye decided she wanted to read one of them herself—a book explaining how the levees breached after Katrina hit that was called, simply and eloquently, *Failure*.

She should have realized which aspect of the past would grab Joe's attention. He was always fascinated with the intersection of history, technology, and the natural world. How did Paleolithic people make spears? How did the moundbuilders make piles of dirt the size of Egyptian pyramids that had lasted for centuries? Millennia, even? Of course, he'd want to know how people had managed for three hundred years to maintain a city that was constructed below sea level.

"Put down the books and come back to bed, Faye."

So Joe hadn't turned into a complete bookworm. Well, he didn't have to ask her twice.

Chapter Fourteen

Faye began earning her consultant's fee before she even took a lunch break from her nine-to-five job. She'd watched Nina grow slowly more animated through the morning. When her skin grew pink and she started glancing frequently toward the parking lot, Faye used her coffee break to call Jodi. A heads-up seemed to be in order.

"I'm pretty sure Charles Landry will be stopping by the battle-field about lunchtime, if you want to talk to him. He's the person who told Nina where Shelly spent the days after Katrina."

"I remember," Jodi said. "I'll be there. And I'll bring the man a po-boy, so he won't have any reason not to sit down and spend his lunch hour with me. Joe's not on your payroll, is he? I have some questions, but if he's available after lunch, I can ask him, instead of you, so I can avoid taking you away from your real job. Or do you have…plans…for Joe?"

"I wish. But I'll be working and you know it. Joe's just killing time until my workweek ends this evening."

"Good. I need a tutorial in aerial photography and satellite imaging. And I need to know how Shelly used those things to find flood victims. All I know right now is that the technique is called geoaddressing. I saw Joe reading aerial photos yesterday like a pro. I bet he can get me up to speed. Tell him to take a short lunch and meet me in your office afterward."

◇◇◇

Faye was pretty sure that she and Jodi had just wasted an hour. And it had been Faye's lunch hour, so she couldn't look forward to any time to relax and get rid of the slimy aura that pervaded any room where Charles Landry was. She'd choked down her lunch, but it hadn't been pleasant.

Charles was one of those people who seemed so patently untrustworthy that she wondered why people even bothered to listen when he talked. It made her twitch to think that his job put him in charge of large engineering projects that involved huge sums of other people's money. Even worse, they were civil engineering projects—bridges, levees, roads—and when that kind of project failed, people died. Faye wanted to be able to trust the people who built them.

He smiled constantly. He laughed frequently. He was just so darned pleasant. Faye had no doubt that he had the trust of his five hundred closest friends. Faye just didn't believe that any of his excessive pleasantness was sincere. And if he called her or Jodi "darlin'"or "sweetheart" one more time, she was going to slap that burnished tan off his smiling face.

Sheriff Mike, along with most of her other male friends back in Florida, called her endearments like that all the time, but they'd earned them with their friendship. And they meant them. This guy just didn't know when to turn off the sweet-talk.

Nina clearly didn't have the same reaction to Charles and his studied charm. Maybe most people didn't. But Faye didn't like him, and she could tell that Jodi felt the same way. His voice was soft, so Faye couldn't say it sounded like fingernails on a chalkboard. But listening to him talk felt somehow like *licking* a chalkboard.

"After Katrina," he said in unctuous tones, "there was a good little handful of my co-workers from Pontchartrain Engineering working with Shelly and me at Zephyr Field. It never occurred to me that the police would want to know that Shelly was there during those terrible days. I was…well, pretty busy during that time and for a long time afterward. We all were. I know you remember." He turned expressive eyes on Jodi.

"And even if it had occurred to me that it was important for you police to know where she was last seen, I guess I assumed that you *did* know. We were on the phone with you guys—and with all the other first responders—constantly. Looking back, I know that there was no way for any of you to know who you were talking to, or that any of us would turn up dead, but I just never gave the question any conscious thought." He sighed deeply. "I'm sorry."

"It's not your fault." Jodi's voice sounded like it was stretched a little thin. "If our investigators had done a better job, they'd have found you and asked you those questions. Of course they were…pretty busy, as well."

"I don't know if I can help you much at this late date, but this is what I remember."

Faye noticed an awkward pause at the end of this sentence, as if his lips wanted to form the word 'sweetheart,' but he'd figured out that saying it might prompt Jodi to reach out a hand and smack the smarmy grin off his face. The most successful manipulators could read people just that well. Garden-variety con artists just kept saying 'sweetheart' until they got slapped silly.

The smarmy grin lingered, and Charles continued. "I don't know when Shelly arrived at Zephyr Field, but we were all there within twenty-four hours after the levees started breaking. I don't know when she left, or how she left. The streets were dry, more or less, out where we were, but she would have needed a boat to get too far. Certainly, she would have needed one to get to the house, where she was found. If I'd been trying to get anywhere that week, I'd have tried to hop me a ride with one of the rescue boats. Maybe Shelly went and helped with the on-site rescue work until she got herself on a boat headed to wherever she wanted to be."

"So you don't think she left on foot?"

As soon as she said it, Faye realized that the question was repetitive. And it was naïve. Nobody who watched the news was unaware of what the streets of New Orleans were like that week.

"I sure wouldn't have done that. The police had already told us that there were criminals running loose, looting and stuff. I hear some of the police did a little looting themselves."

Charles was still speaking in that chocolaty-smooth voice, but there was calculation in his decision to twit Jodi about the bad apples in her profession. After faltering on the word 'sweetheart,' he'd changed his tactics, coming to the decision that he wanted to make Jodi mad, after all. Faye wasn't so sure it was a smart strategy, but he had clearly done it on purpose. Maybe that controlled exterior was merely a camouflage for a risk-taker. It didn't take much imagination for Faye to see the man as the modern incarnation of a riverboat gambler.

He plucked a piece of ham out of his po-boy and ate it with his fingers, eyes fastened on Jodi. "There was no law on the streets of New Orleans. Not that week, and not for a long time after. If Shelly went out on those streets by herself, she might have gotten herself murdered over her wristwatch."

"She was wearing her wristwatch. And her wallet was still in her pocket. With money in it."

Jodi was doing a good job of keeping her temper. Faye could see that it was hard.

"So maybe she wasn't murdered by a thief. Or maybe she was wearing a cheap wristwatch. But it could've been a rapist. No way to know that now, is there?"

This time, he picked a tomato slice out of the wreckage of his sandwich and popped it into his mouth. Thinking about the reason that evidence of rape would no longer exist—a completely decayed body—made Faye want to run outdoors and think of something else. Anything else.

Jodi's nerves seemed to be holding up well enough. "Did anyone else who was working with you and Shelly that week disappear?"

"You've gotta be kidding me. Do you have any idea what Zephyr Field was like? It was probably the sanest place within a twenty-mile radius, and it was still nuts. We had volunteers coming in from all over the country. There was no way to coordinate all the things that needed to be done, but people found a way to get a lot of 'em done anyway. There were a lot of heroes hanging around that week but no, Detective, nobody was keeping track of their comings and goings."

Faye knew that Jodi couldn't argue with that logic, though she would probably like to try. She kept plowing ahead. "Is there anything you can tell me about Shelly's behavior during the days after the storm that might help me find out how she died?"

"Not that I can recall. It was a very busy week. Like I said."

"I know. You've told us that several times. And I do remember." Jodi pushed back from the desk and stood up. "Please make me a list of anybody who might have seen Shelly after the storm, dead or alive. Make a note of the ones who worked at your engineering firm, including their job titles and contact information. Oh, and list anybody else who you think might be helpful to the investigation. After that, you're free to go."

Charles was still smiling as he left, like a gambler who'd just bet on an inside straight and won. But what had he won?

Maybe he was just one of those people who didn't like the police and made as little effort as possible to be helpful. If Faye were to practice psychology without a license, she would have added that he seemed like one of those men who enjoyed putting women who had reached a position of some power back in their places. Even if both those things were true, that didn't mean that he wasn't keeping an important secret to himself.

Jodi had an oddly triumphant look on her face, for someone who had just been jousting with an arrogant jerk.

Faye waited for Jodi to speak, but she didn't. Finally, she said, "What? Why are you smiling? What can you possibly have learned from that interview? I'd say it was a waste of sixty nice minutes."

"No, I didn't learn anything from the interview, but I just had a killer idea."

"And it was…"

Jodi picked up Charles' list and perused it a minute. "I think I need to talk to that man's secretary."

"I didn't hear Charles say that his secretary was one of the co-workers who was with them at Zephyr Field."

"No, he didn't. But he didn't say she wasn't, either, and she might have been. And yes, I know a secretary can be a man, and I know they're called administrative professionals. But not that man's secretary. He lives to lord it over women and he likes power. Any administrative professional working for Charles Landry is going be a woman, and she's going to get treated like a secretary in a bad black-and-white movie."

Faye couldn't argue with that.

"Anyway," Jodi continued, "Nina and Charles have both told us that Shelly was at Zephyr Field with a big group of people from Pontchartrain Engineering, and here they are."

She waved the paper in front of Faye's nose.

"I think I need to question a whole slew of these people. They may be able to shed some light on Shelly's last days, true. They can help me compile a list of everyone who had contact with her, which will be an excellent addition to my very short suspect list. Mainly, though, I need to question every person on this list—starting with his secretary—because it'll annoy the hell out of Charles Landry."

Faye liked the way Jodi thought.

Chapter Fifteen

Faye's work team was moving so slowly that they seemed to be traveling through molasses. When she considered the wet heaviness of the air, she realized that they might well *be* slogging through something as syrupy as molasses. And it was still "springtime," if a weather this oppressive could ever really be considered springlike.

She had not considered that there might be a climate damper than the weather at her home on Joyeuse Island. Logic suggested that water in all four directions would keep the air pretty saturated. Here, though, water on all sides meant that it was underfoot, too.

Nobody was talking, because there was nothing to say. Nobody's trowel had uncovered anything of importance all day. They hadn't even found anything mildly interesting. Monotony had become the enemy.

Nobody was happier than Faye when Dauphine crowed, "Hey! This is a pretty thing."

She had turned up a fragment of pottery, a tiny little find considering the size of the endless piles of backdirt that were piled around her.

"It's majolica, I think," Nina said, cradling it on her palm and letting light play over its colorful and iridescent glaze.

It was indeed majolica, decorated marineware, unless Faye missed her guess. Lustrous colors on the pure white ground of a tin glaze led her to agree with Nina. "You're right. It *is* pretty."

Joe came to look over her shoulder. "So, is this good news? Were you hoping to find Spanish pottery in this spot?"

"Yup," Faye said. "The great house for the Beluche plantation was near here. It's likely that it was destroyed in 1792 or 1793, which was still during the Spanish period. Not that there weren't any Spanish goods in the area during times that the French were in charge. But for something so small…" It was hardly bigger than her fingernail. "For something this small, that's a very tidy connection. I'd love to find the kitchen. It was probably somewhere near here. Maybe this sherd came from a platter or crock used by the cook."

Everyone went back to work, but a moment with an old but pretty chip of pottery had lifted some of the boredom. Even the air seemed to be made of a thinner grade of molasses.

When a group of people is looking for something, whether it be artifacts or a place to stop the car so a child can visit a rest room, the laws of probability do not seem to apply. Hours or days or miles can pass with no sign of something that the lookers know just has to be somewhere close. But the moment comes when probability and statistics have been completely violated for so long that the pendulum swings the other way. Suddenly, there are pottery chips and bathrooms everywhere.

Faye's team was overdue for one of those streaks of good luck. Within half an hour, Faye had found two more sherds of majolica, one of them fairly sizeable. Within an hour, something way more significant saw the light of day. Dauphine, who seemed to be having a lucky day and should probably buy a lottery ticket, raked away a thin layer of dirt with her trowel and, in so doing, uncovered the brick foundation of something old.

"Anybody want to bet me that's not the Beluche house's kitchen?" Faye asked as she whipped out her camera. "We could have a pool. A dollar a guess."

"I'll take that bet." Dauphine looked at the battered old bricks like a proud mother. "I think it's the *Rodriguez* kitchen."

Joe ambled over in time to jump in the pool with, "My money's on a smokehouse."

Nina scooped up some soil with her snub-nosed trowel and spoke without making eye contact. "I think it was an ice house."

There was a second of silence before Faye said, "In eighteenth-century Louisiana? I haven't read about any ice houses here earlier than the 1830s."

Nina's deadpan cracked, and everybody laughed, because they all had a soft spot for geeky history jokes.

Faye took a step toward the bit of foundation that Dauphine had uncovered. She heard an unwelcome "sploosh" underfoot and stifled a completely unladylike word. On cue, the asthmatic pump that she'd been nursing all week coughed and expired.

"Take a break, guys. I need to resurrect Old Wheezy. Again."

Her workers scattered like confetti on a gusty day.

Faye stared morosely at the damp (and growing damper) soil at the bottom of the excavation. She knew it could have been worse. They were working near the river, so the water table was conveniently far from the surface, especially for south Louisiana. This had seemed paradoxical to Faye until Joe had looked it up just that morning and explained to her that the land was shaped the way it was, because the river had flooded every year, forever.

A few eons worth of mud had settled out of the river's flood-waters, lifting the level of the nearby land a little bit every year. This raised ground spread out so gently from the riverfront that the difference in elevation wasn't obvious, but the dirt she stood on was higher than land further away from the river by several feet. This was called a "natural levee," and land on that God-made dike had come at a premium for all of recorded history. It was no coincidence that the New Orleans neighborhoods left unscathed by the post-Katrina floods had been the oldest neighborhoods, constructed on the natural levee before all the high ground was gobbled up.

Even though Faye was lucky enough to be looking for arti-facts that should be above the water table, there was still a slow constant ooze of groundwater that collected in the bottom of her excavations. This was because, as she was constantly being reminded, every last thing was damp all the time in this part of the country. Old Wheezy had been sufficient to keep things dry, but its decrepit condition had cost her some valuable work time. Faye was the only team member with any mechanical skills whatsoever.

Joe was lying on his stomach, with most of his top half hanging down into the excavation so he could get a good look at… something. Faye got the impression that he was looking for the source of the water, because he was poking first at one stratum of earth, then at another, as if he were looking for a soft, wet layer that was serving as a conduit though drier soil. He was probably correct in his theory about the source, though practical Faye hadn't given the matter much thought. Even if she could find the offending layer of dirt, there was no way to stop its ooze, so she saw no point in wasting her time on it.

Instead, she was wasting her time on a pump. She aimed a kick at a sturdy part of its housing that she knew she couldn't hurt. She wanted to express herself, but she didn't want to break it. Faye was frustrated, but she wasn't stupid.

Joe lifted his head out of the unit at the sound and asked, "You want me to take a look at that for you? You could go get a Coke and calm your—"

A dark look from Faye sent him scrambling to his feet. "I'll just take myself a walk till you get that thing fixed. Want me to bring you back a Coke?"

Faye knew that he would interpret her wordless grunt as what it was: a plea for understanding from a woman who needed a quiet moment with her recalcitrant pump, and then a Coca-Cola. He hastened to oblige her.

Faye threw the lid of her toolbox open, hard. It made a satisfying clang. Newfangled tool totes could be bought cheap these days, with pockets that kept tools organized. They didn't weigh a ton like old-style metal toolboxes, either.

Nevertheless, Faye had not invested in one. "Cheap" was not the same as "free." Plus, those wussy canvas totes were completely unsatisfactory when a mechanical problem required her to make some noise. She picked up a pair of channel-lock pliers, decided they weren't the right size, then dropped them—okay, threw them—back into the metal tray. The resulting clang was just loud enough to be satisfying.

Later, when she was asked how much time passed between the time the work crew scattered and the moment when she heard Joe call her name, she couldn't hazard a guess. For Faye, mechanical work involved disassembling the offending objects and scattering them around her, willy-nilly. Then she sat cross-legged among the far-flung pieces, like the survivor of an explosion, until a solution to her problem magically appeared. She was deep into the rumination portion of the process when she heard Joe.

His voice was muffled, indistinct. Still, she was deep-down certain she heard him call her name. And she sensed a looming darkness in the sound, as if a cloud had passed in front of the sun.

Where was he? The sound seemed to come from the levee, but if six-and-a-half-foot-tall Joe were standing on it, then she'd have been able to see him. She hurried that direction anyway, breaking into a run when she couldn't shut out her deepest fear.

What would life be like if something happened to Joe?

Faye's earliest memory was of an old photo of her father in her mother's hands, and the sound of her mother's voice as talked about what it would be like when Daddy came home from the war. When the bad news came, her mother had locked that photo away and refused to look at it again or show it to Faye, for the rest of her life.

It was Faye's now, and she kept it on her bedside table. She never wanted to live through that kind of loss again.

What could have caused Joe to call out to her in that dreadful voice, then fall silent? She almost stumbled at the thought. There were so many terrible possibilities. Climbing the levee, she prayed to find Joe safe on the other side.

There was no Joe. There was nothing but the river.

Seen up-close, the Mississippi River was unfathomably broad. Its muddy blue-brown water rushed past her, swollen by spring rains. Whole trees spun slowly in invisible eddies.

She was startled to see that the water lapped just a few steps from where she stood. Faye was accustomed to seeing large rivers at a distance, from the span of a high bridge, while she was safe in the comfortable confines of a car. It was disconcerting to realize that she could just walk down there to the most notoriously treacherous river on the continent and wade right in, boots and all.

Where was Joe? The only thing in her field of vision that was moving was the rushing water.

Logs and clumps of trash floated past. After a long moment, two of those fast-moving objects caught her eye. They were both downriver from where she stood, past the park's dock, and getting further away by the instant. She had been staring at them for five seconds, maybe ten, before she realized that they didn't belong where they were.

They were gasping faces. One of them was Joe's.

His long, powerful arms were cutting into the roiling water as he swam toward the other face—Nina's—but Nina wasn't reaching out to Joe for help. She just hung motionless in the water, passively letting the insistent current carry her out to the Gulf of Mexico.

In horror, Faye watched as Nina sank beneath the water, then, buoyed by an eddy, bobbed back to the surface, perhaps for the last time. She was sinking again when Joe grabbed her and Faye's heart rose with Nina, until she realized the truth. Even Joe couldn't fight that current.

Nobody human could swim against the Mississippi, dragging dead weight. Certainly, nobody could do it long enough to regain the park's dock, which is where Joe must have jumped in to help Nina. And what about Nina? Did she slip? Or did she jump?

That seemed like a silly question. Nina's career and schoolwork seemed to be going well. She was clearly crazy about Charles, and he'd walked back into her life. Why would Nina jump?

Faye looked downriver, hoping to see something Joe could grab while she rushed to fish them both out. No luck. The next dock was way too far downriver. There was no sandbar, no curve in the bank to catch them.

Faye's first impulse was to just jump in and help. She owned an island, for God's sake. She was a strong swimmer.

No. If Joe couldn't fight the mighty Mississippi, then neither could she. She had to do something to help him. But what? There was no boat tethered to the dock where she stood, and Joe and Nina were way too far to reach with a pole, even if she had such a thing.

One of Faye's grandmother's old sayings popped into her head. "Tools are the thing that separates man from the beasts."

Nice try, Grandma, Faye thought, *but my toolbox would take me straight to the bottom,* yet all the time she was being disrespectful to her dead grandmother, she was looking around. There was a wooden sign advertising an upcoming park event near the end of the dock. She yanked it out of the ground.

It was about half as tall as Faye, and almost as wide as it was tall. It wasn't much of a boat, but it would have to do.

Faye sat down and yanked her boots off her feet. Trying not to think about what she was doing, she held the sign tight against her stomach and ran, launching herself as far in Joe's direction as she could muster. Like it or not, she was going on a riverboat ride.

Faye didn't weigh much, so her makeshift boat dipped underwater when she landed, but quickly surfaced. It held her up, until a slight shift of her weight toward the front sent it submarining, and she swallowed her first gulp of river water for the day. Why did she think it wouldn't be her last? She leaned back and her craft righted itself. Fully realizing that the action was insane, she started to paddle away from the dock and safety, and toward Joe.

If his mouth hadn't been full of muddy water, Joe would have cursed. What was that woman thinking? *His* woman. What was *his* woman thinking when she jumped in the Mississippi River?

She certainly couldn't be thinking that she'd be able to swim out here and save him. Because he had been in the process of accepting the fact that he wasn't going to be able to save himself.

He certainly wasn't going to be able to save Nina. He'd clamped an arm around her waist—an arm he really wished he could use to help himself swim—but she just slumped in the water like a woman who was dead already. He knew she wasn't, because he could feel her shallow breaths against his ribs. So there was no way he was letting her go. Unfortunately, this meant that they were probably both going to die.

Then, just as he was working to accept that unpleasant fact, his woman—his Faye—had launched herself into a river swollen by spring floods.

Now he was going to have to suck it up and fight back against death. This river wasn't going to let him go easily, and it probably wasn't going to let him go at all, but he couldn't just quit. Not if it meant that Faye was going to die with him.

He saw her. Faye could see that Joe saw her.

She saw him give a few strong scissor kicks that brought him slightly nearer to Faye and her stupid little boat. The fact that his kicks were proving effective encouraged her to try something different—something besides just hanging on for dear life. She eased herself back, hanging her legs into the water behind her. Mirroring Joe's form, she kicked with all she had.

Shifting her body so far back caused an interesting effect when she hit a good-sized eddy. Faye and her improvised boat spun slowly around their combined center of gravity until she found herself floating down the Mississippi backwards. She thought that no good could possibly come of this.

Then she remembered that her legs were remarkably long for a short woman, and they were now pointed in Joe's direction. It was an odd way to extend her reach, but Faye would take what she could get.

Shaking water out of her eyes, Faye scooched as far off the back of the sign as she dared and found that her legs were just long enough. Joe grabbed her right big toe so hard that she nearly lost her grip on the sign that she hoped would keep them all afloat. She held on, though she feared she might lose that toe.

Joe started climbing her leg and torso hand-over-hand. Under other circumstances, this might have been fun, but not today. When he reached her waist, he grabbed hard, straining to maneuver Nina's limp body onto the sign.

Faye had lived her entire adult life on the Gulf of Mexico, but she'd never once had so much water driven deep into her sinus cavities. She could hardly breathe. She could hardly see, The out-of-control shaking of her arm muscles signaled imminent failure. Still, Nina and Joe were slightly safer. And she wasn't dead yet.

A dock was looming, but it was too short. On their current course, they were going to float right past it. Joe was already kicking hard, trying to move their pitiful craft cross-current. It was working, but Faye didn't have to do calculus in her head to see that their progress was too slow and their speed downriver was too swift. They were going to miss the dock.

Nina was draped across Faye's sign, unmoving. If Faye's mouth hadn't been underwater, she'd have been shouting, *Wake up! Breathe! Do something!*

Nina did none of those things except continue taking breaths that were so shallow that Faye didn't see how they could help Nina at all.

Faye found herself thinking about Joe's hand-over-hand trick. Without warning him, she let go of the sign and grabbed him around the waist with both hands. Joe knew her so well that he could tell what she wanted him to do, simply by the way she shifted her body in the water. He extended his legs as far as they would go, while still steadying Nina's unconscious form, then he relaxed and let her maneuver herself into position.

She'd just had time to grasp his feet with both hands and stretch her whole body out into the water, before her own feet struck a metal piling holding up the dock that just might save them. The pain was an electric thing, but she was able to hook a foot under that piling, willing it to hold them all. The current pulled inexorably, and her foot was screaming at her, but she clung to Joe. Now what?

Joe was pulling Nina closer to his chest, sliding her off the wooden sign that had served them so well. Faye swallowed hard. This was either going to work...or it wasn't. He eased Nina into the water and let the sign go.

Relieved of Nina's weight, the sign jumped to the surface and headed quickly downstream. Joe jerked his legs and Faye knew he wanted her to let go. It wasn't easy, but she forced herself.

With Nina under one arm, Joe battled the last few feet toward the dock. With her foot still hooked around the piling, Faye grabbed Joe and drew him to her until he, too, had a grasp of something solid. A few lungs full of air helped Faye's feelings considerably.

This was the moment when Faye realized that she had a cell phone in her pocket, and that it had been there the whole time. Damn.

Calling 911 wouldn't have prevented the need for Faye to launch her rescue voyage. Nina and Joe would certainly have drowned by the time help arrived. But if she'd called first, they would be topping the levee's crest right this minute, like the cavalry in an old B-movie.

Ah, well. It wasn't that far to the shore. Too bad she and Joe had to get there while dragging an unconscious woman.

It worried Faye that Nina had never opened her eyes. She was still breathing. But she wasn't doing much else.

Joe battled his way toward shore, dragging two women with him, and he wasn't sure he had what it took to get to dry land. Not any more. Not since he'd gambled that his muscles could take on inexorable, unyielding Mother Nature.

Nina hung limply in one arm, so she was no help.

Faye was conscious. Oh, Faye was more than conscious. She was struggling in his other arm, squawking at him to put her down, blubbering like a baby, and pretending like she wasn't crying at all. She was a big girl, and they don't cry. Except she really wasn't a big girl. She was five feet tall.

He couldn't put her down. The water came up to his chin, so he could slog slowly toward shore, fighting the current all the way, but Faye couldn't do that. If she tried to touch bottom, the water would close over her head. He wasn't sure she had enough strength left to swim. Joe thought he could get the three of them closer to shore, close enough that they could maybe walk the rest of the way. He had that much power left in his muscles, and no more, but it would sure help matters if Faye would quit struggling and let him carry her.

Somehow, he doubted that she was capable of such a thing.

Soon enough, Faye found herself lying face-down at the water's edge, Joe and Nina beside her. Their legs still dangled in the river, all six of them.

If Faye opened one eye, she could see a crushed red-white-and-blue beer can. If she opened the other eye, she could see something unidentifiable and plastic that she hoped wasn't medical waste. She would have been content to lie there for hours surrounded by the garbage of a continent, but getting Nina out of the river wasn't the same thing as getting her out of the woods.

Faye managed to raise herself to all-fours and crawl to the levee, tottering to her feet at its top. Pointing herself in the general direction of the visitor's center, she began to walk. She knew what she looked like—muddy, half-drowned, near-collapse. There was no chance that anyone who saw her coming would fail to dial 911.

She took one long look over her shoulder before she descended the far side of the levee and lost sight of Joe and Nina. Joe was pushing at the ground with both hands, trying to raise himself to a sitting position. Nina wasn't doing anything.

Catching Joe's eye, she found that she had only one thing to say to him.

"Christmas. At home. At Joyeuse."

Faye had always wanted a Christmas wedding.

Chapter Sixteen

Faye didn't like the intensity of the paramedics' efforts to revive Nina. She crouched on the ground beside Joe and gave the medical team a sidewise glance now and then. It seemed somehow indecent to intrude into a scene where a human being's life hung in the balance.

"Did she jump?"

Joe's gaze was directed inward. If he'd heard her question, he gave no sign.

She reached out and touched him on the forearm.

Her touch seemed to revive him. Faye wished it were so easy for the paramedics. Another sidewise glance told her that the paramedics hadn't given up on Nina yet.

"Did she jump? Did you see her go over?" She was asking too many questions, but the adrenaline that was still shaking her arms and legs wouldn't let her stop. "Is that why you went out to the river? Did you see her cross the levee and get worried?"

"No. I was poking around at the end of the canal, trying to see where it went into the river back when Andrew Jackson was around, and I heard something on the other side of the levee."

The questions kept coming. They were completely out of Faye's control.

"Did she call out for help? Do you think she tripped and went in?"

"I don't know. I just heard a splash that didn't sound right."

...a splash that didn't sound right. If Nina survived, it would be because Joe paid attention. If he could see it, hear it, feel it, touch it, or taste it, he paid attention to it.

A drop of water trickled from his hair onto his forehead. He left it there. "She fell off the dock, I know that. But I don't know whether she jumped or slipped."

"Or whether she got pushed."

Faye didn't like the way those words tasted in her mouth.

"I don't like to think that way," Joe said.

"I don't either. But think...how much time passed between when you heard the splash and when you got over the levee?"

"Not a lot. But it wouldn't take long for someone to run up the dock and hide in the trees on the far side of the levee down there."

"Nope. We're just talking about a few seconds, tops." Faye tried to picture someone running, imagining how long it would take. The dock wasn't that long.

"Besides," Joe said, brushing wet hair out of his face, "I didn't look downriver toward the dock right away. I checked out the area close to the canal first, then I looked down toward the dock and saw Nina in the water. It didn't take long—a few seconds, like you say—but there could have been somebody down there that I missed. Still, I don't like to think that way. I'd rather believe it was an accident."

"Me, too, but I can't help wondering what happened. I've never seen Nina out on that dock. Did she just go out there for a look at the river, then fall in? That doesn't usually happen to able-bodied adults who aren't drunk. Did someone walk out there with her, then give her a push? Was she suicidal? I'd say she was depressed until this week, but since Charles came back she's been...well, I guess giddy's the word." Faye sneaked another look at the paramedics as they tried to revive Nina. "Yeah, giddy. I'd like to presume this was an accident, but facts are facts and I can't ignore them."

Jodi, who had walked up behind them while they spoke, said, "I know. That's why I hired you."

◇◇◇

Intensive care waiting rooms are usually full of people who wish they were at their loved one's bedside. Unfortunately, the patients being visited are, by definition, too sick to enjoy having visitors. There are limited visiting hours, it is true, but they're more for the benefit of the patient's frantic loved ones than for the patient.

Friends and family without the magic title of mother, father, children, or spouse gather in the waiting room and try to be helpful. They tell stories of people who have been similarly ill, but are now happy and whole. They hold hands. They ask, "Can I get you anything to eat?"

Nina's parents were dead, so a female cousin was playing the role of closest kin. Faye remembered Nina saying that she had slept on her cousin's couch since Katrina demolished her home. Charles sat beside the cousin, with his head bowed, and Faye liked him better because he seemed to really care about her friend Nina.

Matt had followed the ambulance from the battleground to the hospital. He was sitting with Joe, face taut, with his elbows resting on a small table in the corner of the waiting room. Empty candy wrappers and chip bags were piled in front of them, because young men eat when they're under stress.

Matt seemed to be keeping a constant distance between him and Charles, which Faye found interesting, since she was sure that Matt knew him pretty well. She remembered that he'd dated someone who worked with Shelly. There was no woman in sight, so he was either no longer dating her, or she didn't feel close enough to Nina to have rushed to the hospital.

Actually, "no woman in sight" wasn't quite accurate. There *was* a woman in sight, and she worked with Charles, but Faye devoutly hoped young Matt wasn't dating her. She was thirtyish, just a few years older than Matt, but she seemed so unsuited for the outdoorsy park ranger. The young woman had the impeccably coiffed hair and not-subtle makeup of a Southern belle of the old school. She was not so old-school, however, as to have avoided working for a living.

Charles had introduced her as Leila, his executive assistant, and Faye recognized the light in her eyes that marked her as her boss' most zealous fan. Leila had a planning calendar open across her lap, a pen in one hand, and a cell phone in the other. Faye couldn't hear what she was saying, but her body language said that she wanted people to understand that it would take forty phone calls to reschedule all the important meetings that Nina's unfortunate accident had interrupted.

Jodi sat alone, in a chair that gave her a vantage point for viewing the entire room. Faye remembered that she'd wanted to question Charles' secretary, and here Leila sat. Nina's tragedy had probably shoved Jodi's desire to annoy Charles off the top of the detective's priority list, but Leila's day in the hot seat would surely come.

Faye watched Jodi scan each face, one after another, and she wondered whether the detective had serious concerns that Nina's fall off the dock had not been accidental.

Faye walked over to Jodi, "Any word?'"

"The latest news on Nina has been…okay. She's alive, so that's good. She's conscious and responsive. That's good, too. But her speech or her cognition or maybe both seem to be affected. No one's been able to conduct an intelligible conversation with her yet."

Faye watched Matt as he stood and walked over to Leila, murmuring, "I'm going to get some coffee. You want some?" His touch on her elbow was intimate. So was the angle of her head when she looked up from her work and nodded. So this *was* the girlfriend. Well, nobody ever said love was predictable.

"So we don't know yet about Nina's medical condition. How's she doing from your perspective?" Faye asked Jodi. "Is she recovering from a suicide attempt…or did somebody push her? Why would somebody want to hurt Nina, anyway? It would be like attacking a…field mouse."

Jodi shook her head. "You underestimate your friend. You saw Nina on TV yesterday. You think she didn't make a few people mad? Politicians on the levee board, maybe? Engineers working for the Corps who've heard just one criticism too many? It's not like she just started being a community activist yesterday when the television crews pointed their cameras at her. You should read her blog. Nina's like an avenging field mouse with fangs."

"Any hard evidence that this wasn't an accident?"

"Just like a scientist, aren't you? If you don't have hard evidence, then something isn't true. Well, we detectives kinda operate that way, too." Jodi gave a half-shrug. "Nina's body shows no signs of a struggle. No strangulation marks around the neck. So this isn't Shelly all over again. There are no bruises that anyone could say for certain were made with a fist or a weapon. But there's a humdinger of a wound on her head."

"Could she have slipped and fell?"

"Yep. But she could also have taken a big wallop upside the head, right before somebody shoved her into the Mississippi. No way to tell. Yet."

Faye liked the determined glint in the detective's eye.

Joe wondered if his hair was ever going to dry. It had soaked up a prodigious amount of river water. He also wondered if his brain would ever clear.

Faye had said something about a Christmas wedding. That was real nice but, right that moment he wasn't altogether sure he remembered what month it was, or even what year it was. He wasn't clear on where he was, either. Nearly drowning tended to mess with a man's mind.

May. It was May. He remembered that now, because he'd just finished an endless semester at school—a semester made still more interminable by the problem of Faye's absence.

Christmas was a hell of a long time away, but Joe didn't seem to have much voice in their wedding date. Faye had announced her decision, then walked away. This was a common state of affairs. Under ordinary circumstances, Faye was going to do what Faye was going to do.

But these weren't ordinary circumstances. Joe had cheated death in a big way just a year before, and he'd just had another near-miss. He could just as easily have lost Faye in the rushing river. Such things tended to focus the mind.

Joe wanted Faye, he wanted a family, and he wanted her to stop stalling, because he knew she wanted a family with him, too. She was just scared.

Fear was not something that Faye would ever admit, but facts were facts. Her age, too, was a fact. She would be forty soon. Waiting until December to get married and start trying for a baby was only going to make it harder to get that baby. If Faye didn't want him to know that, then she shouldn't have made him take biology.

Joe knew that if he let her be a coward for very much longer, there wouldn't be much chance for children, and Joe wanted kids. They both did.

Telling Faye what to do was generally a bad plan. She didn't react well at all to being bossed around, so he wouldn't be doing that. Sooner or later, though, he'd need to find a way to inform her—gently—that she was being irrational. The question of when to get married wasn't hers alone to answer, and she knew it.

Joe intended to get Faye to budge on this issue, but he had the uneasy feeling that softening her stance was going to take dynamite. He'd rather use a gentler approach. It would sure help if he could figure out why she was so damn scared.

Excerpt from *The Floodgates of Hell,*
The Reminiscences of Colonel James McGonohan
1876

*I am reminded of a story I heard more than fifty years
past. It was purported to be true. It has the ring of
truth. Still, I cannot swear that everything happened
in just this way, nor that any of it happened at all.*

*Everyone who has told this tale to me has given
its hero the same name: Deschanel. Monsieur
Deschanel was a wealthy man with extensive upriver
land holdings planted in indigo. He spent his youth
consolidating this empire, marrying late to a belle
named Geneviève, twenty years his junior. Wealthy
men who marry children can be indulgent, and for a
time he neglected the plantation so that the two of
them could live in his opulent New Orleans townhouse and attend balls and operas and glittering
dinner parties.*

*When the social season passed, he was anxious to
make the annual move upriver to his other home on
the plantation, so that he could personally supervise
the agricultural business that supported these frivoli-
ties. It was the custom of the day. Planters kept one
house in town for entertaining and to impress their
friends, and they kept a second house on the plantation for those times when work could no longer be
avoided. The wives—the dutiful ones, at least—left the
city each year to live with their hard-working men in
the hinterlands.*

*The huge plantation houses lining the Mississippi's
River Road were extravagantly decorated, and there
were well-trained house slaves to ensure that the
family was well-cared-for during their exile, but each
was built on a plantation that must perforce be vast.
How else could such a lavish and gracious life be*

supported? *Sheer distance curtailed social activities during the agricultural season and convivial New Orleans aristocrats were often lonely in their River Road plantation houses.*

As I told you, Geneviève was young, too young to know where her duty lay. She told her doting husband, "No." (Or, I presume it would be more accurate to say she said, "Non.") She refused to leave the city, weeping and raving and declaring that she could never live in the filthy and uncivilized wilderness.

Knowing what I know of him now, I imagine that Monsieur Deschanel looked out the window of his sumptuous home and saw streets heaped with kitchen offal and worse, and wondered if she understood the meaning of the word "filthy." But, as I have said, wealthy men who marry children can be indulgent, so he traveled up the Mississippi alone many times during that growing season, so that she could live in the city while he earned the riches that she so enjoyed.

The legends say that the young Madame Deschanel was breathtaking, with coils of black hair that set off the milk-white pallor of her skin. This dramatic coloring must have made her suffering all the more striking when yellow fever spread its sallow veil over that exquisite face. It is said that Monsieur Deschanel returned from yet another business trip just moments before she passed into the next world. The fever took their infant son that same day, and she was buried with him cradled in her arms.

There were those who said that the man lost his mind the day he buried his wife and child. Others have said that he was a genius, born too soon to see his visions take shape. All the legends agree that, from that day, he turned his attention to the mud, the swamp miasmas, the bugs, and the filth harboring the pestilence that destroyed his family. It is said that he slept little in the days remaining to him. His every waking hour was spent tinkering with strange and fantastic machinery with but one purpose: to lift New Orleans out of the muck.

Chapter Seventeen

Thursday

It was Faye's day off and here she was, looking at an archaeological site. This wasn't because she had workaholic tendencies, though sometimes she did. Okay, a lot of times she did. But that wasn't the reason she was peering down into yet another excavation.

If she was going to be of any help at all to Jodi in finding out what happened to Shelly, it only made sense to check out the site where the woman was working just prior to her death. Joe was on Jodi's payroll, too, so he was peering down into the same excavation. So much for their vacation plans, but the weekend wasn't over yet. Faye was sure that there was some fun yet to be had.

As fortune would have it, work at the site had been stopped by Hurricane Katrina and had only now resumed. Under ordinary circumstances, these pits would have been long-since backfilled and the soil re-sodded. Faye and Joe would be standing in a grassy lot. Instead, Shelly's work was continuing as if she had just stepped away for a minute.

An SUV with "Pontchartrain Engineering" emblazoned on its side was parked on the street, just as it would have been when Shelly was alive. The same workers were on-site, except for Shelly. The colorful shotgun houses, with their Victorian woodwork and their inviting porches, hadn't changed since Shelly worked here. They had hardly changed in a hundred years. Paint had peeled and flaked away, and windowglass was flowing slowly into ripples, but the houses were what they were. They reminded Faye of the houses on Dauphine's street, just blocks away.

Faye had the dizzying sense that time had not passed. The storm had never come. A thousand people had not died in the floods. The city where jazz was born was unchanged, and it never would change.

A short conversation with the archaeologist in charge, Dr. Al Britton, brought her back to reality.

"The flooding wasn't too bad here in Tremé—which makes sense. It's one of the oldest neighborhoods outside the Quarter, and our ancestors weren't stupid. They built on high ground until there wasn't any more high ground. So our work here wasn't directly affected by the storm but, like everything else around here, the project suffered some setbacks indirectly traceable to the storm. For instance, we lost Shelly."

A shadow fell over his face.

"Shelly was my right hand. Her work was technically flawless, and she had a generosity that sometimes eludes my professional peers. Even outside of academia, people are jealous of their reputations. Some of them aren't big on giving credit where it's due, not when keeping that credit for themselves might advance their career. Shelly wasn't like that."

He motioned with his head, and Faye and Joe walked with him over to another unit that was being excavated as they watched.

"The flood didn't do our work any good, but it wasn't as bad as it might have been. Lots of times, we have to use pumps in these parts to keep units dry, even under the best of circumstances, so standing water in the excavations wasn't the end of the world. We had some problems with saturated soil just slumping down into the units, but nothing that completely destroyed the validity of our work here."

"Yet you've lost years in getting this work done."

"Our personnel were scattered hither and yon, and the client corporation had plenty of better places to spend its money. Pontchartrain Engineering has had to scramble to get all of its projects back on a solid footing, and this is far from their most lucrative job. It took awhile for our project to rise to the top of anyone's priority list, no question. But I expect it'll be on a lot of people's minds pretty soon. You would not believe the stuff we're finding here. Layer on layer of cultural material."

Faye hopped down into the unit with him and listened as he interpreted each stratigraphic zone. The significant finds had been stacked up like layers in a wedding cake.

He read the evidence to her in no particular order. Pointing to a black smear in the clay at about shoulder level, he said, "There was a housefire here in the mid-1800s. The city was rebuilt in brick, for the most part, after the 1788 fire destroyed most of the *Vieux Carré*, but brick houses can burn, too. At least their contents can, not to mention the wooden beams holding up a roof shingled in cedar. And people were still cooking in open hearths. So fires continued to be a problem, especially since the closest thing they had to a fire hydrant was a bucket brigade stretching all the way to the river."

He pointed at a less distinct layer, further down the unit wall. "Down here, we found some evidence of Native American activity. I'm not sure whether anybody was living this far out on the natural levee in those days. The elevation is zero here— exactly sea level. That's higher than most of New Orleans, but it wouldn't have been all that desirable back when there was still space close to the river, around the cathedral. I'm thinking that the scattered artifacts we found at this level date back to the years when local tribes carried their canoes across a portage that was probably right near here. If you could tote your stuff from the Mississippi to the Bayou St. John, then you could get to Lake Pontchartrain and the Gulf of Mexico without dealing with the twists and shoals of the Mississippi south of here."

This tracked with everything Faye had read, so she just nodded her head. Joe had disappeared, lured away by a site worker offering to show him the stone tools found in that stratum.

Joe appreciated stone tools. He made them. He used them. He treasured them for their beauty. He knew so much about them that he'd likely be able to add to the information the site team had already gleaned just by giving them a good lookover. If anybody needed to know how a stone tool was used or how it was made or why the maker chose that particular rock to knap, then Joe was the one to ask.

"We're even finding a few things below that level, from a still earlier period. It makes sense. New Orleans is sitting on a site that has always been strategic. Even way back then, before the Europeans arrived and mucked things up, those guys traded all over eastern North America."

Faye nodded, and said, "They needed efficient shipping lanes, too. They just used smaller boats."

"Precisely." Dr. Britton grinned the way people do when they're talking to someone who's interested in their work.

"What's this? And this?" Faye asked, pointing to areas of dark soil just below the level of the house that had burned.

"We're finding a number of features related to drainage at all levels during the historical period. Cesspools were everywhere in those days, because sewage had to go somewhere. Over there—" he said, straightening up in the excavation and pointing toward the street, "we've found something that looks like one of the ditches that surrounded each block in the city's original design. And over there, if I'm not mistaken, is what's left of a canal from the years just after that. It's not on any historic maps that I know of, which is pretty cool, since we have a lot of them. Whether it was for drainage or navigation, I can't say yet."

The image of an old map was swimming in Faye's mind's eye. She stood up and looked around her, as if she expected to somehow translate the houses and trees around her now into the bird's eye view of a map drawn in 1815.

"You say you found a canal that's not on the maps. Wasn't there a major canal around here somewhere? If I close my eyes, I can just see it on the old drawings. It ran diagonally to the southeast. I think it started at the Bayou St. John."

"Amazing. Do you have a photographic memory or something?" Britton asked.

Faye shook her head. "I just remember things that I think are interesting."

Joe appeared, leaning down into the excavation to say, "She thinks everything's interesting."

Britton laughed. "Photographic memory or not, you're exactly right. There *was* a canal nearby, but it was west of here. Well, I think it's west. I've lived here all my life and haven't figured out the curve in the river yet. Anyway, over there."

He waved a hand in a direction that Faye thought might be west. The Crescent City and its crescent-shaped streets had been confusing her since she hit town.

"It was called the Carondelet Canal," he said. "Aren't place names just...pretty...around here?"

Britton was still looking in the direction that was probably west, thinking about an old shipping channel with a pretty name. They waited a second for him to continue.

The archaeologist shook himself and said, "Why don't you people just tell me to get to the point? The Carondelet started over there close to Basin Street and Congo Square and, you're right, it went as far as Bayou St. John. People with goods to sell could float from Lake Pontchartrain down the bayou to the canal, then it was a straight shot to the city's back door."

Faye squatted down to study the dark soil from the 1800s, so Dr. Britton shifted his attention back to that century. "Like I said, we see drainage features everywhere, but that stratum from the early 1800s has more of those features than you'd expect. At least it does here, on this piece of property."

"You talking about drainage and water and stuff?" Joe had an intent expression one would expect in a conversation about something more obviously appealing than sewage and rainwater. "I've been doing some reading about a spot right near here. There's a story that's been floating around for a long, long time about a man by the name of Deschanel who was trying to learn how to stop the flooding. Died trying, as a matter of fact."

Dr. Britton's eyebrows had risen halfway up his forehead. "Deschanel? Where'd you hear that story?"

"I got an old book out of the library. It's full of stories about the early years of the city. Especially about water. The guy that wrote it was all about water. Lately, I am, too."

Dr. Britton's words were calm, but Faye could tell he was one step away from demanding that Joe get him that book *right now*. All he said was, "Wait until you see the title search for this piece of property." His voice rose, in spite of himself. "One of its earliest owners was a man named Deschanel."

His workers had gathered round as they noticed that their boss was losing his composure. When they learned that two old documents carrying a single name—Deschanel—tied this property and its unusual collection of ditches, cesspools, and canals to a real human being who built things like ditches, cesspools, and canals, all anybody could say was "Cool." And that included Faye and Joe.

Faye sat on the front stoop of the Victorian shotgun house that occupied the land where Monsieur Deschanel's house had once stood. She rested her hands flat on the old bricks beneath her, because she liked their chalky feel. Joe sprawled on the grass at her feet, leaning back on his elbows and stretching out his long legs.

She wiped a bead of sweat off her jaw. "It's been an interesting morning, but I swear that I can't see how Shelly's work could've had anything to do with her death."

Louie Godtschalk, the writer who had upset Nina so, was puttering around the site, gazing curiously into the excavations and just generally getting in the way of archaeologists who were trying to work. Faye could not believe that Joe had called a virtual stranger and urged him to come tour the site with them. Joe hardly spoke to people he *knew*.

It seemed that Joe had cornered Godtschalk after his ill-fated television interview because he'd sensed that the man shared an interest that was growing into a mild obsession for Joe—how the heck did the water here work, anyway? When Joe learned that he and Faye were talking to archaeologists who could actually *show* him the remains of canals and cesspools and such, he got on his phone and told Godtschalk to get himself over there.

Joe had always seen nature as a logical thing, a web of interlocking habitats that made the world go 'round. Once he noticed that rainwater in these parts flowed *away* from the largest river on the continent, he wasn't going to rest until he understood the oddities of this strand in the earth's web.

Water seemed like such a simple subject, but in New Orleans, it just wasn't. It was, at rock bottom, the only subject. Stave off the omnipresent danger of flood, and the city lives. Fail to stave it off, and the city dies.

Joe's fascination with the subject had driven him out of nature and into the library. It took a lot of doing to convince Joe to go indoors.

Louie Godtschalk, who looked like he was born in a library, had been so seduced by the watery history of his hometown that he'd been driven outdoors. Faye had spent the past hour talking to Dr. Britton, while watching Louie and Joe out of the corner of her eye. They had never once stopped talking.

They'd done more than talk, really. They'd walked the site, chatting about slight changes in elevation. They'd stood in each excavation and tried to read history from the earthen walls, then they'd squatted under a tree and pored through the stacks of books they'd each brought with them.

"Looks like you've made a new buddy," she said to Joe, nodding in the direction of the pasty-faced academic, whose face wore a smear of mud and a beatific smile. Faye hoped the man had remembered to put on some sunscreen.

"I can't believe we've read this same book." Joe looked down at his library copy of James McGonahan's *The Floodgates of Hell.* "And I mean the *same* book. Louie says they're not printing it any more, and there's only this one copy that he knows about. He turned it in last week, just in time for me to check it out."

Godtschalk poked his head out of the excavation and beckoned excitedly to Joe, who loped over for a look. Faye couldn't help smiling at the contrast between tall, lean, dark Joe and the pudgy little white-haired author.

Dr. Britton was seated in a lawn chair, with a sheaf of over-sized papers spread across his lap. Faye watched as he leaned close to one, squinting, then beckoned to Faye with the same intellectual excitement as Godtschalk had just shared with Joe.

"You're interested in the work Shelly did for us? Well, this is it." He slapped at the paper in his lap. "She could discern the most telling details from an old map or an aerial photograph. Any idiot can see the route of the old Carondelet Canal cutting diagonally across these neighborhoods north of the Quarter, even though it's been out of service for seventy years."

"The whole canal's out of service?" Faye distinctly remembered reading otherwise.

"Well, pieces of it are still used for drainage, which is fairly remarkable, considering they started building it in 1794. But for the most part, it's gone. Filled in and covered over. But that's beside the point. I wanted you to understand that Shelly saw things in these photos that nobody else could. Look. You and I can see the scar left by a big ol' canal stretching across miles and miles."

He tapped on the paper, where anyone with eyes could see the Carondelet Canal's mark on the cityscape.

"Well, Shelly could see evidence of little tiny things—a ditch or a wall or a pathway that's been gone for a century. She was that good."

Godtschalk walked over to see what they were doing. When Dr. Britton pulled another photo out of the stack and spread it atop the others, the writer grabbed his glasses excitedly, lifting them a quarter-inch off the bridge of his nose so that he could focus through the proper section of his trifocals.

Joe looked at him with an expression that said, "What the heck are you doing with your glasses?" and Faye wanted to say, "Yeah, people get old. Even you will, someday." She had recently invested in a pair of reading glasses, but they were hidden in her shirt pocket, waiting to be used at times when she just couldn't manage without them...and when nobody was looking.

If she squinted, she could see the photo perfectly well. Okay, not perfectly, but well enough.

"Would you look at the resolution of that thing?" Godtschalk enthused. "You can see cars. You can almost see them well enough to identify a particular car. You can even see people, but they're just blobs walking down the street." He shifted his glasses a quarter-inch to the right and Faye wondered whether he needed a new prescription. "Hey! You can even see the fortune-telling gypsies sitting at their tables in front of the cathedral!"

That did it. Faye wanted to see the gypsies.

She broke down and pulled the glasses out of her pocket, despite the fact that she hated for Joe to see her wear them. It was a bit startling to be so visibly reminded that satellites and airplanes and helicopters—the world's eyes in the sky—never slept. And they didn't need trifocals, either. Most people never gave a thought to the hardware zipping around the Earth until their GPS went on the fritz. Faye knew somebody who could be seen on Google Streetview, calmly riding her bicycle down the street with her dog at her side.

"Shelly's talents were as psychic as any of those fakers on Jackson Square," Dr. Britton said. He raised his own glasses off his nose, and rubbed a handkerchief over his eyes. "Losing her was such a waste." He took a moment to gather his composure. "She was no gypsy, though. Shelly's skills weren't magic. After she'd shown me an anomaly on one of her photos, I could see it, too. She just had an incredible eye for detail. And not just with aerial photography, either. Let me show you something."

They followed him to his car, where he pulled a heavy file box from the back seat. Shuffling through junk that seemed to have been thrown in there randomly, he pulled out an old copy of *Archaeology* magazine.

"Most high-profile article I ever published," he said, smoothing the cover possessively. "We found a very early habitation site not far from here, but maybe I shouldn't say 'we.' Shelly turned that job from an absolute bust into some of the most interesting work I've done."

He opened the magazine and went straight to the page he wanted. "See this photo? See the silhouette where a wooden post decayed in place?"

Faye did. Of course she did. The darkened soil enclosed within straight vertical lines was hard to miss.

"Well, this is what it looked like when Shelly first saw it."

He pointed to another photo that showed an excavation cutting down through apparently undisturbed soil. A small black arrow in the middle of the photo pointed to a smudge only slightly darker than the surrounding dirt. "Shelly crawled down in the hole and studied the stratigraphy until that dark spot caught her eye. She told me she thought it was something interesting. I said, 'Yeah, right,' but we enlarged the unit...and found what was left of a hut that dated to the early 1700s. I never doubted her after that."

The handkerchief took another swipe under his glasses.

Faye studied the photo with its tiny telltale smudge. Yes, the woman had indeed been good.

"Since we resumed work at this site, I've wished for someone with Shelly's skills. You've seen some of the remnants of water storage and drainage features that we found. We've done the best we could at reading the soils' permeability and texture and color, then imagining where people would have wanted their water moved. We've done okay, I think. Still, I have to wonder what she could have done with the very same information. The only comfort is knowing that she used her skills to the very end, saving lives. My friend Bobby worked with her at Zephyr Field. It takes a lot to earn Bobby's respect, but Shelly did."

It occurred to Faye that Shelly sounded a lot like Joe in her feel for the way the natural world worked. Joe was, at that moment, head-down in the open unit, scooping up chunks of soil and smelling it. She took off her glasses. If he was going to taste that dirt, she didn't want to see.

Chapter Eighteen

Faye wished her cell phone hadn't rung. Well, it didn't ring, actually. It played the memorable strains of *The Sorceror's Apprentice*, because they were just bombastic enough to catch her attention when she was deep in an excavation, hard at work. She couldn't believe that Jodi had gotten her cell phone company to honor her maintenance contract and get it replaced so quickly. Badges were handy things to have.

If her phone had just stayed silent or if Jodi hadn't managed to get it replaced or if Faye had managed to somehow ignore those bombastic strains, then she could have gone a little longer without knowing the truth about Nina's accident-that-wasn't-an-accident. As it was, she wished she had just switched the phone off, instead of listening to what Jodi had to say. But Faye was a realist. Given a choice, she would always opt for the truth, no matter how grim. Jodi's voice had sounded tight—choked, even—when Faye answered the phone, so she'd had early warning that this was one of those times when the truth was grim.

"My divers found some things in the river, under the dock where Nina fell in."

Faye's analytical mind reflexively began trying to figure out what the divers found. She decided that it had to be something heavy enough to sink, and shaped in such a way that it dropped to the bottom before the mighty river moved it far downstream… then she stopped herself. Some of the possibilities were icky enough that she didn't want to think about them. Besides, Jodi was going to tell her anyway.

"The most important thing we found was an archaeologist's trowel."

Jodi sounded like she wished she didn't have to tell Faye that.

Faye didn't like the direction her thoughts were taking her.

"At least, I think it was an archaeologist's trowel, but it doesn't look like the ones I saw in your office."

Faye's answer was slow in coming. "There are other kinds of trowels out there in the marketplace. It's just that archaeologists are just a boring bunch, so most of us use the same kind. Was it…did it have a blunt end, like a spatula?"

"Yes. And the shape of the cut on her head and the bruise around it matches that odd shape. At least my forensics people say so. You've seen one like it lately?"

"It was Nina's." The anger surged so quickly that Faye was hard-put to say where it had come from. Apparently, it had been there all the time. "Who did it? Who did this thing?"

"We're a little short on clues, other than the trowel. You and Joe tracked the dock up with your old dirty boots, so I can't say whether anybody else was out there who might have pushed Nina."

Faye said, "I'm so sorry—," but Jodi wouldn't let her finish the apology.

"Crap, Faye. If Joe hadn't tracked mud out there, Nina would be dead right now. And if you hadn't left another trail of grime, Joe might be dead, too. Let it rest."

Nina had been attacked with her own trowel, a tool so intimate that it rarely left her hand during working hours. Faye groped for words—just for a second, but it wasn't like her to be at a loss for words, ever. She came up with one.

"Things." The word was important, so she said it again. "Things. You said you found 'things' in the water. What else did you find besides Nina's trowel?"

"Um…weird stuff."

"I'm coming to think that everything about this town is weird."

"Well, it is. But usually it's weird in a good way."

"Are you going to tell me what you found, or not?"

Jodi expelled a stream of air from her lips that was audible even over the staticky cell phone connection. "Yeah. I'll tell you. But remember that I told you it was weird."

"I'm waiting."

"Five coffin nails. And a handful of pennies. And they went in the water recently, because it wouldn't take too awful long for the Mississippi River to wash some silt over the top of 'em."

Faye couldn't think of any logical response to this, other than, "How do you know they were coffin nails?"

"Do you know how many voodoo shops there are in New Orleans? And how many hoodoo practitioners we've got?"

"No. Do you?"

"No. But it's a whole lot. I've run across coffin nails before. And a whole lot of other hexes and spells. I went out to your work site to ask Dauphine what she knew about those nails. She wouldn't say much, other than that coffin nails were used to bind things. She allowed as how maybe somebody wanted to bind Nina to this life. The way she said it, I'm thinking that Dauphine threw them in the water and that she was doing what any voodoo mambo would do for a friend. I never got her to actually say so, though."

"Maybe somebody wanted to bind Nina to the bottom of the Mississippi."

Faye didn't like being so relentlessly negative, but it was just how she felt at the moment.

"Heck if I know. Now pennies…" Jodi's voice turned speculative. "As far as I know, they're usually good luck pieces. Lots of people carry a penny in their pocket all the time to keep from being bewitched."

"Really? These days? In the twenty-first century?"

"Yes, really. And don't get all high and mighty on me. Your family's been in the South for a long time?"

"You know it has." It rankled Faye to think Jodi was implying that being southern was inextricably linked to being ignorant. And it made no sense, since Jodi's people had probably been in south Louisiana since Napoleon was a boy.

"So what does it mean when you drop a fork?"

"Company's coming."

"When you step over a child lying on the floor?"

Faye wished that she didn't know the answer, because knowing it meant that Jodi was right. "She'll stop growing."

"You don't sweep dirt out of your house after dark, do you? Because you'll sweep your luck out the door. And you do know that sweeping under a woman's feet means she'll be an old maid."

"I don't sweep. I like dirt."

A smug laugh told her that Jodi knew she'd won this round. "You archaeologists are all about culture. Well, superstition's a part of that. Isn't it? There's a bit of Africa in every corner of this part of the country. You can call it voodoo, if you're into the formal religion stuff. *Voudon*, if you want to be plu-perfect about your spelling. Or you can call it hoodoo, if you prefer your root magic passed down from mother to child. But don't tell me you think people don't still believe in the power of coffin nails."

Faye grunted, wishing she could think of an argument that would deny the truth. People are superstitious and they always will be. They just shift their irrational beliefs into a modern form…hence the proliferation of fortune-tellers who plied their trade by telephone, television, and internet.

Jodi laughed again. "Faye. You're a fraud. I bet you don't even shake crumbs out of your tablecloths outside after dark. Somebody might die."

"I don't own a tablecloth." And it was a good thing, because there was no way she'd be shaking any crumbs outside after dark, not while Nina's life hung in the balance. "How's Nina doing?"

"Not much different. Doing better all the time, physically, but she still doesn't make much sense when she talks. You know, it could have been worse. If Nina had been attacked by a strong assailant with a pointy trowel like yours, it might have punctured her skull."

Faye paused again. The notion of being attacked with her own trowel, the tool that rarely left her hand on the average workday, felt like an utter violation. Thinking of it gave her the same sick shudder that came of imagining a stranger putting a gun in her hand and forcing her to point it at her own head and pull the trigger.

Faye couldn't talk, so she just mumbled, "Later," and thumbed the phone off.

Jodi's call had taken just minutes. Dr. Britton had stepped back into the open excavation, pointing to soil thats only claim to fame was the fact that it was the wrong color. No one had even seen her leave, except Joe.

Joe didn't miss much, and he didn't miss the look that Jodi's news had left on Faye's face. He locked his sea green eyes on hers and rested a comforting hand on her shoulder. Faye remembered that having Joe made her a lucky girl, if a female person on the verge of forty could ever be considered a girl.

"This band of goopy clay here," Dr. Britton was saying, sticking the point of his trowel into a ribbon-wide layer of black soil, "is something we have to watch. It's a conduit for water, because rainwater seeps down through the more porous layers and gets stopped by the clay. Then it moves along the surface of this layer and oozes into the excavation, flooding it slowly. If it weren't for this goop, we could probably work without a pump."

Pumps. Faye hated pumps.

"It's a weak point, too. We have to watch what we're doing, because the soils can slip along that plane, caving into the unit and leaving us nothing but scrambled eggs."

Faye knew that she would hate that metaphor forever.

"Shelly's the one who identified that layer as the source of our seepage problems."

Why wasn't Faye surprised to hear that?

"If Shelly were still working with us," Dr. Britton continued, "we'd understand all those ditches and sumps and cesspools. She'd have read the soil better than any of us can, checked old maps, then somehow put herself in the place of people in those days until she guessed where they wanted their water moved. And why. And how they would have done it. We'll manage without her, but it won't be the same."

Dr. Britton crawled out of the excavation and took Faye by the elbow. He reached out the other hand and grabbed Joe's elbow, carefully steering both his captives toward the single picnic table sitting outside the trailer that served as his field office. Godtschalk followed them, and Dr. Britton didn't shoo him away.

"I've nattered on about how good Shelly's work was, and I sure don't mind my workers hearing that. But there are some other things I wanted to make sure the detective knew, things that maybe should stay just between us. You did say you were working with Detective Bienvenu?"

Faye and Joe both nodded and settled themselves at the picnic table. Godtschalk hesitated, but Dr. Britton flapped a hand at the picnic bench. "Go ahead and have a seat, Louie. I've got some thoughts I'd like to share with the law, but I've got some sense that I'd also like to share them with a writer...someone who's chronicling what happened to our city. Somehow, I think Shelly's story is important in a way that might belong in your book. Please join us."

Dr. Britton picked up his sandwich and leaned over it, speaking quietly. "Shelly was worried about one of the levees." He paused for emphasis. "Before Katrina."

"What was she? Psychic?" Godtschalk asked. "You make her sound supernatural."

"No, not supernatural. Not psychic. Just a very smart girl who never missed the smallest detail. Also, she was tenacious as hell."

"Why was she worried about the levee?" asked Joe.

"Not long before the storm, she was testing a new pump at the company's Lakeview branch office, within site of a canal levee. Try as she might, she couldn't get that test pit dry. Water was coming into the test pit as quickly as that pump could get it out. Lots of people would have blamed the pump. Sometimes the new ones are so flimsy that our ugly old ones leave them in the dust."

Faye felt a new appreciation for Old Wheezy.

Dr. Britton set down his half-eaten sandwich. "I know other people who would've said, 'Hey, the whole city's under sea level' and given up. Shelly got down in that waist-deep water, so she could find out where it was coming from."

Faye didn't like the sound of too much groundwater so near a levee. A grim possibility—actually two grim possibilities—were coalescing in her mind. "Was it a slippery clay layer like the one you have here?" she asked.

"You got it. Now nobody sitting here is a civil engineer, but this isn't rocket science. All that groundwater was probably coming from the canal, beneath the levee. That's called 'under-seepage,' and it isn't a good thing. A levee's just a pile of dirt. If an extra-permeable layer lets canal water undermine it, then the whole levee could go."

"The slippery layer—" Joe began, but Dr. Britton kept talking.

"Underseepage can destroy a levee, even when the water level in the canal is normal, but think about what can happen when that level rises. The levee is put under stress by the increased water pressure, and that stress is directed straight out."

Joe nodded. "If there's a slippery layer underneath, then the levee's going to slide sideways. Probably break apart while it's doing that. The whole thing would be shoved back from the canal."

"That's a recipe for failure," Godtschalk said. His voice was tight.

"What did Shelly do?"

Faye hadn't known the woman, yet she was confident that Shelly had gone to someone who she thought could help.

"She called the levee board. She called the drainage commission. She called the Corps of Engineers. She told them that the situation was one step short of a sand boil."

Faye saw by his expression that Joe had the same question that she did, so she asked it. "And a sand boil would be…?"

The third person listening to the story, Godtschalk, didn't have the same question on his face, but then he was local. "Water seeps under levees all the time," he said. "It's terrifying when you think about it, but engineers design for that underseepage. I've seen an open field with dozens of wet spots, even little tiny upwellings like fountains. When the water's clear, all's well. But when those upwellings start bringing up sand—in other words, when they turn into a sand boil—watch out. That sand is coming out of the soil supporting the levee, or even the levee itself."

Now, Faye could get a glimpse of the extent of Shelly's concern. "Did anybody listen to her? Or did they brush her off?"

Dr. Britton gave a short bark of a laugh. "They didn't get a chance to brush her off. In my heart, I believe that they would have told her that the design was sound and that she shouldn't worry her little head about it, but I've got to give them the benefit of the doubt. They didn't have time to return Shelly's calls. Katrina was already roaring our way and anybody who was able got the hell out. Within days, we got a chance to see how well those levee designs held up."

Godtschalk grunted. "Days? If I know politics around here, it would have taken years to get action. Maybe if Shelly had made her discovery when she was a little girl making mud pies, something could have been done in time…"

"In time?" Dr. Britton started to laugh, and it looked like the laughter hurt him. "In time? Hurricane Betsy blew through in 1965, when I was in first grade. It was bad. People who weren't here then have forgotten Betsy, but it was bad. My grandmother's house flooded up to the eaves. The government told us, 'Never again,' and they drew up a flood control plan that was supposed to stand behind that statement…only they put that plan on a fifty-year schedule. It wasn't finished when Katrina made her appearance. Do you want to know how long fifty years is? Just look at me."

Faye studied his grizzled beard and the deep lines carving into his forehead. Fifty years was a long time.

"When a government makes a promise to a few hundred thousand people," she said, "I don't think it should take nearly that long to deliver."

"No kidding. But a lot of levees *did* get built, and there's an irony there. People—lots of people—died after Katrina, because they told themselves, 'My house didn't flood during Betsy, and they've built the levees up since then. It'll never be that bad again.' They could look out their windows and see nice, tall levees, and they trusted them. It's easy to trust that a humongous pile of dirt won't go anywhere."

"Did that levee fail?" Joe asked. "The one Shelly was worried about?"

Dr. Britton shook his head. "No. It held. It was the Orleans Canal. It didn't fail because there was a two-hundred foot gap in it."

Faye remembered Nina grieving on live television over that mystifying hole.

With trembling hands, Dr. Britton wrapped his unfinished sandwich in a napkin. "I don't know why the levee system on that canal was never finished, but that's the way it was. They say it happened because of political infighting, but it hardly matters now. Water just poured out of the gap and into the city. It didn't get deep enough in the canal to put the kind of pressure on the levees that Shelly was worried about. So we don't know whether she was right."

His voice dropped to a whisper. "Dear God. I hope we never have another chance to find out."

After a half-hour spent studying Dr. Britton's detailed maps and aerial photos, the simple and colorful city map stuffed in Faye's pocket began to look a little silly. She'd found it on a rack of brochures catering to tourists and, silly or not, it had kept her from getting lost for months now.

She unfolded it and spread it across the picnic table. "I could sit here and talk shop with you all day, but Joe and I should probably try to do something else today to earn our police consulting fees. You told me on the phone that your friend Bobby was one of the last people to see Shelly alive?"

"Yep, Bobby was working with her, side by side, making maps to guide rescue teams through the flood. Bobby's a funny guy. He's no older than you, but he's a history scholar of the old school. Bobby likes to read about the past. He doesn't like it to get him dirty."

Dr. Britton looked ruefully at the ground-in dirt on his knees. Faye didn't look at hers, because she knew they were just as grubby.

"Bobby's made a career of studying historical maps of New Orleans, which gave him enough knowledge of the modern city to save lives during the flood. Helping the rescue teams after Katrina was the only practical thing the man has done in his life. The time he spent at Zephyr Field…I'd call that his finest hour. There are a lot of people walking around alive today because of Shelly and Bobby."

"It seems like everybody but the police in Missing Persons knew what Shelly did after the hurricane," Faye observed. "I bet they're feeling stupid about now."

Dr. Britton shook his head. "I didn't know, not until this week, when they found her dead and everybody started talking about it. If the police had talked to the right people back then, they'd have found out right quick. Nobody was keeping it a secret on purpose, and everybody in these parts likes to talk."

"Where does Bobby work now?"

"He works for the Department of Culture, Recreation, and Tourism. He's all about culture, but he really hates the recreation and tourism part of the department's work. I should probably tell you that Bobby's a bit of a snob. He can't help it. His family was high and mighty in this town for decades before Napoleon got around to selling it to us. Sometimes a family like that hands down money, and sometimes they don't. In Bobby's case, they didn't. But that sense of utter superiority…it must be on a dominant gene."

Faye folded up her crummy tourist's map, resolving not to let Bobby the map connoisseur see it. "You said he's working near here?"

"Walking distance, actually. In the Quarter. At the Historic New Orleans Collection. Their map collection is amazing, and if a man can fall in love with a sheet of paper or ten, Bobby's managed it. He just got back from some time in Texas—went there to get some work and to live in a house that hadn't ever been wet. But his family goes back more than 250 years in this town. A little water ain't gonna keep Bobby away forever."

Chapter Nineteen

Faye liked the way Joe looked, walking through Congo Square, where people had gathered to trade and sing and dance and socialize for a couple hundred years. Faye's boots made a clatter on the cobblestones, but Joe never made a sound when he walked.

Sometimes, Joe wore traditional Creek garb, from head to toe, right down to the moccasins that he sewed for himself. Other times, like today, he traded jeans for his buckskin pants, but there was almost always a feather plunged casually into the nape of his ponytail. And the moccasins were non-negotiable. Whether Joe wore buckskin or a tuxedo to their wedding, she knew what would be on his feet.

Faye had spent a year trying to decide what kind of wedding she wanted, but her ambivalence extended even to that subject. It would be at home, at Joyeuse. That part was non-negotiable for her. But would they invite a crowd of their friends? Did she want to sew herself the dress of her dreams? Or should they load Magda, her husband Mike, and a handy preacher on a boat, haul them out to Joyeuse, and just do it?

She didn't want to think about it, so she looked around Congo Square, instead. The shade of Louis Armstrong Park's old oaks, which had lured her on this detour, was inviting, but the square itself felt alive with the ghosts of all the people who'd passed before. The slaves of New Orleans had precious few freedoms, but Sunday gatherings in Congo Square had been one of them.

The rhythms and melodies played here on African instruments—*bamboulas, banzas,* and gourds—would one day morph into jazz and blues and rock-and-roll, and even in that long-ago time, such music could draw a crowd. Tourists in powdered wigs and whale-boned corsets had gathered like rock groupies to watch dancing like they'd never seen before and would never see anywhere else.

According to Dr. Britton, they were just downriver from the site of the former turning *bassin* for the Carondelet Canal, a basin of water where loaded boats made a U-turn and headed back to Lake Pontchartrain. It was no surprise that one of the most famous streets in this wet city, Basin Street, was named for an oversized mud puddle.

Faye had spent so much time reading up on the history of her temporary home that she found it easy to imagine that time had stood still. The fact that so many houses and cobblestoned streets in the old parts of town were right where the colonial French and Spanish had put them made it even easier.

If she squinted, Joe could pass for a tribal chieftain, striding proudly through town when the old city was new, ready to negotiate as an equal with the fledgling territorial government. She could have been…well, in all likelihood, she would have been a slave, but she might have been lucky enough to live in the social no-man's-land of a free person of color. She figured it was her fantasy, so she could be a free woman, if she pleased.

She imagined herself strutting proudly through the Congo Square marketplace, dressed in varicolored calico, her hair wrapped in a fashionable *tignon*, with a certain spectacular-looking Creek chieftain by her side. As an archaeologist, Faye's daydreams tended to be remarkably colorful.

Crossing Rampart Street and entering the French Quarter did nothing to detract from the time-blurred sensation of this very pleasant walk. Faye shifted her focus to her feet, as she tried not to trip over two centuries of bumps and cracks in the sidewalks of the old city. Shopkeepers still started the day by washing down these sidewalks, just as they always had. Maybe the custom went back to the days when ditches ran around each block, catching whatever the rainwater sloshed into them.

Everything in sight, except for the people on the street and some of the expensive goods in the shop windows, had the worn patina of great age. Time passed slowly here, if at all.

As they walked down a street lined with antique stores that had once been banks, Faye heard little beyond the occasional clinging bell announcing that a customer had come in the door. The Historic New Orleans Collection was, fittingly, housed in one of the few buildings that survived the widespread fires that ravaged the old city in 1788 and 1794, so it was about as old and historic as a building could get in those parts.

Faye mentally shed her *tignon* and morphed back into a 21st-century woman as she walked through its old door. Joe never changed, no matter what century she imagined him in.

Dr. Britton had called ahead to let his friend Bobby know they were coming, but Dr. Britton neglected to give Faye and Joe Bobby's full name. Surely, he would introduce himself, because Faye couldn't see herself calling him "Dr. Bobby" indefinitely.

Dr. Bobby was slow to look up from his work when Faye and Joe walked into the room. He eventually focused a pair of soft brown eyes on them, but he was a millisecond late in doing it, as if to communicate that he was in control of their interaction. It was a very aristocratic thing to do.

He was of average height and slender. Faye thought his skin would have been pale, even if he hadn't spent all his adult life in map libraries. His facial bones were chiseled and his long-fingered hands, though uncalloused, still managed to be manly.

Bobby's hair was thick, wavy, and dark, and he moved with the languor of the very rich. Still, his dark-rimmed glasses didn't look expensive, and neither did his well-shined shoes. It was entirely possible that Dr. Bobby had no assets whatsoever, and no more income than the average historian. Which wasn't much.

In New Orleans, an old family was an old family. The fact that your old family lost everything in the Panic of 1837 was completely immaterial.

Faye took a deep breath. She'd been dreading this moment. It was time to talk to the person with the most intimate knowledge of Shelly's activities in her final days.

The oppressive pall of death over those days gave her the shivers, and not just Shelly's death. While the rescue team had been working feverishly at Zephyr Field, lives were being snuffed out, one by one, by the dank, rising water. Stopping to sleep, eat, even visit a stinking and overloaded portable toilet could have slowed rescuers just long enough to leave the world dimmer by just one light. Then another. Then another.

Maintaining his faintly superior air, Bobby shook their hands and said, "I'm pleased to meet you. My name is Robert Longchamp, but I'm known far and wide as Bobby."

He gave his name as "Lawnshaw," or some such French pronunciation, so it took Faye a few seconds to realize what he had said.

Releasing his hand, Faye looked closely at his face as she said, "Well, I pronounce it like a rural Floridian—'LAWNG-champ'—but I do believe we have the same last name. I'm Faye Longchamp, and this is Joe Wolf Mantooth."

The soft eyes lingered for a single extra millisecond on Faye's medium brown skin and glossy black hair, but he was too well-bred to show chagrin or even surprise at the suggestion that he might be related to someone so racially ambiguous. "What was your father's given name? And his mother's maiden name?"

"Earle. And my paternal grandmother was a Carr."

"Her mother?"

"I have no idea."

He gave a small nod, eyes fastened on her face as if he were trying to comprehend a family that didn't catalog their connections back to 1600s France, and beyond.

"I'll look at the family tree. And I have a cousin who's fairly obsessed with genealogy. She may know whether we're connected."

Wow. The first thing Bobby said to her, directly after stating his name, had been two questions: "Who's your daddy?" And "Who's his mama?"

If this man called his cousin "fairly obsessed with genealogy," then the cousin must be immersed in the subject to the point of insanity. Not that Faye had any room to talk. She might be ignorant of her father's family, but she knew as much about her maternal ancestors' roots in slavery as Bobby did about his high-falutin' family. Faye had read her great-great-great-great-great-grandfather's journal dozens of times.

The old, yellowing map on the table behind him caught her eye, and Bobby noticed. He finally smiled. "That one's nice, but take a look at this one."

He motioned for Faye and Joe to come look at a framed map on the wall that was even older and yellower. "I love this thing. It's an early drawing of the original layout of the city, and there's a bazillion copies floating around, but I just like to stand right here next to the original and breathe its air."

Yep. Bobby was a historian.

Faye scrutinized the map. The old, original city plan had been an orderly thing, with its neat gridwork of streets surrounding the cathedral and town square, the Place d'Armes. Fronted by the irregular sweeping curve of the Mississippi, and backed by swamps and bayous reaching all the way to Lake Pontchartrain, this tiny spot had been a misplaced piece of Europe, dropped down on a spot where life couldn't be so tightly controlled.

Joe reached out a finger and traced a long diagonal line in the air over the map, from Lake Pontchartrain to Rampart Street. By the time this drawing was made, the Carondelet Canal already sliced its way from the bayou to the back side of the city, neatly marking the general vicinity of the excavation she had just left.

Given a few seconds to count the blocks between where she stood and St. Louis Cathedral, she could have precisely plotted her current location on this two-hundred-plus-year-old map. It was amazing. The New World began its metamorphosis in 1492 and it had continued to this day. Few places on this side of the Atlantic had been so little changed as New Orleans over so great a period of time. But that wasn't why she was here.

"Al Britton called to tell you we were coming?" she asked.

Bobby nodded slightly.

"He tells me that you and Shelly Broussard spent a few harrowing days right about...there."

Faye pointed at a spot of swamp where Zephyr Field would be built in 1997.

The slender archaeologist pulled his glasses off and looked down at her, squinting. The motion shook the loose dark curls that dangled almost to his shoulders. He was attractive in a bookwormish sort of way. Before she met Joe, Faye would have said he was her type. One of her types. Truth be told, she was a fan of men in all their forms.

"Now why'd you have to take me out of 1798 and dump me into 2005? I was having fun in 1798. There wasn't a lot of fun to be had in 2005. Not the last part of it, anyway."

"I'm trying to help the police by talking to people who might have seen Shelly in her last days. Joe and I are archaeologists like she was, and we've been asked to chat around and find out what people remember."

"You're an archaeologist? No wonder you gave that map more than a passing glance. Sweet little thing, isn't it?" Then the rest of her statement hit home. "Shelly? Last days? Are you telling me they found her? Or did someone just finally give up and declare her dead."

"They found her. We found her, in a way. I was there. That's how I got involved."

Bobby had sunk into an elaborately upholstered chair. Joe dragged over a couple of matching chairs. He and Faye sat and waited for Bobby to go on.

"I'd hoped…" He swallowed. "Everybody had hoped…"

There was nothing to say.

He put his glasses back on, as if to hide behind them, and cleared his throat. "You asked how Shelly spent her last days. Well, I should know. I was right beside her. We were just cogs in a big, lopsided wheel, but we got some things done. Has anybody explained to you the convoluted way we rescuers found a lot of the victims? It's amazing, really, the ways that technology worked, and the ways that it didn't."

Faye shook her head and said, "I know so little that you might as well just tell me."

"Well, first of all, the rescuers were working in a zoo, but that's because Katrina walloped us where she wasn't supposed to. There were rescue teams staged in places like Shreveport, waiting for the clouds to clear so they could rush in…to Biloxi. All night long, the weather instruments were telling people that it was going to be bad in Mississippi. And it was. It was awful. But nobody expected the New Orleans levees to break, so we started out behind the eight-ball here, and we stayed there. Still, a lot of good things happened. It all started with the victims and their cell phones."

Faye, who had seen what happened to a human body when it was shoved off a cell phone tower, knew more about how they worked than she would have liked. "Their cell phones stayed functional after the storm?"

"To an extent. Voice calls were hard to place but, lots of times, text messages would go through. Some guy would be standing on his roof, thinking he was about to drown, and he'd send a good-bye text to his mama in Texas. Then, Mama would get on the phone to the Texas emergency people and tell them in no uncertain terms that they needed to, by God, send somebody to go get her baby."

"So the Texas people called the Louisiana people and told them where to find the missing person?" Joe asked.

"Hold your horses. Didn't I just say the cell phones weren't working too well here?"

Faye nodded to concede his point.

"So volunteers—say, at the University of Texas—took each text message and they found out the latitude and longitude where it was sent. Then they found a satellite or aerial photo taken after the flood and marked the coordinates of the victim's last known location. Well, really, the coordinates were for the victim's cell phone."

"And the volunteers would use that info to send out a rescue team?" It all sounded reasonable to Faye—except for one small detail. "But…how did they get the data into New Orleans? There were no regular phones at all, and no cells to speak of. Not enough to bet lives on, that's for sure. I'm guessing internet service was a pipe dream."

"No kidding. How did they send us the info? Good question. Some of it came in by satellite phone. And they actually flew in some of it in the form of data bricks."

Faye hated to display her ignorance, but she had no choice. "And data bricks would be…"

"Really, really, *really* big jump drives."

"Gotcha. I can see how that information would be enough to send out a rescue boat."

"No, it's not."

Faye was tired of being the idiotic half of this conversation, but she went along. "What am I missing here?"

"The water was all different depths. But our friends at the university in Texas could compare known water levels with detailed laser measurements of the city's topography—its *texture*, if you will. Using that information, they could tell the rescuers how deep the water was around the victim. Maybe they needed an airboat to get there. Or maybe a flatboat would do. Or maybe a simple high-axle vehicle."

Faye was struck by the tiny gap between pure research and feet-on-the-ground practicality. Jodi had told her about the days she spent after Katrina, trying to do police work with no way to call for help. Her descriptions of being hip-deep in sewage while chasing murdering low-lifes would stay with Faye a long time.

"God, how it would have helped the police if they could've had an eye-in-the-sky like that."

"And we shared our eye-in-the-sky with anybody we could find who needed our help. Police. Paramedics. Coast Guard. National Guard. Volunteers who hauled their fishing boats to town so they could help. Anybody. But first we had to find 'em. Communication was just…gone. It was as if Alexander Graham Bell had never been born."

Bobby's hand went unconsciously to the cell phone he wore on his belt, as if he half-expected modern communication to vanish again. Maybe he'd never again completely trust that somebody would be there when he picked up the phone.

"Anyway," he said, patting the phone absently. "When those data bricks got to us, Shelly and I could look at the information and send out an effective rescue team. Somebody brought us computers and some fantastic printers that we used to make maps of the routes for the rescue boats to take." He sat a little straighter in his chair. "And it worked. The rescuers found people, yanking them off rooftops and out of floodwaters, and they survived. It may be the only time I have ever felt like my own arcane little skill set was worth something to anybody outside academia. I somehow doubt that it ever will be again."

"I understand Shelly could handle a map pretty well, herself."

"Oh, yes. She was amazing. And she had the stamina of a Mack truck. We both sat stooped over those maps for days with hardly a nap. Hell, hardly a cup of coffee. All I had to do was to look at the latest satellite photo that showed the extent of the floodwaters and I was wide awake. Thinking about it now probably means I won't sleep tonight. Maybe not for a week."

He looked like he *needed* to sleep for a week.

"I understand that Shelly had a personal reason for working so hard. She didn't know whether her parents had gotten safely out of town."

Tears welled up in Bobby's eyes. "Every time we handed a map to another boat captain, she asked whether they'd been to Lakeview, and whether they'd seen her parents. She burned up the battery on her cell phone, trying to get a text message to them. She was a tough woman, but sometimes she was crying while she worked. And she wasn't the only one."

He gave up pretending that he wasn't crying and went fishing in his pockets for a handkerchief. "I was actually ashamed to tell people that my parents were okay. My whole family left for Shreveport before the first raindrop fell. It seemed…indecent… for me to even mention that to people who were terrified. Or grieving. You don't know what it was like here that week. And I don't know how to tell you."

"When did Shelly leave?"

"I wish I knew. After we'd been working about seventy-two hours straight, somebody snatched both my hands off the computer keyboard and dragged me to a cot. It was still warm from the person who just got out of it. I fell on my face and didn't move for hours…I don't know how many hours. When I got back to work, somebody else was in Shelly's chair."

"No one knew where she was?" Faye couldn't imagine that anybody was alert enough by that time to know where they themselves were.

"I heard that she'd completely lost it. She was heard yelling and screaming. Shrieking, even. Calling somebody names. Bad names. If you'd known Shelly, you'd know how far gone she must have been to behave that way."

"Who was she yelling at?"

"Nobody knows. It was hours in the past before I even heard about it. Frankly, I can't imagine there was a single calm person within a hundred miles of here that week. I figured she was sleeping it off on a cot somewhere, but she never came back. Still, I just thought somebody gave her another job to do. There wasn't really anyplace else to go. I had no idea that she was gone forever. It's horrible to just…lose…a human being."

Faye wished this conversation had never happened. She wished Bobby had never been forced to peek out of his ivory tower, because she didn't think he was built to weather tragedy. Somehow, he'd managed.

She offered an empty sentence designed to gloss over the enormity of what he'd seen. "I know things must have been busy and confusing for everybody that week."

He studied his soft and immaculate hands for a moment, then turned a surprisingly steady gaze on Faye's face.

"You have no idea. And I don't know how to tell you."

Chapter Twenty

Faye had spent the rest of her afternoon in the office Jodi lent her, following up on the things she'd learned from Dr. Britton and Bobby Longchamp. She'd made three important phone calls so far, and each of them had been a bust. Dr. Britton had told her that Shelly'd hoped to draw attention to the potential sand boil situation she'd uncovered in Lakeview. Maybe she'd been treading on some professional toes with some of her questions. Faye had thought it was time to find out.

Faye would have given a lot to know what Shelly had said to those people, and what they'd told her in reply. She'd made calls to every flood-control agency she could think of—the Corps of Engineers, the local levee board, the drainage district—trying to get that information. No luck.

If only Dr. Britton had known who Shelly had called at any of the agencies, Faye might have made some progress, but he didn't have a clue. Shelly's notes had drowned in the flood, which could have been predicted, but Faye was disappointed anyway. She was reduced to taking shots in the dark, calling random government employees, hoping to find someone who knew something. Anything.

The response had been predictably puny. An unheralded call from a stranger like Faye wasn't going to shake any lethargic bureaucrat into action. She might eventually hear from one of the people who had talked to Shelly about the underseepage problem, but it wouldn't be soon.

While she reached this disappointing conclusion, Faye had strewn notes and files and maps and photos hither and yon, following up on things she'd learned from Dr. Britton and Bobby Longchamp. Sometime during the afternoon, she'd officially bagged the idea of a relaxing weekend vacation with Joe. He would understand.

Joe was, in his way, as obsessed with finding Shelly's killer as she was. He carried his obsessions quietly, and nobody knew about them but her, but he could pursue the truth as implacably as Faye. He and Godtschalk were at the library, investigating the newspaper clipping Shelly had been carrying in her pocket. Its date could help them pinpoint her time of death.

Faye had elected to spend most of her remaining time and energy on Shelly's aerial photos. Everybody kept talking about how good the dead woman had been at reading the things. And there had been aerial photos found on her body. There had to have been an excellent reason for that. Shelly had wrapped those photos in plastic like precious heirlooms, then she had waded into a flood. Why was she carrying them?

Bobby had rooted through his collection, looking for the original of the pre-Katrina map of Lakeview that had been in her pocket. Until he found those actual prints, he'd lent her copies of other photos of the same area for comparison, a later version and a fifty-year-old print, without being asked. Faye could see that Bobby was thrilled that his little corner of the scholastic world could harbor things that were so useful in real life.

The original photos were much larger than the fragment Shelly had been carrying. More than two feet square, the three of them draped over the sides of her borrowed desk. They covered the central part of the city from the Mississippi to Lake Pontchartrain. The rectilinear street layout of the French Quarter, nearly three hundred years old, stood out among the curving streets of the Crescent City. Dauphine's neighborhood hid under its trees nearby. Congo Square, by contrast, was easy to spot. It had been there almost as long as the city had, lying just outside the Quarter, giving revelers a place to sing and dance out under the sky. Now there were planes and satellites in the same sky, looking down on those revelers and taking pictures.

In the newest photos, post-Katrina devastation was still evident, even down to the blue tarps on roofs. This made the photos interesting and depressing, but probably useless, since Shelly likely didn't live long enough to see them.

Faye turned to slightly older photos, taken just before Katrina. She could make out throngs of tourists on Bourbon Street. Horse-drawn carriages could be seen clip-clopping down Decatur Street, carrying still more tourists. She could see delivery trucks blocking streets that were designed for horses and buggies. Normal scenes of everyday life were visible in amazing detail, but what did that tell her?

Motives for murder could so easily be masked by everyday routines. Something as simple as a car parked in the wrong place could reveal that somebody's husband was somewhere he shouldn't be. There could no doubt be something in one of these photos that had gotten Shelly killed. Faye just didn't know enough to see it.

As she was putting away the photo taken just before Katrina, an odd cluster of activity caught her eye. Large construction equipment was parked alongside a levee, presumably for maintenance or for improvements. She knew such construction was still going on even now, because Joe had seen it. Maybe she'd get him to take her over there for a look. She could think of no useful reason to do that, but she didn't know how levees were built and Faye liked to understand how things worked.

Faye gawked at the clarity of the image, thinking, *Sweet Lord, these photos are amazing. In ten years, we'll be able to see people pick their noses.*

A long straight line stood out to Faye's eye, as clearly as if someone had marked the photo with a yellow highlighter. It was different somehow from all the short straight lines and natural curves of the scene. Even when she looked away, it drew her eye as soon as she returned her focus to the photo. Surely this was how Shelly's gift had worked. She'd simply been incredibly sensitive to details that were visually different from their surroundings, more so than most people.

Now Faye was having the same experience. Once she noticed that straight line, she couldn't have ignored it if she'd tried. It was a sheet piling being driven into a levee to form a metal extension that raised the effective height of its earthen berm, just like those that Joe, the self-trained water resources engineer, had seen pounded into the ground not long before.

If she'd thought about it beforehand, she'd never have imagined that the piling would be visible from so far away, but it made sense. To bite far enough into the soil to hold back raging floodwaters, the thing would have to be lots longer than a car, and cars were easily visible on photos of this scale. People had been driving past the levee at the instant this photo was shot, and the piling was longer than their cars were. But not enough longer. The fact that it was too short was obvious to Faye in the same way that Shelly's observations had been obvious to her.

How long *should* that sheet piling have been?

Shelly hadn't been doing a major geological study when she hit the mucky layer of soil that had scared her so badly. She'd just been trying out a new pump. Faye sincerely doubted that she'd dug a hole halfway to China to do that. She'd have bored down to the water table, and then gone just a little deeper. In that area, Faye'd guess six feet, give or take.

Dr. Britton had said that Shelly was working very near a levee. How tall would that levee have been? Faye conjured one up in her mind's eye and guessed eight feet. And how much sheet piling would stick out of the top? Four feet, maybe? So it would take twelve feet or so of piling just to reach ground level. Then it would take another four feet to reach the top of the mucky soil that had worried Shelly so. That was sixteen feet of piling, and who knew how thick the worrisome layer of soil was? To keep water from seeping through it, the protective sheet piling needed to go all the way through it, with extra length to spare to anchor it into something stable.

Faye was no engineer, but she wasn't altogether sure she was looking at pilings that were long enough to protect against the seepage that had driven Shelly to get on the phone and look for help. And even if they *were* long enough, was it possible that Shelly had seen something else? Something that nobody else saw? Something that doomed a levee and the people it was protecting? Had someone cut corners while installing this levee? And maybe others?

Not long after this photo was taken, Shelly got worried about a levee and started asking questions. And not long after that, the world watched one levee after another fail catastrophically.

Shelly worked for a firm that did civil engineering. Levee construction was high-stakes work for a business like that. Any design engineer working on a levee project—not to mention every last one of their contractors—would be shaken to hear the questions Shelly was asking. If one of those people had already known that the levee might be inadequate, then Shelly's questions would have been troubling indeed.

Would those questions have been a motive for murder?

Before August 2005, it might not have been. After more than a thousand bodies were fished from the floodwaters? Yes. Shelly could have died for those questions.

Faye was out of her league here. She'd better call Jodi. The detective probably needed to add another consultant to her payroll—a pricey one. Faye had a feeling that civil engineers cost a lot more than archaeologists.

The phone rang. Faye answered it, expecting to hear Joe's voice explaining how he and his new buddy, Louie Godtschalk, needed to work real late at the library. If she'd looked at the screen before flipping open her cell, she would have known that the caller worked for Pontchartrain Engineering.

"You need to lay off the calls to the Corps of Engineers." It was the opening salvo of a woman whose tone brooked no impertinence.

"Who is this, and why do you care that I'm talking to the Corps? They're a government agency and I'm a taxpayer."

Faye felt like she paid a lot of taxes, just like everybody else. The more she thought about it, the more this woman had pissed her off with a single twelve-word sentence. "They have a public information officer who has nothing to do all day but make sure we taxpayers know what's happening to our money."

"This is Leila Caron, Charles Landry's assistant. The Corps pays my paycheck and everybody else's here at Pontchartrain Engineering. They're our biggest client, and I'm on the phone every day that rolls, talking to that public information officer and to the contracting officer and to their purchasing department. People are talking."

"Already? I just called them. Those people are getting paid with my tax dollars. If they've got time to talk about me, then they need some more work to do."

"Yeah? Well, they've caught a lot of flak they didn't deserve these last few years. Sometimes things just happen, things that nobody can foresee, not even the best engineer alive. Those people are hurting, too. They asked me who you were and why you were stirring up Shelly's old paranoid business at this late date." Leila's voice dropped three semi-tones. "I told them I'd find out."

Faye was hard to intimidate. "You're not paranoid when they're really out to get you. Shelly saw the levee failures coming a week before they happened, and she called over there to talk to an engineer who would know something about the design. I wanted to know what she said to that engineer, but I can't find out who it was."

"For all you know, she's dead. Drowned." Leila's voice had been steadily rising, but she caught herself. "It's over, and the Corps has been patching up those levees ever since."

"So the Corps of Engineers is your biggest client. Have they been paying Pontchartrain Engineering to repair those levees? Did your company build them in the first place?"

"Shut up." It was the spiteful voice of a high school cheerleader who wasn't accustomed to having the school dweeb get in her face. "Just shut up."

"Didn't you lose anything in the flooding? Didn't you lose any*body*? Don't you want to know why it all happened?"

Leila Caron hung up the phone.

Somehow, Faye wasn't surprised when the phone rang again. She had clearly hit a sensitive spot with her calls to the Corps and the other flood control agencies. When Shelly had made the same calls, she would have hit the same tender spot. Only it would have been worse. Faye was just looking for information. Shelly had been calling with hard questions about questionable design and other uncomfortable issues.

There was a soft, firm woman's voice on the other end of the line.

"I'm Chloe Scott, with the Army Corps of Engineers, New Orleans District."

Faye remembered that, somewhere in Leila's diatribe, she had spewed out some reference to the fact that Shelly's contact at the Corps had been a woman. She'd said, *For all you know, she's dead.* She figured that this meant Leila's statement was about a specific person.

If Leila had said, "For all you know, he's dead," while speaking about an engineer, then she might have been speaking about a hypothetical person. But Leila had said, "For all you know, *she's* dead." Even now, in the twenty-first century, Faye couldn't think of a single workplace where a design engineer would be automatically presumed to be a woman.

"Ms. Longchamp—" the woman continued. "I heard you called and asked about my friend Shelly."

"Can you tell me about her? I can come to your office, if—"

"I'm at a coffee shop called the Rue de la Course on Magazine Street. Can you find it?"

Faye checked her wristwatch. It was already past five.

"I'm on my way."

◇◇◇

Chloe Scott's accent said that she hailed from somewhere north of the Mason-Dixon line. Faye was thinking maybe Ohio. She had apparently been in the Big Easy long enough to like her coffee strong, black, and laced with chicory.

Chloe would never be able to find coffee to suit her now, if she were to decide to move back home. She was trapped here forever, below sea level, because now she knew that no one anywhere else in the world knew how to brew coffee properly. She would never again be content with Ohio-baked bread or with food cooked without sufficient seasoning, either. If Chloe had not yet learned how to make a roux, moving back north would mean that dinnertime wouldn't be a happy time for her, not ever again.

If Faye weren't engaged to marry a handsome man who was a brilliant cook, she'd be in the same boat as Chloe.

Chloe was getting a refill when Faye arrived. She sat across the table and knocked back half an unsweetened cup while Faye loaded hers with sugar and cream.

"So why did you call the District asking about Shelly? There's been whispering among the office gossips all afternoon. I heard that her body was finally found." Chloe took another swallow and added, "God rest her soul."

"I was told that Shelly was worried about the levees. I just wanted to know more."

"What are you? A reporter?" Chloe's icy blue eyes looked away from Faye's for just a second, but they flicked back and held steady.

"I'm an archaeologist."

"Those levees aren't that old. Some of the ones along the river are old enough to interest someone like you, but not those."

"The past is the past. I'm interested in all of it. But I just wanted to learn more about Shelly's fears as a...private citizen. An interested private citizen."

Okay, that was sort of a lie, but she figured that saying she was a contractor for the police department was a quick way to make Chloe shut up. So maybe she was a plain-clothes archaeologist/detective now?

Chloe didn't seem to care who was on the other side of this difficult conversation. She just wanted to talk.

"I spoke to Shelly myself, right before the storm. I told her that she might be right. There could be a danger that the levee was suffering from underseepage, or that it would slide sideways under the load of significant floodwaters. But the geotechnical work didn't predict it, and you've got to base a design on something."

"So you think the design was sound? The levees were tall enough and thick enough? They were well-maintained—"

"I can't speak to maintenance. That's not what the Corps does."

Faye nodded, then casually asked the question that interested her most, adding it to her list of more general questions as if it were no more important. "Do you think the design used sheet pilings to a sufficient depth?"

"Based on the geotechnical models I've seen, yes, I do. Models are based on assumptions and limited knowledge, so they can fail, but that's not necessarily the fault of the design engineer."

And now for the most sensitive question. "Did the contractors build the levees exactly as they were designed?"

This was when Faye learned what to say if she should ever want to make an engineer mad. Chloe was a pale-skinned blonde. When her cheeks flushed, she couldn't have hidden her fury if she'd wanted to.

"They better, by God, have built those levees to spec. I've been on-site for many construction projects over the years. Whenever I was involved, the taxpayers got the structures we designed for them. I don't have any colleagues I'd suspect of allowing anything else."

"Then what happened?"

Chloe took a controlled sip of her coffee. Her flushed cheeks began to pale. The military engineer was marshalling her thoughts. In a second, she would marshal her words.

"An engineer is held to prescribed design parameters. A bridge, for example, cannot be made a hundred percent safe. It's not possible. And it can't be made ninety-nine point nine nine nine..." She made a gesture to indicate that those nines would go on forever. "...percent safe, because it would be cost-prohibitive. Society has to make a decision on the balancing point between how much it can spend and how infallible a design must be. This is the difference between an applied science like engineering and a theoretical one like...oh, I don't know...cosmology."

"I understand. Everybody has to balance a checkbook. We all have to put our resources where they will do the most good."

"Yeah." Chloe stared into the bottom of her empty cup.

"So I'm just a rank-and-file engineer. Someone else gives me a safety factor, and I apply it to my work. For the New Orleans levee system, we design for the hundred-year storm. In other words, the storm that we would expect to cause the system to fail will come along every hundred years."

"But...New Orleans has been here for nearly three hundred years, and I presume it'll be here hundreds more."

Chloe set the cup down and pushed it away from her, but she kept staring at it, as if it held some kind of design secret that would make everything clear.

"You think like an archaeologist, and of course you're right. We can expect a design based on a hundred-year flood to fail over the life of a city. Maybe not as badly as it did here, but still. The odds favor it. It doesn't have to be this way. The Dutch live underwater, too, you know."

"I never thought about it, but they do. I guess I was thinking of New Orleans as unique."

"Well, yes. Good heavens, yes. There's no place in the world like it, in terms of history and culture. But from an engineering standpoint, the Netherlands sits on land that was once under the sea, and I imagine the sea would like to have it back. Care to guess what their design criterion is?"

"More than a hundred?"

"Um, yeah. They design to a thousand-year flood and, in heavily populated areas, they do better than that. They design to the ten-thousand-year flood. This is where they've chosen to balance cost and benefit. To an archaeologist, that means that many cities will never see a flood while they stand. Do you know what it means to an engineer?"

Faye was getting an inkling, but she said, "No."

"When I design any project to a hundred-year model, it means that the odds are very good that I will see it fail within my lifetime." She took her eyes off her coffee cup and fastened them on Faye. "I'm thinking of getting into another line of work."

Chapter Twenty-one

A rusty wrought-iron lawn chair, a sweating glass of iced tea, and good company. Faye was pretty damned content.

Her garage apartment was set well back from the street. This meant that the cracked concrete pad in front that served as a makeshift front porch was far enough away from traffic to assure private conversation, yet near enough for a smiling nod and wave at neighbors as they passed by. They streamed in and out of gently aging shotgun houses, socializing and just generally enjoying one of the last cool evenings before summer's onslaught. Faye could see why whole families stayed in neighborhoods like this one, generation after generation.

The houses were painted every conceivable pastel color, and their sagging porches were loaded with pots full of flowers in every conceivable non-pastel shade: scarlet geraniums, creamsicle-orange impatiens, purple petunias, and lemon-yellow marigolds. Picket fences leaned like sleepy drunks against head-high rosebushes planted by somebody's grandmother. The flowers alone were proof that money couldn't buy beauty. A dry brown lily bulb, passed over a fence from friend to friend, could light up a garden for the rest of its giver's life.

Twilight was coming on. The squealing kids on tricycles had already been scooped up by their young mothers, and Faye could hear those mothers now as they stood on the front steps and called for their older children to come in the house. It was suppertime and cars were passing even more infrequently than they had been in the hour since Faye sat down to chat with Jodi.

The detective rattled the ice in her glass and Faye reached for the pitcher sitting on the tray table beside her. Jodi looked around for a second, as if she'd just noticed where she was, and said, "Didn't I tell you to take my money and get you a nice place to stay with that pretty man?"

"It's not your money any more."

"Too true. Which is sad, because I'd know how to make much better use of it than you seem to, darlin'."

"Besides, what's wrong with this place?" Faye gestured at the live oaks, the Spanish moss, the festive parade of slightly decayed houses lining the street.

"It's not so bad, though I'll be honest and tell you that I don't know many folks who'd stay here if they had the money to be anyplace else."

"Depends on where you want to put your money. Don't worry. I have some expensive plans for Joe. I'm just not ready to spring them on him yet."

"That's more like it. Care to tell me about them, or are you talking about some seriously kinky stuff?"

Faye rolled her eyes and didn't answer the question, because she knew Jodi's imagination could outdo any scenario she might dream up. "I just spent the day talking to people about maps and history and, well…my kind of stuff. One in particular was definitely worth the time I spent on him—Bobby Longchamp."

Faye was careful to give Bobby's last name his preferred French pronunciation. If Jodi noticed that his name was the same as Faye's, only with a Francophone spin, she didn't say so.

"So," Faye continued, wiping iced-tea-glass sweat on her pants, "what's the latest word on Nina?"

"Well, I'd love to talk to her about what caused her to go in the river, but I can't."

"Has she gotten worse?"

"Nope. She didn't make any sense when she talked yesterday. She didn't make any sense when she talked this morning. And she doesn't make any sense when she talks now."

Faye thought of Nina's articulate plea, asking for help for people who had been suffering for years. It had been broadcast to all of New Orleans and probably, through the modern miracle of all-news cable networks, to all the world. She didn't like to think that her friend might never be able to speak her mind again. "Will her speech improve?"

"She took a bad blow to the head and breathed in a lot of muddy water, so it's possible that some of the part of her brain that makes her talk is just…gone. The MRIs and CAT scans and what-have-you don't show any obvious damage, so everything may come back by itself. If it doesn't, well, they say speech therapy can do a lot. Maybe it's a good sign that she can speak as well as she can. Like I said, she talks a lot."

"What does she say?"

"I spent a few minutes with her this afternoon. Her mind just wanders and, when you're an archaeologist like Nina, it has a lot of ground to wander over. She talks about saints and kings…"

"Don't tell me. Catholic school."

"Bingo. And streetcars and Americans moving to town. Did you know that she thinks Americans should be segregated into their own part of the town, away from the French and Spanish folks?"

"That was the majority view among Creoles a hundred-and-fifty years or so ago. The neighborhood we're sitting in was well-established, even then."

"Yeah, it's plenty historic, if you like slums."

A dark look from Faye prompted Jodi to backtrack. "Okay, I take back the slums comment. Let's call it 'a neighborhood ripe for gentrification.'"

Faye gave a surly grunt.

"Anyway," Jodi went on, "Nina would probably love it here. She's all about old-fashioned stuff these days. And so's that boyfriend of hers, Charles. He's acting like an Edwardian suitor who just wants to breathe the same air as his beloved."

"Spending five minutes with that man makes me want to go home and take a bath."

"Me, too. But I'll give him credit. He hasn't stirred from Nina's side. Nobody in my life besides my mama would be that attentive, if I were in the same shape."

An image of herself watching over Joe just twelve months before, while he hovered between life and death rose in Faye's mind. Being a no-nonsense kind of person, she squashed it down and promised herself she'd deal with that pain later. "Well, just because I don't like Charles doesn't mean he's not a good man. I am hardly an infallible judge of character."

"Nevertheless, I want to hear what you think of young Matt the park ranger."

"Huh?" Faye blinked. "Matt? He hardly speaks to Nina."

"Nowadays, he hardly speaks to anybody. He's a very quiet young man, I notice. Anyway, he hasn't left Nina's side, either. Well, I exaggerate."

"Really. I'd never expect such a thing from you."

Jodi wrinkled her nose in Faye's direction. "The hospital's enforcing visiting hours on Nina, and they're being pretty strict about them. Her parents are both dead, so Charles has muscled himself in there by calling himself her 'fiancé.' Still, he spends a lot of time in between those visits in that waiting room down the hall, sitting a few feet away from Matt and pretending he's not there."

Faye wasn't sure what to say about that so she sat still and enjoyed the sweet and astringent taste of her tea. She could see Dauphine through her open bedroom window, rearranging the shells and candles on her bedroom altar. Joe and Louie Godtschalk were upstairs in her apartment, but the windows were open, too, so she could hear their animated conversation as an unintelligible buzz. Faye didn't care what they were saying, not so very much. She just enjoyed the sound of masculine voices.

Joe leaned out the window and called, "Hey, Faye!", then he waved the book in his hand at her, and kept talking.

His face and voice were animated, but Faye couldn't understand a word. She shrugged at him, and he hollered, "I'll come down there."

If Faye had taken a snapshot of the world surrounding her at that moment, she could hardly have imagined a more contented scene. She and Jodi were lounging in their chairs, drunk on sweet tea and pleasant conversation. The love of her life was bounding down the stairs clinging to the outside of Dauphine's cottage, anxious to share something exciting with her. Dauphine's lit candles were fending off the coming dark.

She always thought she remembered slow-moving tires on the street in front of her at that moment, but she was never sure. Everything was slow-moving that evening. She remembered that much. When gunfire erupted, life slowed almost to a stop.

A bullet slammed into the metal chairback beside her chest. That was the first thing that happened when the world spun out of control. She would always remember the first bullet.

There was another bullet, and another, but they were just background noise, accompaniment to the frantic movements of people turned prey.

Out of instinct, Faye grabbed Jodi as she lunged for the ground. Out of training, Jodi grabbed for Faye as she dropped flat to the dirt shouting, "Get down! Get down! Don't move!"

As Jodi groped for the weapon and radio concealed beneath her fashionable street clothes, Faye turned her head toward the street. There was no car, and she couldn't be sure there ever had been.

Then Jodi was barking, "Get down!", again. And "Get on the ground now, you idiot!", as something dark and lean dropped on top of them both.

It was Joe. He had run full-tilt, wide-open and without cover, to protect Faye and Jodi with his own body. Of course he had. That's who Joe was.

"Now that you're here, get her someplace safe. Idiot." Jodi sounded like she wanted to take the gun in her hand and pistol-whip Joe until he promised to quit doing heroic but stupid stuff. She slithered off on her belly, gun in one hand and radio in the other.

Faye crawled alongside Joe, remembering something she'd heard an old soldier say as he recounted tales of his service in World War II.

When there's bullets whizzin' over your head, you find a way to get real friendly with the ground. I remember a time when I was so scared I started cussin' the buttons down the front of my uniform. They kept me further up off the ground than I wanted to be because they was so damn thick.

Joe persisted in lifting his head a millimeter now and then, so that he could glance left and right and call out, "Louie!"

Faye figured that Louie was huddled safely upstairs in her apartment, but there was no way to know. He very well could have taken a stray bullet. The same was true for Dauphine.

Faye was crawling—oozing?—across the ground as fast as she knew how, but Joe had an arm around her so he could haul her faster still. When they reached the far side of Dauphine's garage, she started to sit up, but got no further than a twitch in that direction. Joe's arm was welded to her back.

"We should be safe now," she whispered. "We've put a whole garage between us and the street."

"Are you sure that the shots came from the street? Dead sure?"

No. She wasn't.

"Are you dead sure that the shooter isn't on foot? That there isn't somebody hiding behind the house next door, waiting to get a clear shot?"

No. She wasn't.

"Then lie still."

He reached out a fist and knocked on the garage's wood siding, still calling, "Louie! Louie! Knock if you can hear me."

There was a faint rapping. Faye didn't so much hear it, as feel it through the skull she was resting against the garage's exterior wall.

"Knock again if you're okay."

The wood siding vibrated again. So Louie Godtschalk had survived the shooting. Faye knew of no way to get the same information from Dauphine.

There was nothing to do but wait and listen to Jodi describe the situation to several armed officers who had arrived within minutes of her call. They fanned out through the neighborhood, searching for someone who was probably out of sight within seconds of shooting the third bullet.

"Joe?" He had thrown himself so completely over her body that her voice was almost totally muffled.

She could hardly hear herself speak, but he must have heard her, because he said, "Don't even think about going out there to help Jodi. Or to look for Louie and Dauphine. Or to do something else stupid. Because you're not big enough to shove me off you."

Oh. So he was allowed to do stupid things because—why? Because he was bigger than her? And she wasn't allowed to do stupid things because—why? Because he was bigger than her. It was logic like this that made her despair for the male half of the human population.

She answered the "you're not big enough" part of his statement by saying, "Yeah, I know," but with oversized Joe on top of her, it sounded to her more like, "Ehmmph. Ah-oh."

Joe gave a mollified grunt. This gave her the fortitude to keep talking. "Thanksgiving. I don't want to wait till Christmas."

He raised his shoulder up a millimeter, which made it easier to talk.

"Let's get married in November, before it turns cold."

"You know I'm ready whenever you say so."

The shoulder dropped back down, and Faye gave up trying to talk. She lay on the ground, with Joe's massive bulk weighting her down. Though she'd have never believed it, she dozed now and then during the long wait until Jodi said, "You can come out now. The situation's under control."

When the immediate danger was past and the other officers had dispersed, there was nothing to do but hug Jodi and Joe and Louie and Dauphine, who had jumped into her broom closet when the first gunshot sounded. After Louie had disappeared into the night and Dauphine had begun occupying herself by lighting candles placed strategically around her garage and yard, Faye had tugged Jodi toward the steps that ran up the side of Dauphine's garage and into Faye's apartment.

"I need to show you something. I saw this stuff when Joe and I were crawling around in the dirt. It's nothing out-and-out dangerous, and I didn't want to bother you with it until you'd dealt with the immediate crisis, but come look."

Tucked out of sight, under the bottom step leading to Faye's home, lay an odd assortment of objects. Jodi's department-issue flashlight did an excellent job of illuminating them. The stump of a red candle. A stone cradled in a scrap of blue cloth. A pair of scissors, open as if to cut a harmless piece of paper.

Jodi grinned. "You don't know what this stuff means? Your grandmama didn't do a good job of passing folklore down to you and your mama, did she?"

"Apparently not."

Jodi glanced over her shoulder at Dauphine, who was concentrating on a sweetly scented cloth bag balanced atop her palm. "Somebody thinks you need a baby. And apparently she thinks you don't know how to go about getting one."

Joe snickered. A withering look from Faye sent him into the shadow of the staircase so that he could enjoy the rest of his good, long laugh.

Jodi stooped over the pile of worthless objects and trained her flashlight over the dirt around them, lighting a halo of dark dots half-buried in the dirt.

"What are those?" Faye asked.

Jodi flicked off her flashlight, leaving them with only street-lights and Dauphine's candles to light the night.

"They're coffin nails."

Excerpt from *The Floodgates of Hell,*
The Reminiscences of Colonel James McGonohan
1876

I have told you the sad beginning of the story of Monsieur Deschanel, whose riches could not buy the lives of his wife and child. His end is sadder still.

It had long been whispered that he enjoyed working with his hands in a way that was not becoming to a gentleman. In fairness, he may have owed the great wealth that the whisperers envied to that menial labor. His facility with pumps and sluices and canals would doubtless have been useful in guiding the proper amount of water to his crops. And it is said that the levee guarding his plantation never failed during his lifetime.

City society did not mind that he amused himself like a peasant with these toys when he was on the plantation, out of sight. It was a different matter when he moved his gadgets into town, where delicate sensibilities could not ignore the sight of a gentleman in grease-stained clothing.

It did not take long for his wealth to attract another lovely young bride. That wealth made it possible for him to purchase menial labor and to hire an educated but impoverished young gentleman to help with the work that obsessed him.

Why did it obsess him? Because he refused to lose this cherished new wife as he had lost the first one. And he refused to bring children into a world where such things happened. Monsieur Deschanel would not rest until New Orleans was a clean, dry, and safe place to nurture a family.

Let us not forget that love of family was at the root of the man's obsession. This fact renders his fate that much more poignant.

Every hour of daylight was spent in his workshop, and many candles were burned as he labored over intricate drawings of miraculous pumps that used the power of moving water to move more water. And, oh, how the municipal government tired of his public railing against the design of the city's drainage system. Draining rainwater and human waste was not a proper job for a gentleman, and the government consisted entirely of gentlemen.

Never mind that he was right. Water does not run uphill and the government's well-intentioned canals could not carry excess water to Lake Pontchartrain, which any fool can see is situated higher than the city. In particular, Monsieur Deschanel argued against the Carondelet Canal, which encroached on the city's very ramparts, if you will, ending as it did at Rampart Street. He maintained that torrential rains or tropical cyclones could easily raise the lake until it flowed down the canal and into the city. He was ignored.

Fortunately—or unfortunately—Monsieur Deschanel's expansive property abutted the canal to which he so objected. He was, as I have said so many times, a very wealthy man, and this property encompassed more than one full city block. Fortunately—or unfortunately—this gave him ample space for his experiment.

There were few passersby to watch as his vision took a mechanical shape. Those men who did pass walked hurriedly, and the women drew their skirts to them in their reflexive desire to have no contact with a man rumored to be mad. City dwellers shunned Monsieur Deschanel and his wife. When plantation business required them to leave New Orleans, they were more isolated still.

Is it any wonder that his young wife began to chafe under her loneliness? Her husband would not even give her children to occupy her time.

I can imagine Monsieur Deschanel, happy in his obsession, barking orders to the clever young man, Monsieur Beaulieu, who had become such a satisfactory assistant. In time, their contraption was complete, and there was nothing to do but wait for a torrential storm. Knowing the climate here as I do, the wait could not have been long.

The legends are vague about the machinery Monsieurs Deschanel and Beaulieu built. Descriptions of a flooded ditch and massive gates are all that survive, but my experience as an engineer gives me a concrete image of what they were trying to achieve.

I believe that Monsieur Deschanel's laborers had dug a canal that cut deep into his property and stopped just feet from the Carondelet Canal. Across this dry canal, they had constructed gates that would swing shut when overflow from the Carondelet Canal threatened to flow into his small canal and onto his property. When the rains came, he intended to have his laborers breach the narrow dike between his canal and the public canal, then set his floodgates into motion.

If those floodgates functioned properly—and he was accustomed to his machinery functioning as designed—then they would serve as a prototype for the protection he had begged the city government to install. Scaled up to full-size, they could be installed at the mouth of the canal that he believed was a danger to the city. And that would be the first step to building a New Orleans where he was willing to rear a family.

I am sure that you've guessed the nature of Monsieur's Deschanel's tragedy by now. His floodgates failed under the stress of tons of rushing water. Some say he was crushed under their weight. Others say that he drowned.

All accounts say that two of his laborers also lost their lives in the accident and that Monsieur Beaulieu was the sole survivor of the tragedy. It is only logical to presume that any description of the events that has come down to us can be traced back to him. Reason tells us that it is dangerous to make judgments on the word of just one witness. Perhaps this is why I instinctively doubt that the full story has survived.

In this engineer's judgment, Monsieur Deschanel was right. The city needs those floodgates, and it didn't get them. It doesn't have them yet.

As clever young men often do after a tragedy, Monsieur Beaulieu landed on his feet. Monsieur Deschanel's widow married him after a scandalously short period of mourning, but city society quickly forgot that impropriety. Attractive young couples blessed with great riches are easy to forgive.

Monsieur Beaulieu is said to have settled quickly into the life of his former employer, even to the extent of building and patenting marvelous inventions in his workshop. He was more handsome in his rich man's clothes than Monsieur Deschanel had ever been, and he was much more skilled at making his wife smile.

Why does this bother me? Why does my damnable engineer's logic taint this happy ending with the conviction that the collapse of those floodgates was no accident? Is it because Monsieur Deschanel's reputation for skill has survived the centuries?

I find it difficult to believe that such a man would try to close those floodgates without being utterly sure they would hold. It is impossible to ignore the fact that their collapse brought Monsieur Beaulieu all that any man could want—a beautiful wife and fabulous riches. Monsieur Deschanel strikes me as a man who knew machinery, but not human nature. Was he unwise enough to trust his life to a man who knew the floodgates' design well, but who had everything to gain from their destruction?

Is this why I look at a simple engineering failure and imbue it with the dark stain of murder?

Chapter Twenty-two

"So…who was shooting at us yesterday?"

Faye knew that there were only a few answers Jodi could give to this question that would make her feel a single particle better. One of them was *Never fear. We've got the culprit locked up so far from daylight that he'll never need sunscreen again.*

Jodi kept munching on the breakfast burrito she'd just nuked in the police department's microwave. Shuffling nonchalantly through the manila folder lying open on her desk, she mumbled, "Who was shooting at us?" Another piece of the burrito went in her mouth. "Hell if I know."

This was far, far from Faye's hoped-for answer. "Am I supposed to stop worrying, just because you're so blissfully unconcerned about us both staying above-ground?"

"I'll be above-ground, regardless. My family plot is in the Metairie Cemetery. It's a mausoleum. We don't bury our people."

Faye spread her slender brown hand flat on top of Jodi's paperwork. "My people like to plant their dead in the dirt. And I don't think staying above-ground is worth much if I'm not breathing. How are you planning to make sure none of us acquires any bulletholes?"

Jodi nudged her hand aside and kept perusing the file. "You don't think this was just another drive-by in just another crummy section of town? My supervisor does. Why don't you?"

"For starters, I didn't see any other targets standing around. Just us. Aren't drive-by shootings usually related to gangs or drugs or something? It's not like some drug dealer was shooting at a client who stiffed him, and we just got in the way. As far as I could see, we were alone."

"As far as you could see. So maybe there was an obvious target standing around there somewhere—maybe in that woodsy area around the ditch that runs behind this row of houses—and maybe we got in the way of somebody trying to hit that target."

Faye decided to let Jodi be obtuse. "Yeah. Maybe. If you say so."

"You don't think so? Just who do you think they were trying to plug? And why?"

"You? If they were after you, there could be a thousand reasons for a person to pull the trigger."

Jodi finally looked up. "I'm glad you think I'm so popular." After a few seconds, the detective's deadpan face failed and she cracked a smile full of small, perfect teeth. Faye hoped the woman never took up poker.

"You know what I mean, Jodi. Every crook you've ever sent to jail could be gunning for you. And his brother. And every crook who's afraid of someday crossing your path and being sent to jail."

"I see. It's an ordinary thing for me to be shot at. The rest of you, on the other hand…"

"Well, yeah. I've gotten crossways with some people in the past—"

"Crossways enough to get shot at?"

"Um, yeah, once or twice. Joe, too. But I can't think of any-body in New Orleans who cares whether either of us lives or dies. And I certainly can't imagine someone trying to kill Louie Godtschalk. I'm not so sure about Dauphine."

Jodi shook her head. Her golden-brown curls kept moving a second after she stopped. "We take our voodoo practitioners seriously around here. I think most of New Orleans would be scared to put a bullethole in Dauphine. We all figure that mambos are just as dangerous when they're dead as they are when they're alive."

"Did you find all three bullets? Can you tell where they came from?"

"They didn't come from the street. It gave me great pleasure to tell that to my supervisor, who was hell-bent on pigeon-holing this as a garden-variety drive-by shooting. Bad neighborhood, stray bullets, lucky bystanders who didn't catch any of those bullets in the gut…it's an old story, and it wouldn't be the first time such a thing happened on that block."

Faye's feeling of security left her, and it wouldn't be back soon.

"So you've had drive-bys in that neighborhood, but this wasn't one of them?"

"Nope. It came from a back yard somewhere north of where we were sitting."

Faye had to picture a map of New Orleans in her mind, just to figure out which way was north. If the dang river would just flow in a straight line, then the city's streets would be more likely to run straight, though such a logical thing still might never occur to people here in this city where logic slept. "In the direction of Dauphine's house?"

"Correct. Could have been her back yard or the next yard over. Maybe even the next yard after that. None of them are fenced. Anybody could have been standing behind one of those big ol' trees. There's a little canal back there, too. Or maybe it's just a big drainage ditch. Anyway. It wouldn't have taken much effort for someone to sneak in, shoot, then fade into the night."

Faye knew that Jodi hadn't missed the obvious suspect. She had just elected not to mention her, so Faye did it, instead. "Or it could have been Dauphine. I'm not real crazy about the notion of someone leaving coffin nails under my doorstep or in the water where Nina nearly drowned. I like Dauphine, but she's the only person I know who's likely to have access to a steady supply of coffin nails. Do you see her as a plausible suspect?"

"That's what I like about you, Faye. You never stop being an archaeologist. You never stop digging. And you never fail to look at facts, even when you don't like them much. Dauphine is your friend and you don't want her to be guilty of attempted murder, but you're willing to weigh the evidence and look at the truth with an open mind."

Faye looked at her expectantly and Jodi said, "Oh, yeah. I didn't answer your question. Is Dauphine a plausible suspect? Hmmm. She's being questioned right now—Louie, too—but I can't imagine what either of them would have against you or me. Or Nina."

"Or Shelly. Dauphine knew her, too." An odd thought occurred to Faye, a thought that would have made no sense in any other American city. "Do you think the people questioning her are willing to cross swords with a mambo? Maybe she'll threaten to put a hex on them. And don't think I haven't noticed that *you* aren't doing the questioning."

"Oh, Dauphine knows I'm the reason she's being hassled. She's perfectly capable of hexing me *in absentia*. Nevertheless, I was lily-livered enough to assign a couple of Yankees to the task. Besides, I want to find out what she's going to say to people she doesn't know, people who weren't lounging like sitting ducks in the sights of that gun last night."

Jodi leaned against her desk, legs crossed. Then she crossed her arms like a woman fending off a curse. "Those two Yankees may find themselves hexed so bad that their dogs die and their wives run off, but they don't know diddly about mambos. They'll never know what hit 'em. They'll just write it off to bad luck. Nobody's going to be blaming *me* for throwing them in the path of an avenging mambo."

Chapter Twenty-three

"So how's Nina?" Faye asked anxiously, as Jodi hung up the phone.

She'd sat across the desk, listening to half the conversation as Jodi quizzed Nina's doctor. Jodi's reactions hadn't told Faye nearly as much as she'd wanted to know.

Jodi had said, "That's good," and "Can I come back in and talk to her again?" and "Do you think she'll be in the hospital much longer?" She'd given an incongruous laugh, the kind that sounds like it hurts the person laughing. Then she'd thanked the doctor for his time, told him she'd be checking back again soon, and said good-bye.

From this, Faye had inferred that Nina hadn't taken a turn for the worse. She also inferred that Nina wasn't going to be back on the job with Faye any time soon, looking for treasures with her stupid-looking trowel.

The trowel...Faye didn't even want to think about the trowel. She promised herself that she'd buy Nina a new trowel—any trowel, as long as it wasn't snub-nosed—once her assistant was well enough to work again.

"I'd hoped for better news," Jodi said, "but I guess we have to take what we can get. Nina's been released from intensive care. She's doing very well, physically—so well, in fact that her doctors say she'll be going home soon, maybe this afternoon. But her speech is improving slowly, if at all."

She shook her head and gave the same short ugly laugh Faye had just heard. "Remember how Nina seized her moment with a TV camera? Quiet people like her—they must feel like they have plenty to say and no one listens. Well, she really must feel that way now. The doctor says she talks all the time, but it's all random nonsense. Or maybe not so random. Remember how he told us that brain injury patients sometimes fish for one word and come up with another that's related to it somehow?"

Faye nodded.

"Well, Nina's nephew came to visit her, and she talked about chocolate for an hour. The nephew went down to the vending machines and bought her a candy bar. That didn't satisfy her. It's frustrating to be misunderstood, so she got even more agitated. A nurse came in and asked if she'd like some hot cocoa. Nope."

Jodi pursed her lips, took a big sip of coffee and swallowed it hard. "Nina was getting so stirred up that the nurse was thinking of asking the doctor-on-call for a sedative. Then somebody asked if she wanted a chocolate chip cookie, and Nina got so upset that the doctor heard her all the way down the hall and he *did* order a sedative. Good thing it took awhile for it to be delivered, or we still might not know what Nina wanted."

Faye didn't like this story. How awful it would be for someone to drug you, just because they couldn't understand what you were saying. "What was it? What did she want?"

"Nina's cousin came in the room about that time and called the nephew by his name, which was Chip. The nurse had worked with a lot of head injury patients. When she heard the cousin say 'Chip,' she nearly busted a gut laughing. Then she asked Nina if she'd been trying to call the boy by his name. Nina was so relieved that she cried."

Faye heard herself give the same painful laugh she'd heard from Jodi. "Chocolate chip."

"Yep. Her brain is still working and making associations, and she's still a smart woman. Nina recognized the boy. She knew his name. But when she reached in her brain for his name, she got the word stored next door to it."

It was funny, but it wasn't. Faye wanted to hurt the person who hurt her friend this badly. "Why did somebody do this to her?"

"I keep asking myself that. Actually, I keep asking myself, 'Why did somebody do these things to Nina *and* Shelly?' We don't know that the two attacks were related, but the two women knew each other and they knew a lot of the same folks. There's a decent shot that solving Shelly's murder will bring us Nina's attacker. Or vice versa."

"Strangulation's not the same thing as crashing a heavy object onto somebody's skull, but when I imagine doing such a thing, it feels…" Faye stopped herself. She didn't like the way it felt to imagine such a thing. "Um, it feels creepy, but what I'm trying to say is that it feels the *same*. Stealthy. And impersonal. Somebody walked up behind two women and tried to kill them in such a way that they never really had to look them in the face."

"Yeah. The two attacks have that in common. And your observation that Shelly could have seen something on her aerial photos that showed problems with the levees is interesting, because Nina had been ranting about problems with the levees just the day before she was attacked."

"And she's been blogging about the levee failures for a long time, or so I'm told."

"Exactly." Jodi rubbed a finger over the photo Faye had shown her, tracing the line of a long, slender sheet piling. "Don't forget that Shelly had been calling around just before she died, trying to get somebody to listen to her concerns about the levees."

"Everything seems to come back to the levees. But then everything does, around here. If they stop holding back the water, then you've got no city, do you?"

Faye stuck out her mug, and Jodi poured her another cup of Louisiana-style coffee, as interpreted by the New Orleans Police Department. It was so strong it felt thick in the mouth. It was laced with enough chicory to completely confuse Faye's palate, which was expecting…well, *coffee*. And it was as black as Satan's heart.

"Damn, Faye. Can't you think of something a little bit more politically charged than that? A conspiracy to assassinate a major public official, maybe? People around here are kinda sensitive about their levees."

"People kill each other over 'sensitive' stuff. Well? Don't they?"

"Yes, indeed." Jodi stared deep into her cup and snickered.

"What's so funny? Levee failures? The assassination of a major public official? Brain damage? Murder?"

"Nope. Charles Landry."

Faye didn't get the joke. "He's insufferable, but he doesn't exactly make me laugh."

"I called him to ask whether Shelly had ever shared her concerns over the levees with him."

"Had she?"

"I have no idea, because Charles went into immediate ass-covering mode. It seems that his firm has a finger in all aspects of flood control work—levee design and maintenance, for starters. They've also done some work on floodgates to protect against flooding from Lake Pontchartrain. They dredge canals. Right now, they're bidding on a project to upgrade the pumping system. Charles did *not* want to hear me asking questions about why the levees failed. He handed me off to his assistant Leila the Bulldog, so she could put my call through to a so-called expert."

Charles' expert must emit an odor strong enough to travel through telephone lines, because Jodi's nose was wrinkling at the thought of him.

"Not someone you're itching to hire as the department's engineering consultant?"

"Not just no, but hell, no. It was the company's marketing flak, telling me not to believe all the stuff that the independent levee review team said in their report."

"So now you're gonna have to read that report?"

The question made Jodi reach for the coffee pot again. "Again…hell, no. The thing's six-hundred-and-ninety pages long. I've gotta find me an impartial engineer to read it. Until then, I can't even form an opinion on the issue." She held out two sheets of paper. "But I sure wish I had me an opinion on these."

Faye reached for the two pages. They were copies of the most intriguing things found in Shelly's pocket. At least, Faye thought so.

In her right hand was the neatly inscribed list that started with Charles' surname and ended with Shelly's.

Landry
Martin
Guidry
Bergeron
McCaffrey
Johnson
Dupuit
Prejean
Broussard

And in her other hand was a messy list, scrawled in handwriting even worse than Joe's.

Johnson
Guidry
Broussard
McCaffrey
Dupuit
Bergeron
Prejean
Martin
Landry

Jodi and Faye devoted a solid half-hour to brainstorming those names. They got exactly nowhere.

"Pontchartrain Engineering is an obvious link," Jodi said, holding up the company's flashy brochure. Charles Landry was one of the faces on the cover. Either he was a high muckety-muck with the company, or he was the most photogenic engineer they could find. "Shelly Broussard and Charles Landry both worked at Pontchartrain Engineering, and their surnames are on the list. Leila Caron's name isn't there, but Matt Guidry is her boyfriend, so there's another link to the company."

Jodi flipped thoughtfully through the colorful brochure. "I went to the company website and searched their directory. Charles Landry and Shelly Broussard were in it—Leila Caron, too—but none of the other names appears. I'll get hold of a list from the time of the storm but we'll have to wait a while for that information."

"So what do we know for certain?"

"Neither list is alphabetical," Jodi said, ticking off her observations by counting on her fingers. "We've checked professional organizations for a link between these nine names. Nothing."

"We've got an engineer, a park ranger, and an administrative assistant," Faye said. "I guess there might not be too many professional organizations that attract all three of those. Maybe something social, like The Royal Order of the Moose?"

"I already checked that."

Wow. Jodi was thorough. Faye had only suggested the Moose because their name made her smile.

Jodi kept counting on her fingers. "We thought they might have gone to church together, but Shelly, Matt, and Charles didn't live close enough together to belong to the same parish. I even did a web search for all of those names together. Nothing came up but a bunch of genealogies, and none of them showed a family tree that included all those names."

"Have you just come out and asked Charles and Matt about the lists? It'd be interesting to hear their explanations of why their names might have been in Shelly's pocket."

"I asked Matt, the next day after we found Shelly. As for Charles, I was saving that question, so I'd have an excuse to call him again, if it suited me."

"Does it suit you now?"

"Yeah. It's time to bother my least favorite engineer, just one more time. Okay, two more times. Hell. I don't like the man. I'll bother him as many times as I like."

Jodi downed another big gulp of her coffee and an evil, caffeine-fueled grin lit her face. "You know what? That conversation would be a lot more effective in person, don't you think? I can wave these lists around. Make him look at the handwriting. Tell him to look real close at both lists, so he can be good and sure that he's never seen them before. Why don't we go make Mr. Charles Landry miserable, face-to-face?"

Jodi put the car in park and would have jumped out of it, ready to annoy the life out of Charles Landry, but Faye stopped her with a hand on her forearm.

"Before we go in there, you'd better tell me how your last interview with Leila the secretary went."

"She's not a secretary. She's an administrative assistant. She reminded me about that pretty loudly. A couple of times. And she had a valid point. The nameplate on her desk does say she's an 'Administrative Asst.' Me, I woulda left off that last 't'."

Faye heard a little guilt speaking to her. "You know, my mama spent forty years making her jerk of a boss look good, and he never gave her any title other than 'secretary.' I shouldn't laugh at Leila, just because she wants to be taken seriously."

"No. You should laugh at her because she's a pretentious snob. Let me see…within the first five minutes, she'd asked me how long I've lived in New Orleans, where I went to grade school, and who my people were. She made sure I knew that her mother ruled a particularly choice Garden Club with an iron hand. I also learned that, just this past Mardi Gras season, her father was King of Some Mystic Krewe or Other. I believe she was about to ask me what regiment my great-great-great-grandfather served in during the Civil War. Excuse me—the War Between the States. Also my mother's maiden name."

Faye motioned to Jodi to flip the car key toward "auxiliary" long enough for her to roll the window down and let some air into the stuffy car. "If I'd been in your shoes, I'd have told her I was a descendant of Marie Laveau, the voodoo queen. Your mother's maiden name is none of her damn business."

"Yeah, well, it's pretty important damn business around here. The social circles you can enter, the exclusive Mardi Gras balls you attend…'who your people are' is a critical component of those things, and your mama's maiden name figures into all that. I'd say it was more important than what color your mama was, and you can't say that for most places in America."

Faye, whose parents' skin colors couldn't have been more different from each other, wondered why nobody was asking about anybody's daddy's family. She figured it was because people's last names revealed enough information for the asker to go poking around in their father's genealogy, unaided.

"A big, fat civil rights lawsuit or two might fix those social circles and Mardi Gras balls…"

"Did I say any laws were being broken?" Jodi asked. "I'm pretty darn white, and I wouldn't be comfortable at society balls around here. I could attend. You could attend. But if nobody knew who our people were, we might be hard-pressed to find anyone willing to have more than a brief, polite conversation. It would be nothing personal. They just wouldn't be able to think of anything to say to us."

Faye knew these things. Bobby Longchamp had been as obsessed with family relationships as Leila. It had just bothered her less, because she liked him more.

"We only want a few minutes with Mr. Landry."

Jodi was making every effort to use her most official detective's voice on Leila Caron, and she could see that it was working. She liked it when people respected her badge. She liked it better when people respected her as a person, but Leila seemed to be one of those who just respected the badge.

It seemed that she was also more than a little intimidated by the badge. Or maybe it was guilt that was keeping her bright black eyes fastened on Jodi, as she carefully answered questions without really saying anything at all. It was as if Faye wasn't even in the room.

Jodi watched Faye push that envelope a bit, first leaning on Leila's desk, then actually resting her hand atop the stack of papers on the desk corner, just as she'd gotten Jodi's attention earlier that day by laying that same hand flat atop the paperwork she was filing.

Nervous Leila never noticed. She just kept giving Jodi non-committal answers.

It wasn't that Leila betrayed her nerves overtly. Her voice never trembled. Its tone was pleasant but firm. Her hands were steady.

No, she hadn't thought of anything else significant that Shelly had said or done during those tough days at Zephyr Field, the woman had told Jodi as a hand reached up to touch her cheek.

No, she'd never, at any time, seen anyone at the office arguing with Shelly, Leila had said as she brought her hands in front of her, palms inward, in an instinctively protective position.

No, she'd never heard Shelly mention being afraid of anyone or anything, she'd asserted calmly, while she adjusted the position of the bright gold bangle bracelet encircling her wrist, again.

Yes, she'd be happy to let Jodi and her tagalong friend speak to Mr. Landry, but they had to remember that he was a busy person. She was sure he would have contacted the police, if he'd remembered anything that might be helpful.

With that, Leila sighed and turned to lead them into Charles' office, stopping only to alert him by intercom that they were coming.

The woman simply bristled with body language that said she was lying. Or that she wasn't giving them the whole truth. She had more tells than a bankrupted poker player. Her last evasive tic cost her, though.

By moving toward the door of Charles Landry's office with the liar's stereotypical facial expression, eyes locked straight ahead, she never saw Faye drag her hand across the desk, raking a single piece of paper into her other waiting hand.

◇◇◇

Charles Landry was a better liar than his administrative assistant, or at least Jodi thought so. His hands were relaxed. His body position was open. His voice was blandly pleasant.

Too bad his speech patterns were skewing way more formal than the ordinary conversational style of a good ol' boy from the Big Easy. Jodi had learned early in her career that liars always reveal themselves. Maybe they *wanted* to be revealed, although Jodi highly doubted that. In her experience, liars and criminals were convinced that the rest of the world owed them... everything.

"No, I do not recall ever seeing this," he said, as he perused the neatly inscribed list of names that had been retrieved from Shelly's pocket. He reached for the second list with its hurriedly scrawled handwriting, and said, "Nor this."

"How about the names? Are any of them familiar to you? Other than your own name, I mean, and Matt's. And Shelly's."

"Yes. That's my last name. It's also my brother's and my father's and my mother's. All my aunts, uncles, and cousins, too. And lots of people that I'm not related to, as well. Would you like to talk to all of them?"

In Jodi's peripheral vision, she saw Faye continuing her trick of hovering just outside the interrogant's field of vision, forcing him to choose where to focus his eyes. Like Leila, Charles chose the woman with the badge, because he perceived her as the biggest threat. The man had no idea who he was dealing with.

Jodi waited patiently while Charles studied the two lists and made noncommittal noises. Then she took her leave of him, but Faye did something. She showed that she was done with silent observation.

"May I ask you a personal question?" she said, speaking softly so that Charles had to turn an ear in her direction in order to hear.

"You can ask," he said. Wariness put an audible edge on his voice.

"Nina's my friend, and I know she has been so glad to spend time with you again. She told me that she had no idea why you'd come back into her life so suddenly. Could I be so bold as to ask why you did? You don't have to tell me, but Nina's my friend and I..." Faye's voice trailed off and she looked at him expectantly.

"I couldn't...well, I..." Charles' smooth manner was now thoroughly ruffled. Finally, he just blurted it out. "Nina's not what I pictured for myself. I plan to head up this company, or one like it. I wanted a wife who could make cocktail party conversation, and Nina doesn't even own any hairspray. But you know her. There's not anyone like Nina. I just couldn't stay away."

He signaled to Leila that the interview was done. As she led them through the door, back into her own workspace, Charles turned toward his own desk. In that instant, Jodi felt Faye press a scrap of paper into her hand. She glanced at it and blessed the day that she hired Faye Longchamp to help her with this investigation.

It was a simple to-do list on a piece of paper that said *From the desk of Leila Caron* across the top. The clear round handwriting on that paper was utterly familiar.

Leila Caron had written one of their two lists.

Chapter Twenty-four

Faye's face was expressionless, but Jodi could read her body language as well as she could read a liar's. She was smugly proud of handing Jodi something she could use to pry a little truth out of Leila.

"Ms. Caron," Jodi said, holding out a copy of Shelly's sloppily written list, "does this look familiar to you?"

The mouth said no, but the eyes said Leila wished she knew whether this lie was safe to tell.

"How about this one?"

Leila hesitated, then raised her eyes to the bulletin board hanging three feet from Jodi's left shoulder. Jodi glanced that way and saw three pieces of paper covered with neat round handwriting identical to that on the list in her hand. Leila saw the glance, and she was a good enough gambler to know when to fold her hand.

"Yes, I've seen that before. It's my handwriting."

"Do you remember making this list?"

"I'm an administrative assistant. I take notes and shuffle people's paper for them. I make lists like that one every day. I can't possibly remember them all."

Jodi knew that the woman was feeling cornered, if she was willing to acknowledge the menial labor that was central to her job. She decided to press her a little. "But do you remember *this* list?"

"No. I don't."

Well, at least Leila had given her a straight answer, even if her body language screamed out that it wasn't true.

"Did you ever make a list like this for Shelly Broussard?"

"Shelly worked for Charles. Charles is my boss. Of course, I gave her notes and lists of things that he wanted her to do. I did that for all his employees."

This was true. But Jodi was well aware that most of that kind of work was done on computer now. She didn't know why the fact that this note was hand-written seemed notable, but it did.

"Why would you make a list of names like this? Hypothetically, I mean."

"Umm…"

Leila was thinking too long. Instead of throwing out a few random reasons for listing nine surnames, she was reviewing her alternatives and taking the time to mentally throw out the one that was true.

"Maybe it was a list of potential clients that Charles wanted her to call. Or subcontractors. Yeah, they could be subcontractors."

Jodi was so dead certain that Leila was lying that this was actually useful information, in a backhanded way. There was no way in hell that these names referred to clients or subcontractors.

"Well, if you remember anything about any of the people on this particular list, or if you think of something that reminds you why you wrote it in the first place, you've got my card. Have a good day."

Jodi turned to Faye and nodded that it was time to go. The look on Faye's face, even more smug than before, caught her attention.

Jodi's eyes followed the line of Faye's slim arm downward to the desk, where she was again resting her hand. This time, however, the hand was not lying flat. Three fingers and a thumb were curled into her palm, leaving an index finger pointing…at what?

Jodi's own body language nearly slipped when she followed that index finger to its target. Faye was pointing at Leila's desk plate, which Jodi had seen before. It announced to the world at large that she was an Administrative Asst. It also broadcast to the world that her professional name was Leila Martin Caron.

Leila was not married. Jodi presumed that she never had been, but she'd have to check. She wagered that "Martin" was Leila's middle name and that it had been her mother's maiden name. She and her ilk did not let go of their family relationships easily. It was the most natural thing in Leila's world for her to continue letting the world know who her "people" were, even though her mother had presumably been married to Mr. Caron for decades.

And Martin was one of the names on Shelly's lists.

Leila waited for the woman cop and her poorly dressed, dark-skinned flunky to leave the room. Then she counted to sixty before opening her office door and peeking out. They were gone.

She turned around and surveyed her desk from this angle. The two women had been looking at something. What had they seen and why had it caught the silent archaeologist's eye? Why had it been so noteworthy that she had lurked right there, in that spot to the right of the desk, until the detective looked her way?

Faye Longchamp had been pointing at something with that hand motion that she'd thought was so damn subtle. What in the hell was it?

Leila turned her thoughts off and just let her eyes drift over the desk. The paperweight was harmless, though she was so rattled that she believed she could just slam it into the detective's head, if given half a chance. The scissors gave out no incriminating information, though they too could serve well as a weapon to ensure that Detective Bienvenu would leave her the hell alone. Ditto for the letter opener.

The papers were all harmless. They'd all been generated within the past month, for innocuous reasons. They had no pertinence to the matter at hand. Well, the handwritten ones in the detective's grasp did, but she'd already admitted the obvious fact that one of those damnable lists was written in her own handwriting. It was unfortunate that she'd had to give up even that shred of information, but not catastrophic. As long as no one ever found out what those lists *were*…

The memories welled up, and so did the adrenaline. Leila closed her eyes and willed away the trembling and the quick, shallow breaths. Post-traumatic stress disorder was for the weak, no matter what her psychologist tried to tell her. After a moment devoted to blanking out memories, Leila opened her eyes again, and she saw it.

It was only a nameplate, and it had been sitting on her desk unnoticed for seven years.

Leila Martin Caron.

The sight of those three names infuriated her. Of its own volition, her hand reached out and snatched up the offending nameplate. Without conscious control, she slung her arm back and overhanded the evidence at her office wall.

The nameplate left a tiny scar in the fashionable taupe paint as it caromed off the wall and slammed to the tile floor, ruined. No matter. Leila was an administrative assistant, which meant that she kept charge of the office supply catalogs. She could simply order herself another nameplate, one that didn't broadcast her mother's maiden name. No one would be the wiser.

◇◇◇

Faye sat with Joe and Jodi, huddling over yet another batch of po-boys, while they studied Shelly's two lists of names with magnifying glasses. Faye was trying a new variety of po-boy—sliced ham, anointed with barbecue sauce. It tasted great, but it was saltier than the Gulf of Mexico. It was so salty that she was pretty sure she could feel a stroke coming on. She drank half a glass of water without setting down the glass, hoping to dilute all that sodium.

"I got a sample of Shelly's handwriting from her aunt," Jodi announced. "She didn't write either of these lists."

"Shit," Faye said, and Joe twitched one shoulder. He hated it when she cursed. "So we have no idea who wrote the scribbly list."

"The 'scribbly' list, as you call it, was written with a pencil," Jodi said. "And I'd say the person was under lot of stress."

"Because the writing's messy?" Faye asked.

"Well, yeah, but I was also looking at how hard the person was pressing into the paper."

Joe pointed to the last name on the list. "Look there. You can even see the pencil getting blunter, the further you look down the page." Picking up the other sheet, he said, "This one's in pen, but the person was bearing down pretty hard, too. See here? The pen nearly punched through the paper in a couple of spots."

"So you'd say that both writers were under stress? I wonder what a graphologist would say."

"I don't think the neat writing means that this other person was calmer or easier in their mind," Joe said, cocking his head to one side as he brought the paper almost to his nose. "I think the writing's neat because the person writing was feeling really..." He considered the paper again. "...really *careful*."

Faye made a mental note to tell Jodi that she should listen to Joe at times like this. He understood every animal that walked. Some of those animals walked around on two legs. And a few of those were dangerous.

"Let me back up and think about what we know about Shelly's last days," Jodi said. "She rode out the storm in a higher area west of town that stayed dry, probably with some of her co-workers. They found out about the rescue work at Zephyr Field, so they went there to help. And they got there...how?"

"By car, I figure," Joe said. "When the rain stopped, you could probably drive just fine on a lot of the streets where it didn't flood. You might have to take the long way around, though."

"But not to the Lower Ninth Ward," Faye said. "That would really have been the long way round. And going there would have taken you through...oh, fifteen feet of water. And we know she was alive for days at Zephyr Field, before she somehow got to the Lower Nine, so never mind."

"Okay," Jodi said. "So she went to Zephyr Field for several days, but we don't know how many. A lot of people saw her there. She worked like a dog. She may have disappeared after taking a nap—"

"Not to butt in here," Faye said, "but don't forget that Bobby said that he heard Shelly yelling at somebody shortly before he lost track of her."

"Damn, I wish I knew something about that argument— who she was yelling at and why." Jodi picked up the lists again. "Anyway, she left Zephyr Field at some point, but we don't know when, why, or how. We don't know whether she was alone. We don't even know if she was alive. We just know that sometime since then, she turned up dead in the Lower Nine."

"I'll argue with you on one point," Faye said. "I think we know why she left Zephyr Field. Think about it. She was looking for her parents. We know that she was agonizing over them for days. Trying to reach them by phone. Crying over her work. If she was alive when she left the rescue operation, then she was going after her parents."

"Reckon she got there?" Joe asked. "We could look."

"Hmm?" Jodi gave him a sharp look. "It would be good to know that, but I don't know how we could possibly tell. Where would you look for that information?"

"We know they drowned in their attic," he began. "If you were in a boat and you floated up to a flooded-out house where you thought somebody was trapped, what would you do?"

Jodi had asked him the question, but Joe looked at Faye like a law professor grilling a first-year student…and she knew why. It was because he knew precisely what she would do in that situation.

Her answer was instantaneous. "I'd try to go through the roof. And if I knew I might have to do that, I'd bring an ax with me."

"We already said she probably hopped a ride in a rescue boat." Jodi rubbed her forehead as if it hurt. "They would have had axes…"

Faye could see Jodi thinking. She could almost see the ideas as she conjured them up, weighed them, and cast them aside.

Joe gave Jodi the answer before she got to it. "If the rescuers— with or without Shelly—got to that house and wanted to see if her parents were still alive, they would have…what? Made an unholy noise by knocking on the walls and roof until somebody answered?" He knocked on the table to give the image a bit of reality. "Is that how they worked?"

Jodi nodded.

"Okay," he said. "If nobody answered and they didn't have a real good reason to think somebody might be alive inside, trapped, I'm guessing they moved on, because lots of people were out there waiting for help—"

Jodi nodded and Joe kept talking without missing a beat.

"—but if somebody answered when they knocked, they would have had to chop through the roof to get to them. I bet we can find out if that happened at Shelly's parents' house without leaving this room." He nodded at the stack of aerial photographs Faye had stacked on the table where they sat. "Do you have their address?"

Jodi slapped the file folder in front of her. "I sure do."

He looked at Faye. "You've pretty much memorized those photos. I watched you. Can you find their house by its address?"

"The Lakeview photos are overlaid with street maps. Yes. I can."

Within minutes, the three of them were gathered around a detailed map of Lakeview taken days after the storm, looking at the roof of the very house where Shelly's parents drowned. Some other houses in the neighborhood had clearly visible holes battered through their shingles, but not the Broussards'. Dark water surrounded them all.

Faye wondered why the photo made her stomach knot. She already knew that Aimee and Dan Broussard had died under that roof. The visual proof of it unsettled her, anyway.

"So the rescuers got there and, even if Shelly was with them, it was too late. They never even tried to get into the house. God rest their souls." Jodi ran a gentle finger around the outlines of the undamaged roof. Then she drew it back and crossed herself.

"Shelly wasn't with the rescuers when they got to her parents' house." Faye heard certainty in her voice, even though the words had come to her without conscious thought. "Of course, she wasn't with them. She would have pried off those shingles with her teeth. She would have peeled back the plywood under them, splinter by splinter. Wouldn't you, if it was your mama and daddy underneath those shingles?"

Jodi's face lost its wistful look. "Yes. You're right. The rescuers had to follow procedures—they had thousands of people to save. If nobody answered their calls or knocks, then they moved on. Shelly had two people to save. She'd have done everything in her power to get into that house."

Faye nodded, more certain about this than she'd been about anything else related to the investigation. "If she'd gotten this far, you'd be able to see the hole she made in that roof from any photograph, whether it was taken by a plane, helicopter, or satellite. You'd be able to see it from space. Sometime between leaving Zephyr Field and arriving at this house, Shelly got off-track. And about the only way she could have gotten so off-track that she failed to go after her parents would be because she was dead."

The three of them sat there silent, eyes focused on the photo, until Joe reached out and turned it over, face-down. It felt like the right thing for him to do, just as it would have been right to gently close the eyes of a person newly dead.

Chapter Twenty-five

Faye wished there was some way to guarantee that she'd never have to smell a hospital, ever again. She didn't think of herself as having a particularly keen sense of smell, but some odors seem to cling to her skin. They lingered, and her body responded viscerally, time and again.

Death. Antiseptics. Sickness and stale sweat. Disinfectant. Institutional food. Fear. Hospital air carried layers of bad smells. How lucky for Nina that she was escaping those foreboding odors.

Faye and Joe had just stopped for a quick evening visit. Dauphine had done the same thing, so she stood with them now wearing a puzzled expression that reflected their own thoughts:

Going home? That's great...but...

Where will she go?

Can she care for herself?

Can she make herself understood in a world that doesn't wait for people to grope through their memory banks for the right words?

Is she ready for this?

Faye didn't think she was ready. Not at all.

Nina's face should have been radiant as the orderly pushed her wheelchair toward the elevator and freedom. If she were really ready to go home, she would have been casting girlish glances at the man walking beside that wheelchair. Under ordinary circumstances, Charles' mere presence would have made her pale cheeks glow.

Instead, she canted her head nervously in Faye's direction and reached a tentative hand toward the bandage wrapping her head. After a few seconds' stammering, she came out with, "Head… water…save. Thank."

Faye put a hand on her arm and said, "You're very welcome. Joe and I are just happy we were there. You would have done the same for us."

Nina nodded without speaking, but she seemed determined to try to communicate. Nothing but a groan came out of her mouth for a hard second, but the groan finally coalesced into recognizable words. " Mmmmuh…mom. Da-aaa-aad. Save."

Faye looked at Joe, then Dauphine. What was there to say? Nina's parents had been dead for many years. Had she forgotten that? Who knew what random damage was done by a powerful blow to the head?

It would be a long time before Faye let go of the image of Nina, who had challenged authority on the evening news with such strength and vitality, being wheeled toward the elevator. She had lost so much weight in the few days since the attack that she looked shrunken, with her arms wrapped tightly around her breasts.

When the bell sounded to signal the elevator's arrival, Nina turned around in the chair, looked at Faye and reached a hand just a few inches in Faye's direction. Her mouth worked for a second, but all that came out of it was, "Save." And again, louder, "Save!"

Then the orderly pushed her into the elevator, Charles stepped in, and the door closed behind them.

◇◇◇

"You've got to get some sleep, Faye."

Joe said this as if he thought she was unaware that the human body needed sleep. Or as if he thought she was lying in bed awake because it was a fun way to spend the hours between midnight and three a.m.

Maybe Joe had total control of his autonomic nervous system. Maybe he could wake at will and sleep when he wished. Maybe he could consciously slow his pulse so that no pesky heartbeats would jostle his arm as he pulled back his bowstring and took aim.

Faye could do none of these things. She couldn't do anything but stare at the ceiling and pretend like she didn't know that dozens of candles lit the open yard between her apartment and Dauphine's house.

Dauphine had begun setting those candles hither and yon, muttering to herself and singing, as soon as she, Faye, and Joe had returned from the hospital. She had spoken to them as they walked past her on their way from the car to Faye's apartment, but her speech was hardly distinguishable from the mumbling she'd been doing before they approached.

A heavy fog was settling like a miasma over the scene, but the candles burned despite the dampness. Their flames set small globes of gray mist alight.

Dauphine had glanced over her shoulder as Faye passed, and kept up her unintelligible speech. The quiet words had prompted Faye to move closer, but Joe had just drifted on upstairs, perfectly willing to let her have a few minutes of girl talk with her mambo friend without his supervision.

If he'd known about Dauphine's brand of girl talk, he might've stayed, just to get a chance to compare Haitian ceremonial magic with his own Creek ways.

"My blood is flowing," Dauphine had crooned as she wiped the top of a broad stump clean and spread a red cloth over the worn wood.

Faye had thought the woman was oblivious to the wet mist dropping from the sky, but maybe she wasn't, because she turned her face skyward. The song changed to, "When you see Dantò pass, you think it is a thunderstorm. My blood is flowing, Dantò."

In mid-song, Dauphine's voice had quieted to a hum, then gone silent as she watched Faye approach.

Faye had thought at that moment that it had been a mistake to approach Dauphine. She had no idea what one said to a mambo in preparation for…for whatever it was that voodoo practitioners did. She'd settled for saying the first thing that entered her head. Perhaps that was what voodoo mambos wanted to hear, anyway.

"How are you, Dauphine? Are you feeling as worried about Nina as I am?"

"I give my worries to my lady Ezili Dantò," Dauphine had said, plunking a metal plate loaded with fried pork onto the red cloth.

The odor of the crisp meat, redolent with spices, grabbed Faye's attention and kept it. She'd forgotten to be hungry.

"My lady does not smile when women are harmed," Dauphine declared, slapping an open palm on the altar's red cloth. "She acts to defend victims, always. My lady knows that women and children are so often victims. Lady Dantò and I will dance tonight for our poor Nina. And for our Shelly, too. Always for Shelly."

Dauphine had then set an open pack of Camels on the stump, letting it rest there for a moment before removing one from the pack and lighting it. The cigarette had dangled from her fingers as she poured Lady Dantò four fingers of rum, then lifted the glass to help her lady drink it. She plunked the bottle and the empty glass onto the red cloth, right next to the pack of cigarettes.

The offerings had been stored in a shapeless bag slung over Dauphine's shoulder. Reaching her hand back into its depths, she'd retrieved a large piece of canvas, rolled up and secured with a dirty string. She'd driven a nail through the canvas, nailing it to a tree beside the lady's makeshift altar, then unrolled it and held it flat against the trunk while she fumbled for another nail. Faye had hurried over to help her get it straight.

Once the canvas was fully visible, Faye found that she couldn't look away from the fierce female face emblazoned on it. The face had been splashed across the canvas in Dauphine's trademark shades of brilliant blue and red and black paint. There were scars on the woman's cheeks and she cradled seven infants in her massive arms. Ezili Dantò's image was not a comforting one. If the Madonna had gone to Haiti, watched her children suffer, and worked herself into a towering rage, she might look like this.

"I do not think our Nina's pain is past, no. She cannot tell us her troubles, and that puts me in mind of the Lady." Dauphine drew an endless drag of cigarette smoke. "Lady Dantò carries her pain inside, too, ever since she led the slaves in Haiti to revolt. The masters cut out her tongue for that, you know. She cannot talk any more than Nina can, but she is strong. I cannot talk for our Nina, either, but I can dance for her."

Dauphine had stubbed the cigarette out on the red cloth, leaving a smut-black hole. "Lady Dantò and I will do our best to dance that pain away, if God wills it. Away with you. We do not need your help."

From the bottom of her sack, Dauphine had drawn a jewel-hilted dagger. She'd freed it from its scabbard and laid it carefully with the other offerings on her makeshift altar to Lady Ezili Dantò. After that, nothing Faye said could induce Dauphine to speak. The woman had swayed and moaned and clicked her tongue in a "keh-keh-keh-keh" sound, but she couldn't be induced to say anything more intelligible than Nina's few words. Maybe she really *had* lost her ability to speak as she surrendered to the avenging power of the mute but fearsome Lady Ezili Dantò.

Faye had retreated to her apartment, frustrated by Dauphine's inability to respond to a simple good-night. She'd been looking forward to a quiet evening with Joe, but Dauphine's flickering candles had invaded her windows and the woman's wordless songs could not be quieted. Sometime after three, Faye's eyes had finally slid shut but, so far as she knew, the Lady Ezili Dantò had danced with her faithful mambo all night long.

Excerpt from *The Floodgates of Hell,*
The Reminiscences of Colonel James McGonohan
1876

*After Monsieur Deschanel was killed by the failure
of his floodgates, his widow and Monsieur Beaulieu
lived together for a number of years. I suppose they
were happy, though the gossip that grew into legend
recounts that they were never blessed with children.
They enjoyed her dead husband's wealth, but even
that great pile of money began to fail in the face of
their extravagance. There are always ways for people
to spend more money than they have.*

*For a time, they staved off creditors by selling
shares of the proceeds flowing from the brilliant
inventions that Monsieur Beaulieu concocted in his
dead employer's workshop. He gained a reputation for genius among a citizenry that had forgotten
how they derided Monsieur Deschanel for the very
same kind of labor. That reputation was eventually
tarnished when his business schemes crashed, one
after another, taking the money of his friends and
neighbors with them.*

*It eventually became obvious that Monsieur
Beaulieu needed to keep a closer eye on the plantation, since it was his only venture still generating the
money that they needed for their happiness. This
meant that his wife was once again married to a man
whose business kept him away from the social whirl
that she loved. I wonder whether this turn of events
shows that God was playing His own jokes on her.*

*She accompanied this husband on his trips to the
hinterlands, perhaps because she didn't trust him.
Or perhaps he demanded that she come, because
he didn't trust her. In either case, I wonder again
whether God enjoyed toying with a murderer and
his woman.*

Soon enough, mounting debts forced them to sell the townhouse and live on the plantation, so they were cut off from society year-round. It is at this point, when circumstances force them to be alone with each other, that a man and woman learn whether they were meant to be married.

I do not know how long they lived there, nor whether they were happy. But the night came when a crevasse opened in the levee that Monsieur Deschanel had so assiduously attended while he lived, right in front of the house where the guilty couple lay sleeping. The Mississippi roared through, rapidly opening the narrow gap into a cleft that rendered the levee useless. The rushing waters shoved the house right off its foundations.

Their slaves were able to escape, rowing in small boats to safety, but Monsieur Beaulieu and Monsieur Deschanel's widow were trapped in the house. Their bodies were found in the attic, trapped beneath the impressive but impenetrable slate roof that they'd had installed before they ran short on funds.

If they had only left the original cypress-shingled roof in place, they could have hacked through it in time, but slate roofs were oh-so-fashionable in that day, because they were oh-so-expensive. I see this deadly roof as one of the proofs that my theory is correct: they were guilty of murder, both of them. The roof was another of God's jests, if you will.

How did I reach this conclusion? By faith? No. An engineer may have the faith of an Old Testament prophet, but he always draws his conclusions from pure logic. Allow me to explain.

Consider this. A great engineer—a man capable of creating the inventions that flowed out of Monsieur Beaulieu's workshop—would not have built a house that could not be escaped if a flood should come.

Not on the very bank of the most powerful river on the continent.

I believe that he stole those inventions, one after another, from drawings left behind by his dead benefactor. That is why he was never able to make those inventions profitable. He didn't completely understand them. Perhaps he simply wasn't smart enough.

And consider the fact that all the slaves escaped the flood, even those who slept in the house to tend their owners' nighttime needs. They were almost certainly awakened by the field slaves, whose low-lying cabins would have flooded early. Out of more than a hundred slaves, not a single one had enough feeling for the master and his wife to wake them up and warn them of the danger.

You might say that this is because they hated their owners, because that is what slaves do. But few human beings hate so thoroughly that they will leave defenseless people to die. No, I believe they knew what this man and his wife were—murderers, the both of them— and I believe that they knew that this earth would be a better place without them.

And I believe God knew it when He reached down His finger and carved a hole in that levee.

Chapter Twenty-six

Saturday

Louie Godtschalk seemed to have glommed onto Joe as a limitless source of material for his book. He did at least have enough social grace to lay offerings on the altar of his benefactor, and they were the kind of offerings that were best-designed to get Joe's attention: they involved flour, grease, and a towering pile of powdered sugar.

Joe was incapable of resisting *beignets*—also known as "French market doughnuts" to people with so little poetry in their souls that they weren't willing to even try to pronounce the French word. It wasn't that hard: *ben-yay.*

Louie stood in the doorway and held out the bag of *beignets* with one hand. He clutched a cardboard carrier loaded with cups of coffee with the other. "There should be plenty. I brought enough to feed four, but Dauphine didn't answer when I knocked."

Joe stretched out his big hand and plucked three beignets out of the bag. No food went to waste when Joe was around. "Dauphine's sleeping off a long night of voodoo stuff, I bet," he said. "And all the rum that goes with it."

"Probably. There's burned-out candles everywhere out there."

Faye grabbed some plates and napkins and they pulled chairs up to her tiny table. "So what's the topic of today's research? And how can Joe help you? I'm dead certain that *I'm* not the reason you're here."

"Not unless you know something about drainage canals. Or screw pumps."

"I know quite a lot about pumps. Old Wheezy's been moving water for months, thanks to me."

"I'm talking about pumps big enough to empty the bowl this city's sitting in."

Faye shook her head. "Can't help you there."

"The librarian got me an article that talks about the canals. Says there's something like ninety miles of 'em." When Joe started talking about numbers as big as ninety, and distances as long as ninety miles, he talked with his hands. Even Joe's arms were hardly long enough to communicate his excitement over these glorified drainage ditches. "Ninety miles!"

Godtschalk wasn't easily impressed. "Ninety miles? I'm not surprised. There are canals just...everywhere. I grew up in a house that backed up to one. It was the same one that ran beside my elementary school. There's so many canals that you stop noticing them. They—"

"You didn't let me finish."

Faye was surprised to hear those words come out of Joe's mouth. He never interrupted anybody, and he was so soft-spoken and good-humored that he ordinarily just let people drown him out. Somehow, canals and pumps lit his fire enough to make him want to be heard.

"Sorry. Go ahead, Joe."

"There's maybe ninety miles of canals that you can *see*. Underground? There's ninety *more* miles. And some of those canals? They're big enough to drive a school bus through."

"Get out! That's good enough to put in the book." Louie grabbed his notepad. "You got a reference for that article?"

"Over here somewhere."

Faye wasn't sure how she felt about Joe turning into a geek—he might even qualify for bookworm status soon—but she was proud of him. When her cell rang, she was so distracted by watching him fumble through his stack of reading material that she barely looked at her phone as she thumbed it on.

"Faye?" Jodi's voice had more than its usual edge. "Did I wake you up?"

Faye turned her head so she couldn't see how cute Joe was when he was excited about canals. "No. I'm up. What's happening?"

"It's Nina." Jodi's voice had that foreboding tone, the one that goes along with sentiments like, *I'm so sorry for your loss,* or *I know the doctors did all they could.*

"What's wrong with Nina? Is she back in the hospital? I wish she'd been talking better yesterday, but she looked okay—"

"It's not her health. She's fine. Well, Charles said she was fine when she went to bed last night." Jodi let out a long breath. "She's missing, Faye."

Charles hadn't shaved, and sweat slicked his pasty skin. He had never been conventionally good-looking, but his easy swagger had called attention away from an oversized nose and puffy cheeks. Take away his confidence, and he was just another homely man pushing forty. This particular homely man lived in a house Faye would have killed for—one of the French Quarter's "hidden houses" tucked behind the storefronts visible from the cobbled streets—but that didn't change the fact that he was homely.

"No, I didn't hear a thing. I guess I was just glad to have Nina here, where I could take care of her, because I went to sleep in front of the TV and I stayed there all night. It was nearly nine before I woke up this morning. I haven't slept till nine since I was a teenager. I hardly sleep at all, most nights."

"Insomnia?" Jodi asked.

"Yeah."

"Did you take anything for it last night?"

"I never do. I don't like the way it makes me feel."

"That's not an answer." Jodi sounded like she had officially come to the last millimeter of her patience. "Yes or no, did you take any medication last night that would have made you sleep?"

"No. I didn't. Besides, I wouldn't have done that last night, especially. What if Nina had needed me?"

Jodi wasn't feeling merciful. "Apparently, she did need you."

She swept an arm around the room where Nina had been sleeping. Tangled bedclothes hung off a queen-sized bed, dragging on an unfinished cypress floor burnished by centuries of feet. Behind the bed, a pair of casement windows opened outward onto a courtyard hung with flowering vines. Tremendous clay pots held trees that looked like they'd grown in this garden since the French ruled the city. New curtains sewn from old lace framed the window opening. It was a beautiful spot for a kidnapping.

Jodi pointed at a gate on the far side of the courtyard. "Where does that go?"

Charles found a way to look even more miserable. "An alley."

"Was that window locked?"

"Yeah. At least I think so. This is my guest room, so I'm not in here much."

"Your girlfriend sleeps in the guest room?"

Jodi fastened an "I-don't-believe-you" glare on Charles.

"I just thought Nina would be more comfortable resting in here, instead of sleeping with me like she usually does. She has to be in some pain. It hasn't been that long since she got hurt."

"Did Nina do or say anything last night that would suggest she might have left here on her own?"

"No." He shook his head, then repeated himself. "No. She certainly didn't do anything. She might have said a few things, but they didn't make any sense."

"Do you remember what they were?"

The tone was crisp and decidedly cool. Jodi was making no secret of the fact that she felt no sympathy for this man whose sick girlfriend had gone missing under his very nose.

Charles pursed his lips in anger. Beneath the razor stubble and clammy skin, Faye caught a glimpse of the arrogant man who had so captivated Nina.

"Why are you taking this attitude with me? I picked Nina up from the hospital and brought her home so I could care for her. That's what you do when you love somebody. How could I know someone would snatch her right out of my own home?"

"Maybe she was snatched. Maybe she left on her own. All I'm doing right now is asking questions. Do you remember anything Nina said before she went to bed last night?"

Charles said, "No," but Faye didn't believe him.

If Joe were to lose his ability to tell her what he wanted her to know, she would hang on every last thing he said. She would turn every word over in her mind like a stone imprinted with an unfamiliar fossil, feeling for something, anything that would re-open the flow of communication. So Charles was lying when he said he didn't remember what Nina had said.

Either that, or he was lying when he said he loved her.

The crime scene technicians were hard at work, lifting fingerprints and looking for tiny things like hairs and fibers. The rumpled bedclothes in the unmade bed were no evidence of a struggle, and there were no other signs that Nina's abduction had been violent. They had found nothing but footprints on the courtyard's bricked floor suggesting that someone in sneakers had come in from the alley, walked to the window, then walked back to the alley with a second person, presumably Nina.

"Assuming one set of those prints was Nina's, then she was walking under her own power," Jodi told Faye and Joe. "We've got no proof she was taken against her will. We don't even have any proof that it wasn't Charles who drove off with Nina. He could have walked her across that courtyard just as easily as anyone else. The only tricky part—for Charles or anyone— would have been convincing Nina that there was some good reason to crawl out the window."

"Nina would have done anything Charles asked her to do." Remembering Nina's face when Charles reappeared in her life, Faye was certain of this. "She was recovering from a serious conk on the head, so we can't presume out-of-hand that her actions would make sense to us. But if she was acting logically at all, we should presume that Nina knew the person who took her."

"She trusted the person," Joe said. "She felt like she'd be safe with whoever it was."

"Then where is she?" Jodi demanded. "If she's so damn safe, why doesn't anybody know where she is?"

A movie stub. And another one, identical in every way. They lay on the interrogation table in front of Jodi, mocking her.

She had sent Faye and Joe home, because she'd hired them to help her navigate the world of archaeology—the science, the people, the arcane bits of history—not the world of criminals willing to kidnap a badly injured woman from her bed. This was police work, and she'd let them follow their curiosity too far already.

She should have taken Faye and Joe off the case after someone tried to shoot them, but she'd dragged her feet. They'd both been incredibly useful to Shelly's murder investigation. Besides, she just liked having them around.

Jodi knew it would break her heart if her new friend Faye were stolen from her bed. Also, she knew that Joe would kill her if she let that happen. So she needed to deal with Nina's disappearance on her own, with old-fashioned police work and without the unorthodox assistance of an archaeologist or two.

Matt and Leila had sat calmly across the table from her, with the ticket stubs lying in the center of that table, denying that they'd done anything the night before that could remotely interest the police. Since it was Friday night, they'd gone to the movies. They always went to the movies on Friday night.

Jodi reflected that neither Matt nor Leila was old enough to even give middle age a good long look. They were way too young to be so set in their ways.

The young couple had said that they'd seen no one they knew, but they'd produced these two ticket stubs as if the two scraps of pasteboard were incontrovertible proof that they'd been where they said they'd been. As if it were impossible to go to the movie, buy a couple of tickets, tear them in half, then walk away.

Their alibi was absolutely useless. Jodi would be checking into surveillance tapes, looking for proof of the young couple's whereabouts, but it was a pointless exercise. Even if they'd attended the midnight showing of the latest cinematic celebration of guns and car chases—and these two ticket stubs said they had—there was still no accounting for their activities between two a.m. and sunrise. That was the likeliest time period for Nina's disappearance, and precious few people could ever offer an alibi for that time of night.

Why was she putting so much effort into tracking down two people who didn't bear much resemblance to any of the murderers and kidnappers Jodi had ever sent to jail? Nor any of the ones she wished she could have sent to jail. They were young, attractive, educated, polite. She had no doubt that they paid their bills and that they were good to their respective mothers. In fact, their excuse for going to such a late flick—if two people their age even needed an excuse for staying out late—was that they'd gone to an anniversary dinner for Leila's grandparents earlier in the evening.

It was a fair measure of Jodi's desperation that these two people were even viable suspects. Leila was on her radar screen because she looked nervous and because her mother's (very common) maiden name had been written on a scrap of paper found in the pocket of a corpse. Also, because she worked for the missing woman's slimy boyfriend.

Matt? She'd hauled that poor man in for questioning because he was dating a woman whose mother's maiden name was found on a scrap of paper in the pocket of a corpse. And so had his own name. She was also questioning him because the missing woman had once said that the dead woman called her cousin Matt "weird." This did not strike her as brilliant, groundbreaking police work.

Where was Nina?

Jodi somehow doubted that Nina was enjoying a slumber party with an old friend. Something had prompted somebody to try to crush Nina's skull, before shoving her into a river that had swallowed more human lives than Jodi cared to count. If someone had wanted Nina dead that bad, just a few days before, Jodi figured that they *still* wanted her dead. She'd been missing for twelve hours, so the odds were good that her kidnapper had already found a way to make that happen.

But *why* did somebody want Nina dead? She was sweet, hardworking, unassuming. How could anyone want to hurt a woman like that?

Chapter Twenty-seven

"We've been fired, Joe."

Faye realized that sitting at the kitchen table, sipping morosely on a cup of cold coffee, meant that she had rendered herself completely unattractive to any man alive. This should probably have bothered her, but Joe seemed to love her even when she had mud on her face and sweat in her hair. She was learning to trust that love. "How could Jodi have cut us loose like this?"

"She didn't cut us loose, Faye. She told us to go back to doing what she hired us to do—thinking about Shelly's job as an archaeologist and finding out whether it had something to do with her getting killed."

Faye hated it when Joe talked sense. She walked to the window. Dauphine's altar to Ezili Dantò was a red blotch on nature. The offerings left for the Lady were untouched, except for the empty rum glass. Faye wondered if the candles strewn around the damp yard could be made to burn again when Dauphine needed another favor from her Lady.

The bold strokes of Lady Dantò's portrait cut through the gray mist that had descended the evening before and lingered all night and into the day. The afternoon was winding down, but the gray hadn't relented yet. Faye guessed the day would be over before she ever really saw the sun.

The pack of cigarettes still lay on the cloth-covered stump, beside the empty glass that had held rum before Dauphine helped her lady drink it. Everything was as it had been.

No, it wasn't. The Lady Dantò's knife was gone.

There were no lights in Dauphine's windows, and why should there be? It was her day off and she had spent a long night dancing. Why were Faye's thoughts straying to the coffin nails under her own stairs?

The stump of a red candle. A stone wrapped in blue cloth. An open pair of scissors. A handful of coffin nails.

Faye had taken her share of anthropology classes and she understood the concept of sympathetic magic. She knew why these objects had been placed under her entry stairs. It was because she'd be forced to walk over them, and the magic associated with a person's path was considered powerful.

She knew that open scissors were supposed to protect against witchcraft. The red candle was intended to provoke desire. She suspected the blue cloth was meant to be calming. The stone must be the baby that this spell was conjuring up. The coffin nails...

She knew that coffin nails, to the practitioners of voodoo and hoodoo, were intended to bind, so maybe the idea was to make sure Joe stuck around, presuming all the other magical items worked and she actually got pregnant. But the coffin nails meant something more to Faye, more than the concept of being physically bound.

She did feel bound. She felt bound to this place out of sheer ignorance, because she didn't know where to go or what to do. If she stepped outside, she could be shot dead in her own front yard. Somebody had already tried.

When her cell phone rang and Bobby Longchamp's voice came out of it, asking her to come look at something important he'd just found, she was primed and ready to go. It really wouldn't have mattered who was on the other end of the line, nor what he wanted from her. Right that minute, anyone who offered Faye a reasonable excuse to get out of the house—an excuse to get out of her own head—was going to win out over Faye's fears of invisible gunmen or monsters who prayed on lonely women. As it turned out, Bobby was the one to offer her that chance.

◇◇◇

"Come see!" Bobby had crowed. "I found the precise photos that Shelly had in her pocket. I know who took them and when, so I can tell you that she was definitely alive for at least three days after the storm. I've laid my hands on copies in the original size. Shelly had cut her copies down and thrown away the rest. Why don't you come see my copies, so you can see the parts she *didn't* care about? There's value in negative information, you know. I'm still at the Historic Collection. Come see what I've got here."

"Aren't they about to close? Did they give you a key to the place?"

"When I was a callow fraternity boy, my grandfather donated two hundred years worth of family papers and artwork to this place, along with a small fortune to curate it all. It's been a long, long time since then, but they still give me whatever I ask for, and they do it with a smile. I can't even afford an annual membership to the place, but I'll happily ride on *Grandpère's* coattails."

Faye was in the mood to get out of the house anyway, but the deal was sealed by Bobby's promise to show her the parts of the photos Shelly threw away. She had to appreciate the thought processes of anyone who could understand the finer qualities of data gathering implied by the term "negative information." Maybe she and Bobby *were* kin.

Throwing on a jacket as a safeguard against the damp evening air, she stuck her phone in her pocket, and hustled Joe out the door. It made her flat-out angry to find herself glancing furtively around the yard, looking to see if someone with a gun was hiding there.

As she crossed the yard, she had the inexplicable urge to run her fingers over the leering face of Lady Ezili Dantò, still nailed to her tree trunk, but something—she couldn't say what it was—stayed her hand. Faye would have thought that years devoted to the study of a rational science like archaeology would have driven every last vestige of superstition from her psyche. Apparently not.

Though the sun hadn't set, the moon already hung low in the darkening east. They were both veiled in the same cool mist that had dropped over the city the night before. As Faye and Joe walked through Dauphine's aging neighborhood and reached the even older streets of the *Vieux Carré*, the fog was penetrated by the rhythmic plucking of a guitar being tuned. Those random tones were punctuated by the bangs and crashes of a drummer's warm-up. There would be music at Congo Square tonight.

Since Faye had no desire to go back to her apartment and sit, she thought maybe she and Joe would stroll over there after they finished working with Bobby. Enthusiastic street music would drive her worries over Nina away for awhile. Maybe the jolting rhythms would tie up the conscious part of her brain long enough to let her subconscious come out to play. Because she somehow thought that, deep down, she already knew the answers to the tough questions—*What happened to Shelly? Where on earth is Nina?*—pestering her waking mind.

Suddenly, with a cymbal crash and a free-form trumpet wail, the music started. The hum of human voices told her that a crowd had gathered, ready for a party. If the trumpet player hadn't taken a breath, preparing to play his heart out for the next three hours, at least, Faye would never have heard her phone ring.

She didn't recognize the number on her phone's small screen, other than to notice that the area code was local. Gripping the phone hard against her ear, she struggled to hear the voice on the other end of the line, but it was too weak to stand against the blast of noise coming from Congo Square.

Faye backed away from the music, looking for a courtyard or an alcove or any place where she could shelter her ears from the music permeating the old town. She needed to find a quiet place to listen to this quiet voice…

…because it was Nina's.

Chapter Twenty-eight

"Nina. Where are you? Can you tell me where you are?"

Faye caught Joe's eye and tapped her phone. He whipped out his own phone and dialed. He was calling Jodi. She knew it as surely as she knew he loved her.

The thin, reedy voice had a strident edge, as if the words were being forced past her vocal cords. "Faye…the saints. Sometimes saints do wrong. Sometimes."

And then there was silence.

"Nina! Nina, are you still there?"

"Yes…where is here?" The frail voice drifted away, as lost as its owner was.

"That's what I want to know. Can you tell me where you are? And can you tell me who took you? Where are they now? Are you safe?"

Too many questions. She was asking too many questions for Nina's battered brain to follow. But those questions meant life or death.

"Safe…yes…suh-safe. Are you safe?"

Was Nina safe? Was she asking if Faye was safe? Or was she echoing the words because she wasn't capable of forming sentences of her own?

Faye found a tiny niche in a long line of storefronts, big enough for one body. Stout bricks on three sides insulated her ears from the raucous partiers a few blocks away.

"Nina. If you tell me where you are, I can come get you."

"Streetcar? Mmmm…yeah. Streetcar."

"You want me to come by streetcar? Are you near the streetcar line?"

Faye fumbled in her pocket for the tattered tourist map that kept her from getting lost. The streetcar line ran down St. Charles Avenue. How far away was that?

"Come, Faye."

I'm trying, Nina. I'm trying.

Joe had one hand clapped over his free ear. He'd drawn away from Faye, several paces away, so that he wouldn't bother her as he bellowed instructions for Jodi into his phone.

"The police are coming to help us, Nina."

Could they find Nina if they knew she was talking to Faye's cell phone? Maybe they could if she were talking on a land line. Faye just didn't know what investigators could do with the limited information available. Whatever it was, Jodi would make sure it got done.

"Nina," she said, trying to make her voice soft and reassuring, despite her mounting frustration. "Jodi and her officers are coming to help you. We just need to be able to tell them where you are. It might help if we knew who took you. Do you know who it was? Can you tell me?"

Faye was asking too many questions again, but they were all important. She couldn't choose just one. "Do you know *why* this person has done these things to you?"

"Do anything to have my mama back, Faye…anything. My daddy…whatever it took." The weak voice finally broke. "Anything."

It tore Faye's heart to hear Nina weeping. She'd give pretty much anything to have her parents back, too.

"Where are you, sweetheart? Mama's not here, but I'll come get you. I'll come, if you'll just tell me where you are. Just give me something I can use to find you."

But all Faye got was quiet sobs. And the bricks weren't doing their job, because the music was intruding, still. Faye jammed her hand so hard against her free ear that she heard a roar like the ocean, but the music didn't stop. How could she make it stop?

She had closed her eyes, trying to think, when she finally heard the music clearly...because she could hear it with both ears.

"Nina! Do you hear music? Can you get to the window and open it?"

Faye heard the faint grinding of a heavy window being raised. It sounded like an old window, with many years of thick paint that made the sash hard to operate. This observation didn't help her at all. How many old windows, with their woodwork roughened by years of paint, existed in this city?

"Cold...wet, too."

"Yes!" Faye was laughing, but she didn't know why. "Yes, Nina, it's wet and cold outside. Do you hear music?"

"Music...yeah! Dixieland. Basin Street."

Faye didn't think the song of the moment sounded much like "Basin Street Blues," but that wasn't the point. Nina was within earshot of Congo Square. She might well be in earshot of Faye and Joe, but how were they going to find her?

"What do you see out the window?"

"Trees."

Great. That was a lot of help. There were a lot of those in this town, but none of them were visible from the city street where Faye stood. So maybe Nina was in one of the residential neighborhoods on the other side of Rampart Street.

Or maybe not. There were trees in the French Quarter, too. Some of them were in the courtyard of Charles Landry's house. Could he have faked the kidnapping and hidden Nina, bringing her back to his house while he decided what to do with her?

Why would he do that? Why would he want Nina dead? Was she dangerous to him in some way? Did she know something that he wanted kept secret? No matter. The question of the moment wasn't whether Charles had Nina, nor why. The immediate issue was her safety.

The trees in Charles' courtyard were impressive. They'd probably been growing in their tremendous clay pots for way longer than Faye had been alive. But they were still glorified potted plants.

"Nina…tell me about the trees. Are they big?"

"Pretty trees. Big? Hmmm…maybe…."

Well, Charles' trees were pretty, but so were most trees. And, though there were other trees in the French Quarter, there weren't an awful lot of them. She could go forward, deeper into the Quarter, or she could turn back, toward the tree-lined residential streets in Tremé.

Faye decided to take the better odds. There were a lot of trees in Tremé, so that's where she'd go. She caught Joe's eye and pointed back up the street. They were turning around.

Faye ran with an awkward gait, hefting her feet just a little higher than normal to clear big chunks of pavement that were heaved upward by soil that never stopped settling. She flung her left arm out for balance, but her right hand relentlessly clutched the phone to her ear.

She passed a cross-street and saw throngs of people converging on Louis Armstrong Park, which surrounded the spot where Congo Square had always served as a gathering spot for music and revelry. The music slid from one soloist to another without stopping, as if it had never stopped, not in three hundred years. It shifted again, and the trumpet made its opening call, answered by softer woodwinds.

Faye heard Nina sigh, and say, "Oh, listen."

A leather-lunged vocalist was belting out an old song with such power that Faye could actually understand the words from this distance.

Won't you come along with me?

To the Mississippi?

They were playing Basin Street Blues.

The historic maps, the new photos, the old photos, the tattered tourist map in pocket…Faye could see them all in her mind's eye. She could see the old diagonal slash of the Carondelet Canal with its turning *bassin,* the basin that inspired the name of one of music's most famous streets.

The original location of Congo Square had bordered on the *bassin*, which meant that modern Basin Street passed damn near the park where Basin Street Blues was being played with such gusto, right that minute. Maybe Nina had mentioned the song, even before Faye could tell it was being played, because she was trying to tell Faye where she was. Maybe she was somewhere near Basin Street.

Basin Street wasn't much of a street, in terms of length. Just a few blocks, really. Still, getting there and canvassing the street itself—not to mention nearby side streets—was too much to do on foot.

"Let's start from scratch, Joe. Let's go back to the apartment and get my car."

◇◇◇

The cacophony at Congo Square kept Faye's thoughts scrambled. She ran down blocks that grew scarier as the sun set. What had she been thinking, walking after dark in this part of town?

The streets were deserted, and Faye praised God for that. And she was eternally grateful that someone tall and brawny was running at her side. Not that Joe would be much help if they were attacked by someone carrying a gun.

Every minute or so, Faye mustered enough breath to wheeze a few words into her telephone.

"Keep talking, Nina."

That's really all she could think of to say. Nothing else was important, right this minute.

The faceless vocalist had no idea how hard her song was driving Faye—driving her to run because her friend's life depended on it. If somebody had been willing to beat her and drown her and steal her out of her sickbed, then that somebody would surely be willing to kill her.

"Keep talking. Please, Nina. Keep talking."

So Nina kept whispering nonsense about saints and streetcars, and the vocalist kept singing, sending out a timeless melody to Faye and Joe and Nina and everyone else nearby who had ears.

We'll take the boat to the land of dreams,
Steaming down the river down to New Orleans.
Basin Street...

Chapter Twenty-nine

The band's here to meet us,
Old friends to greet us.
Where all the light and the dark folk meet,
This is Basin Street…

The streets of Tremé were lined with old mossy oaks, maybe the very trees outside Nina's cage. How would Faye know which ones Nina could see?

The massive trees soaked up the music, slowly bringing quiet until Faye could hear herself breathe again. She could hear the thudding of her heart beneath her ribs. The silent calm made her want to run slower, take a deep breath, give herself a moment to think. But there was no time for those things, and Faye knew it.

Nina's doctor had said that brain injury patients could often understand everything that was said to them, but their ability to choose words in response was garbled. Why was Nina talking about streetcars?

The St. Charles Avenue streetcar line was blocks away from Basin Street, at its closest point. It started at the intersection of Carondelet and Canal Street, which was an interesting coincidence considering that Shelly was working along the former route of the Carondelet Canal before she died, but the old canal was many blocks from that intersection. This line of thought was filed away for future consideration, because it was getting her nowhere. Worse, it was adding more streets, stretching for far more city blocks, to the area Faye needed to search—St. Charles Avenue, Canal Street, Carondelet Street…

It seemed worthwhile to concentrate on Nina's obsession with saints, more so than on St. Charles Avenue or its streetcar line.

An echo in that sentence bothered Faye's ear. Saints. St. Charles.

She tried to think like someone whose brain couldn't process language. Was Nina reaching for one word and coming out with the one her brain had filed in the neural cells next-door? Was she saying "saint" when she meant "Charles?"

Charles' patronizing air toward Nina and his arrogant behavior with Jodi had never spoken well for him. Neither did his uneasy manner when he was showing Jodi the scene of Nina's kidnapping.

Faye had suspected Charles of hurting Nina the whole time, simply because she didn't like him. Was Nina trying to tell her that she was right?

Faye's pace flagged, and Joe reached out a hand to steady her and to help her along if necessary. She reached for energy reserves that she might not have, as they turned the corner onto Dauphine's street. Faye knew her car was just a block and a half away. The Pontiac Bonneville had been wrecked and patched together again, but it would get her where she needed to go. Her legs sure didn't have much left in them.

She was trying to think of something else odd that Nina had said about her parents. If she could only make the poor woman's ravings make sense. What was it she had said?

I'd do anything to have my mama back, Faye…anything. My daddy…whatever it took.

Faye knew it was the truth. Of course, Nina would be thinking of her parents at a time like this. But she had said it at an odd point in their conversation. What had Faye said just before that? What had she said to prompt that particular response out of Nina?

Do you know why this person has done these things to you?

Did they do it because Nina wanted her parents back? Maybe not. But maybe they did it because they wanted their own parents back. Shelly had lost her parents to Katrina. Faye believed in her heart that Shelly had gone to look for her parents when she was killed. And she wasn't the only person who had lost loved ones. What had Bobby said about Shelly's last days?

She was a tough kid, but sometimes she was crying while she worked. And she wasn't the only one. I was actually ashamed to tell people that my parents were okay.

Whose names were on the lists in Shelly's pocket? Charles Landry. Matt Guidry. Leila Martin Caron, and Shelly Broussard. All of them had been working at Zephyr Field.

Bobby Longchamp had been there, but his name was not on the list. His family had never even been in danger. What about the rest of them?

Charles Landry had mentioned his parents in the present tense when Jodi was questioning him about Shelly's list of names. Leila Caron's parents ruled the Garden Club and the Mystic Krewe of Something-or-Other. Matt's parents were rescued at the last minute off their roof in Chalmette.

The families of everyone else they knew who had surnames on the lists had survived the storm, except Shelly's. Faye had stared at those names for so long that she could see them swimming in front of her eyes. On one of the lists, the one written in Leila's handwriting, the first three names were Landry, Martin, and Guidry…and the last one was Broussard.

I'd do anything to have my mama back, Faye…anything. My daddy…whatever it took.

When the rescue teams went out in their boats, they had to go somewhere first. How much power would have rested with the person who decided where they went and when?

Zephyr Field was staffed with volunteers. Leadership would have gone to the person who acted like a leader. Maybe Charles? Certainly not Leila or Matt.

Suppose the hurriedly scrawled list had been the first one made, and it had gone through Leila Caron's hands on its way to Charles. How hard would it have been for him to ask her to copy the list over, but put the names in the order he wanted them? How much would people have paid to have their loved ones rescued quickly, while a rescue was still possible? How much was it worth for your parents' name—or your sister's or your grandmothers'—to be high on that list?

Shelly did not seem like the kind of person who would stand for that kind of corruption, and she'd had no compunction about taking her fears about the levees to everyone who would listen. If she'd learned about this scheme, she would have protested... and loudly. She was heard arguing with someone just before she died. Faye sincerely doubted that a person who had perpetuated a scam like this one wanted the city to know about it... this city filled with people who had suffered their own losses to the floodwaters.

If the scammer knew Shelly, then he or she would have avoided letting her know about the scheme at all costs. This would mean that Shelly's parents would go to the bottom of the list, below the loved ones of all the paying customers.

This scheme was nothing more than the sale of life and death for individual human beings. Who could have done such a heinous thing?

Was it Leila? Was Leila the one who took bribes to have certain names given a higher priority?

Maybe. But a huge promotion had been handed to Charles Landry right after Katrina. Perhaps the company president had bought his sister's safety—or his grandmother's or his mother-in-law's—with that promotion. Leila was still an administrative assistant.

Married women usually use their husbands' names. With that in mind, Faye realized that only some of the names on a list like this would be familiar. If Shelly's friends or coworkers had paid to have a maternal grandmother rescued, their own last names would not appear on the list. Just their relatives'.

If Faye read Leila's handwritten list correctly, Charles and Matt made sure their parents were safe. Leila had safeguarded someone on the maternal side of her family, the Martins. If any of the other people on the list had been maternal connections to the people paying Charles off, their last names would be different, and thus very difficult to track.

And how were Charles and his co-conspirators paid? Faye guessed that the company president might have paid Charles with a salary and a job title. Everybody else had been forced to make do with mere cash...which would have been in ample supply at Zephyr Field. Everybody there had fled their homes, certainly with their pockets full of all the cash they could assemble for an evacuation that could last indefinitely.

Charles Landry was the one living in a posh townhouse in the *Vieux Carré*. And his last name was first on Shelly's list.

The goal had been simply to reach Faye's car and drive away, hoping that Nina's location would be obvious once they got to Basin Street. Faye had never intended to climb the stairs to her apartment, so she was never sure why her eyes strayed to the staircase. Maybe she was thinking of the coffin nails.

If she hadn't stopped dead in her tracks—if she hadn't reached out a warning hand that stopped Joe—he might have shot them on sight. Instead, they were standing well within range, but just a little too far away for an easy shot. Darkness was falling, blurring their outlines and making it harder for the man beneath the staircase to raise the gun barrel and fire off a shot that he was certain would find its mark. And then another.

By stopping and turning their faces toward that gun barrel, murder became a different thing. It became the snuffing out of two lives, rather than the simple elimination of a threat. It was harder to shoot people whose eyes were locked on yours, much harder than squeezing off a few bullets in their direction while they were sitting in their lawn chairs sipping iced tea. Even harder than attacking a defenseless woman from behind her back.

Two defenseless women, actually.

The man holding the gun was surrounded by people he needed to kill. Faye. Joe. And Dauphine, sitting beside him on the ground, as stoic as the Lady Dantò.

If he killed them all, what would happen to Nina? Did he have her locked away somewhere? Faye could hear the hum of constant chatter from the cell phone in her hand. Nina was alive, somewhere. Why hadn't he killed her already?

Faye wondered how she could have been so wrong. Charles was corrupt and sleazy, and he may well have sold spots on that damnable list to the highest bidder. But he didn't kill Shelly and he didn't hurt Nina.

Wide-eyed Matt sat in front of her, panting with terror, holding a semi-automatic handgun in his shaking hands.

How could she have forgotten that there was a saint named Matthew?

Chapter Thirty

"It's growing dark, child."

Dauphine waited for Matt to focus on her murky green eyes. "You need light to see your path. That's the only way for you to see what you need to do. There is a candle in the dirt underneath your foot. And I have matches in my apron pocket. You need your hands to control your gun. Please hand me the candle. I will light it."

In a single non-threatening motion, she pulled the matches from her pocket and reached out her hand, just slightly. Matt snatched up the red candle stub that was supposed to bring Faye a baby and handed it to Dauphine. Faye sensed a tremor in Joe, a sign that he had thought about jumping Matt during the instant there was only one hand on the gun. He had thought about it, and rejected the idea.

Matt was too far away. In the time it took Joe to reach him, Matt could put a bullet in his heart. Or Dauphine's. Or Faye's. Or his own. This was a man who had murdered out of terror and shame. Anyone with a glimmer of humanity would be unhinged by that act. And Matt was no inhuman beast who had killed for entertainment or convenience.

Faye couldn't imagine ever making the choice to kill, so she couldn't empathize with his agony. But she understood it, just a little. The things he'd done had left him unbalanced and, in a way, more dangerous than a demon who killed coolly and easily. There was no way to predict what he might do.

To underscore that unpredictability, Matt seemed to find himself inexplicably fascinated by his gun. He turned it slightly left and leaned forward to get a good view down the muzzle. Satisfied, he leaned back and practiced aiming it. In turns, the target was Joe's belly, Faye's heart, Dauphine's head.

Then he checked the muzzle again—for what? dust?—before making the rounds again. Joe's heart. Faye's head. Dauphine's throat. When he had finished with that game and sat again with the gun balanced in two relaxed hands, Dauphine lit the candle.

The match flared more than Faye expected, then settled to a steady glow as Dauphine held it to the candlewick. Her hand was silhouetted by the small flame and, even from a distance of several paces, Faye thought she saw the mambo's hand shake as a faint cloud of powder dropped from her hand into the flame.

A nameless smell reached out for Faye. If forced to give it a name, she would have said, "Warm. It smells warm."

Dauphine held her hands to the flame, humming a gentle song. More sound wafted from an unexpected corner. Joe was humming the same tune, so quietly that no one could possibly hear but Faye, and she wasn't even sure she was hearing it. It seemed that he had been listening on that long night when he had communed with Shelly's spirit, and Dauphine had said good-bye to her in the style of her own religious tradition. What else had Joe learned from this voodoo priestess?

"Young Matthew, my people teach that our ancestors love us." Matt twitched at the word "ancestors." "They want the best for us. They heal us. We can call them to us with good thoughts and a candle like this one to light their way."

Dauphine kept her hands open, showing that there was no weapon in them. She was showing Matt that he had nothing to fear from her. Something about Matt's reaction to the word "ancestors" told Faye that he thought they might be well worth fearing.

"There are clouds all round you, young one. I see them... here." She gestured in a tight circle around her own chest, belly, pelvis. Her hands moved slowly, easily, so that he wouldn't be startled by the motion. "You're bewitched, but you don't have to stay that way. Let Dauphine help you get clean."

He looked at her like an orphaned child. "Nobody can help me. I killed Aimee and Dan."

"Not with your own hands?" Dauphine moved her hands close to the candle. They moved through gentle steady arcs, and the flame made her skin glow from within.

"No! Not them. I didn't kill Aimee and Dan myself. I just gave Charles everything he wanted, and that's why they're dead. I'd emptied my bank account when I saw the storm coming, thinking I'd need money to live until things got back to normal. My pockets, my briefcase, the glove box in my car—they were all full of cash by the time I got to Zephyr Field."

He drew a deep, ragged breath. "I went to Zephyr Field because I wanted to help. Can you believe that? Help. I thought maybe I could help."

He shifted his hands, and Faye could see a shimmer where they'd left sweat on the gun's frame.

"I gave my money to Charles, all of it, so he'd send someone to get my mother and father. I didn't think about what that meant. I didn't think about other people dying just because Mom and Dad didn't. Aimee and Dan drowned while my parents were being rescued, and other people did, too. I'm sure of it. Shelly realized what I'd done before I really understood it myself. She never knew for sure that her parents died because mine lived. I killed her before either of us could know that without a doubt, but the look on her face when she found out what I'd done…"

The gun wavered dangerously as Matt groped for his last shred of self-control. "How can I ever look my mother in the eyes? People are dead because she's alive, because of what I did. As it turned out, one of those dead people was Aimee. I killed Shelly so that Mom would never know that."

Faye recognized the gentle motions of Dauphine's hands. She'd seen them before, but the last time she witnessed these movements, Dauphine had held a knife in her hand. They were the motions that called Ezili Dantò from her slumber. Faye hoped she came. At this moment, she couldn't think of any better supernatural being to call up than a fierce Lady who danced and drank rum and carried a knife.

Faye decided to risk speaking, because there was something she desperately wanted to know.

"Why did you take Nina? Where is she?"

She really wanted to ask *Why did you hurt Nina? Why did you want her dead?*, but the questions might have set Matt off again. Dauphine's candle—and that good-smelling dust she'd dropped into its flame—seemed to have calmed him.

"Take her? I didn't take her." He stroked the barrel of his gun. "Somebody's got her, and she's telling them everything. Charles has been a wreck, ever since you showed Nina those lists. She knew all those people, the ones who paid to get their families saved. She knew what their last names were when they were single. She knew their mother's maiden names. She knew who their children married. Charles said she'd almost figured it out, but he didn't know what to do about it. I did. His problem is that he loves her. But Nina's not going to keep those secrets. She'll tell them on TV. She'll write them in her blog. She'll tell the world. I like Nina, but I'd rather see her in the river than let her tell anybody what I did."

Faye tried to decide whether she believed him. If he didn't take Nina, then who did? Charles? Had Faye guessed wrong? Maybe Nina *was* at Charles' house and Faye could have saved her, if she'd rushed straight there. But maybe that would have meant that Dauphine was shot right here in her own yard.

"But if you don't have Nina—" Faye began, but she stopped at a twitch of Dauphine's head.

Dauphine was right. There would be nothing to gain by pointing out to Matt that he had no reason to kill Joe or Dauphine or Faye. If Nina was out there somewhere safe, there was nothing to stop her from telling someone everything she knew, so there was no reason to add three murders to his list of crimes.

Matt was beyond that kind of reasoning now. He just wanted to silence anyone who knew his secrets. Unfortunately, the three of them were on that list.

Dauphine had closed her eyes. Faye wasn't sure that she was capable of closing her own eyes in the face of certain death. She needed her wits about her. She needed to trust that there was some way to get out of this.

Dauphine trusted something else. She trusted *someone* else.

With eyes still closed, she began crooning a song Faye had heard her sing before. But she only sang two words—*Come, lady!*—and merely hummed the rest. The effect was peaceful, serene.

The tightness around Matt's eyes eased. Faye found it harder by the minute to resist the urge to relax and trust that everything would be okay. But she needed to resist, because she was in no way sure that things would work out okay. The warm smell seemed to be emanating from Dauphine now and the candle seemed to be glowing brighter.

Dauphine murmured—*Come, lady!*—again, and Faye snapped back to attention, because she had remembered the words that Dauphine was being careful not to sing:

> *Seven stabs of the knife, of the dagger*
> *Seven stabs of the knife, of the dagger*
> *Lend me the basin, I must vomit my blood*
> *Lend me the basin, I must vomit my blood*
> *My blood pours down*
> *Come, Lady…*

Joe knew the song. Dauphine had been singing it on the night that he sat vigil for Shelly. He'd sat so quietly while she sang it over and over that it was probably as engrained on his brain as it was on Faye's. But he just kept humming along with Dauphine, pausing only to let her call out *Come, Lady!* alone.

And then calm, rational, scientific Faye saw a spectral lady with her own eyes. She felt alert and wide awake, certainly not like someone who was dazed or drugged, yet there was no question in her mind what she saw.

There was a woman beneath the oak tree in front of her. She was fifty feet away, but there was no mistaking the sinuous curve of a woman's silhouette—of a Lady's silhouette. The setting sun's last few beams of red light highlighted a cheek, a jaw, and a collarbone revealed by a wide-cut neckline.

As for the rest of the Lady's face, Faye couldn't say what it looked like, because it was covered in shadow. She could have been half-bird. Her face could have been scarred or twisted. Faye just couldn't tell, and she had the impression that a voodoo spirit—a Lady—could look like anything she damn well pleased. Over the Lady's shoulder shone silver-white moonlight that backlit her wild and untamed hair.

It also glinted brightly on the edge of an upheld knife.

Chapter Thirty-one

How long had she stood there, watching Matt play with a deadly weapon and grow more careless by the minute? Faye didn't know.

How many times had he pointed that weapon at another human being with an expression that said he was mulling over the consequences of pulling the trigger? She couldn't say.

All she knew was that there was something creeping up behind Matt. It had the form of a woman, but was it a woman? At this moment, she wasn't at all sure she would stake her life on that. It was wearing a robe that hung from a frame so skeletal that it seemed to carry no flesh on it at all. Its head was wrapped in a cloth so red that it glowed in the moonlight. It walked barefoot. And it was carrying a knife.

Step by step, it stalked them. Dauphine and Joe never once looked in its direction, which told her that they both saw it, too.

Dauphine's portrait of the Lady Dantò showed her in a red head cloth. Dauphine had said that the Lady carried a knife that wrought vengeance against men who preyed on women. If ever there was a time for the Lady to show her face, this was it.

Dauphine continued with her hand gestures that were constrained and slow and gentle, but if they'd been done with the power of a fully extended arm moving at top speed, everyone involved would have seen them for what they were—the jabbing and recoiling motion of one person stabbing another, again and again.

Joe and Dauphine were still singing. Matt was still contemplating mass murder, when the Lady reached him. Her face still in shadow, she grabbed his head and yanked it to her left, clearing the path so that she could jab the knife in her right hand deep into Matt's right hand...his trigger hand.

The blow robbed Matt of complete control of his weapon, but it didn't render him defenseless. The gun was still clutched in his left hand. He jumped up, trying to twist around and blow his assailant's head off, but Dauphine threw herself into his legs, trying—and failing—to knock him off his feet. Joe stepped in to help, leaving Faye to do the one necessary thing that required cunning but not brawn. She went for the gun.

The Lady's knife rose again and dropped like a sledgehammer. Matt screamed and reached for his wounded hand—the left one, this time. Faye saw her chance and launched herself at the gun, grabbing it with both hands and twisting its muzzle toward the sky as hard as she could. She felt Matt's grip give way and let herself drop to the ground with the handgun aimed, at point-blank range, directly at his heart. Sprawled there, Faye finally got a good look at the Lady as she threw a skeletal arm around Matt's neck, using her free hand to lift his jaw.

The Lady's prey was immobilized and waiting for her killing strike, but Faye barked out, "Stop! Don't hurt him. I have the gun! *I have the gun.*"

Tortured eyes met Faye's. The knife hand was still upraised, ready to strike.

"He's no threat to us now. He can't hurt you any more, sweetheart. He can't hurt anybody."

This lady had every reason in the world to drive the knife home, but Faye couldn't let her.

"Don't do it, Nina."

Sirens sounded in the distance, and Faye said, "Jodi's coming and she'll take care of this. You're no killer, Nina. Don't let him make you into something you're not. Don't become the monster that he is."

Nina was still deprived of useful speech—robbed of her very voice—but her comprehension was unquestioned. The knife trembled in her hand, but she lowered it slowly, slowly, until that arm hung loose at her side.

"That's a good child. I told you I'd keep you safe, if God willed it."

Nina turned a wordless stare on Dauphine. The knife fell from her hand and stuck, blade-first, into the soil at her feet. She shrank back from Matt, as if he were toxic or contagious or radioactive. Nina couldn't physically say what she was feeling, but her body language spoke for her. She couldn't believe she had actually touched someone capable of doing the things that Matt had done.

Nina's gaunt form was swallowed by Dauphine's voluminous, colorful hand-me-down clothes, and the bandages on her injured head were covered by a bright cloth, tied under her right ear. But what else would she be wearing? Dauphine would hardly have let an honored guest stay in a threadbare, dingy hospital gown. She certainly would have wrapped Nina's battered head in something pretty, knowing that covering her wound would give a woman a sense of dignity and healing.

"*You* took Nina."

Faye gave Dauphine an appraising glance. She could see that the mambo was feeling a little proud of herself.

Dauphine brushed a wayward curl from her eyes, and said, "I did not 'take' her. She went with me of her own free will... though who knows what the child thought when I said we must crawl out of the window?"

Faye got the definite impression that Dauphine thought Faye and Jodi and maybe Joe, too, were certifiably insane.

Dauphine waved a dismissive hand. "Please. Someone had to do it. What were any of you thinking? To leave her in the care of *that* one...impossible. And after she had suffered so much." Her forbidding tone said exactly what she thought of Charles' worth as a human being. "I would not trust him with a cat I liked."

Faye could see her point.

"There was a spell I suggested to you, but you didn't like it."
Dauphine eyed Joe meaningfully.

Faye remembered Dauphine's spell to hold a lover. It had
involved a jarful of urine underneath her bed. No, she hadn't
liked it, and she certainly hadn't given it a try.

Dauphine inched a little closer to Faye, who couldn't move
away from a conversation turned suddenly uncomfortable,
because she needed to keep holding a gun on a killer.

"Perhaps this will suit you better," Dauphine purred. "Take
a half-spoon of sugar, a spoon of peppermint, and a teaspoon-
ful of candied orange peel; stir this mixture into a glass of red
wine and…"

At least this spell sounded tasty. But Dauphine was still being
coy about its purpose.

Faye knew the promise that Dauphine didn't want to say out
loud in front of Joe.

Do these things and he will love you forever.

Joe, unaware that Dauphine was promising to ensnare his
heart, reached out and took the gun from Faye's hand, and she
let him. She looked at him standing in the candlelight, as silent
and powerful and mysterious in his way as Dauphine or even
Ezili Dantò. She could barely make out the outline of his face,
but she didn't need to see him. She knew that his green eyes
were gentle and steady, and she knew that his lips would always
smile when she entered the room.

Why was she dragging her feet on getting married? Now, as
she finally understood her fears, they already seemed silly and
toothless.

Faye had been raised by a grandmother whose husband
abandoned her and a mother whose soldier husband didn't come
home alive. Just a year ago, Joe had been shot, and she'd nearly
lost him, too. Her fear of marriage had felt complicated and
deep, but the reason for that fear was simple, really. Dauphine
had understood it all along, and she was offering to fix it, but
this was a fear Faye had to face and conquer for herself.

She was afraid that, someday, Joe would leave her.

But Joe wasn't going anywhere. She didn't need to cast a spell, whether it contained candied orange peel or urine.

Joe would never, ever leave her, not if he had breath in his body, and she'd never leave him, either. Yes, one of them might die—they both would die someday—but she'd just have to be willing to take that risk.

Excerpt from *The Floodgates of Hell*
by Louie Godtschalk

If Colonel McGonohan could have lived forever, what a book I would have written! Wouldn't you love to see what he would have made of the twentieth century?

Of course, the resulting book would have been his, and not mine, but I cannot bother my head with worries that can never come to pass. Colonel McGonohan *was* mortal. Thus, when we look at the years after the publication of his memoirs, we must rely on witnesses who had neither his keen powers of observation nor, in some cases, his absolute honesty.

The colonel just missed seeing his dreams for New Orleans come true. In the closing years of the nineteenth century, the city at last embarked on a monumental effort to drain the damnable swamps where it was born. Stormwater and sewage systems were built, making New Orleans one of our first cities to separate those two functions and, in the process, making her engineers into heroes.

The success of these heroes can be told in human terms: America's last epidemic of yellow fever happened here in 1905, having taken more than 41,000 lives in this city alone since Colonel McGonohan served Andrew Jackson so ably in 1815.

Yellow fever cannot kill without mosquitoes to carry it, and mosquitoes cannot plague us without stagnant water to live in. The victory went to the engineers who dug endless miles of canals and built the best pumps the world had ever seen. They sent those pestilence-carriers packing. (Most of them. The survivors, as I can personally attest, are fearsome beasts.) Colonel McGonohan would have been proud.

To close my book, I decided to speak with one of the heirs to these accomplishments. And to acknowledge that the world has changed, I chose an engineer Colonel McGonohan could not have imagined...a woman.

Personal interview with Chloe Scott, 2008

I didn't decide to be a civil engineer because I was fascinated with sewage and flood control and bridges. I just fell into the field, I guess, because I was good at math and I liked physics and it seemed like there would always be jobs. I mean, we're never going to stop needing roads and water treatment plants, are we?

Hmmm. I guess we could, but it'd mean that the world had changed so much that none of us would recognize it, and probably not for the better. Let's hope that doesn't happen in our lifetimes. You can't have civilization unless you have things like clean water, and I don't think water's going to start purifying itself any time soon. So I think I have job security.

And I'm glad I've got civilization. Because I got a good long glimpse of what life would be without it. I'd hardly been in New Orleans a year when we lost it all...clean water, electricity, telephones. Everything.

There was chaos in the streets—the ones that weren't flooded. I learned something in the days after Katrina—if our civilization ever goes under, I don't want to be around.

When the water receded and the lights came back on, I found myself at my desk, just sitting. I couldn't think of any reason to do my work. Why did I feel that way? Well, I'm on the team that's responsible for the levees that failed.

Did I prepare faulty designs? Did I screw up the geotechnical work? Did I let a contractor get away with shoddy work?

Of course not. I'd just moved to town. Nobody in the world was going to say that any part of the disaster was my fault. My problem was that I could see no way to ensure that it wouldn't happen again. Even if we rebuilt the levees exactly to specs, a Category 5 storm in the right place could open the floodgates again.

I asked myself if New Orleans even had to be here. Maybe there's no reason for all these people to be in harm's way. Then I drove across the Mississippi River and saw the boats and barges hauling petroleum and grain and...everything. Yes, I do think we have to be here, and we always have. The dollars-and-cents need for this city has been as constant as the river. And the emotional need for it...

Throwing away New Orleans would be like throwing away a family album full of three centuries of pictures. The French, the Spanish, the English, the Indians, the Africans, they're all still here—we're all here—and so is everyone else who ever stayed here long enough to fall in love. Andrew Jackson. Jean Lafitte. Millions of Mardi Gras revelers and jazz lovers. Throwing that away would...well, we have to keep it.

Still, I wasn't sure I could come to work every day and throw my heart into a design that had a decent chance of failing in my lifetime, all the time knowing that I'd have to watch it happen.

But what if I left? What if I went into...I don't know... real estate? Would that help? Would it lessen the chance that I would one day be staring at The Weather Channel again, watching the water roll into town? My town? No.

If I stayed, though...could I do anything to make a difference?

Yes.

I could do my job well. A computer model is only as good as the person running it. I could be that person.

I could be an extra pair of eyes, ready to squawk if some poor soul reporting a sand boil was being brushed off.

I could vote for candidates willing to fight for the money we need to protect ourselves.

I could campaign for candidates honest enough to use it well.

I could speak up.

And if that free speech costs me my job, well…wait until you see what I'll have to say to the blogosphere.

If I were a scientist, I'd have to pack it in, because there's no way our messy political system will ever produce a fail-safe system based on pure, unassailable theory. But I'm an engineer. We take that pure, unassailable theory and turn it into the most practical design possible. We make the best of the tools at hand. We work within the constraints of the money available.

We get things done.

Chapter Thirty-two

Sunday

Faye's cell phone rang and she answered it. This meant that her eggs were going to get cold, but the phone had rung repeatedly all morning, signaling each time that yet another friend had heard that she and Joe had captured a murderer. And nearly died in the process.

This time, it was Bobby Longchamp. "Can I come see you?"

Jodi, Dauphine, Louie, and Joe were already crowded with her around the breakfast table. The tiny apartment couldn't take another body, but Faye wanted to see Bobby. He made her smile.

So she said, "Absolutely."

Then she turned off the phone and said, "Pick up your plates and mugs. We're going to have to move this party outside."

Bobby arrived carrying a big jar of his mother's fig preserves. He set it beside Jodi's offering, a plate of biscuits that was still warm.

His smile had the charm of a man whose manners were taught to him by people whose primary accomplishment, these past three hundred years, had been a scintillating social life. Faye thought it was a waste to lock up that smile in a library, where nobody much ever saw it.

"Hello, Cousin," Bobby said. "I'm glad to hear that you and Joe are alive."

Faye was touched that someone with Bobby's reverence for family would acknowledge that they might be kin, just because they had the same last name.

"Yeah, why don't we consider ourselves cousins until somebody proves us wrong? Thanks, Bobby. I'm glad we're alive, too."

"Ain't nobody going to prove that we aren't cousins. We might never prove that we are, either, but I've got some pretty solid evidence that says it's true. As solid as we're likely to get, anyway."

"Already? How'd you pull that off?"

While Joe got Bobby some breakfast, Faye opened the jar of figs and spread a thick layer of chunky, brown goo on her biscuit. It was the tastiest goo she'd eaten in a long time. The recipe was probably…yeah, three hundred years old. No doubt about it. She hoped the figs themselves weren't that old.

"How'd I find our family connection? Libraries are my life—" Bobby began, then he shifted gears. "Oh, I'm not going to take credit for this research triumph. My cousin Tish—I told you about Tish—well, she's just nuts for genealogy. She started from your father, Earle Longchamp, and worked backward until your family tree ran into ours. A hundred and eighty years, it took. The man's name was Lamarr Longchamp."

"My father's middle name was Lamar."

"I know. Tish told me."

Of course, she did. Tish seemed to know everything there was to know, genealogically speaking. Louie was laughing, which showed that he had cousins just like Tish.

"But you say there's no proof?"

"Well—" Bobby's voice took on the conspiratorial tone of a historian about to spin a good story. Or maybe an incorrigible gossip about to pass on a choice piece of dirt. "Lamarr Longchamp was my great-great-great-great-grandfather. Tish's, too. And we have a document that says he owned your great-great-great-grandfather, Henri."

Joe put a hand on Faye's arm. She patted it, so he'd know that it didn't upset her to talk about her enslaved ancestors.

"Um, Bobby. Slaves aren't blood-kin."

"Not usually, no. But Henri was freed as a young teenager. Tish found the papers. Afterward, he took the Longchamp name. He was educated at an academy for wealthy boys located somewhere near Natchez. There are documents that say he was a landholder as an adult. And he owned land that had once belonged to Lamarr Longchamp. Then, when Lamarr died, Henri Longchamp was included in his will."

Faye wasn't sure how she felt about this information, but she just said, "That's not proof."

"Oh, come on, Faye, don't be that way," Jodi said, waving the butter knife at her. "Sounds pretty close to proof to me. Close enough, anyway. Let the man talk."

Bobby paused to glance at this woman who'd barged into his side of the argument, uninvited. She flashed him a folksy grin that was just as high-wattage as his old-money smile. For a long second, Faye could see that Bobby had completely lost his train of thought, which might have been a first for him. She could also see that Jodi had noticed that Faye's putative cousin was indeed a pretty man.

Bobby dragged himself back to the task at hand, which was arguing with Faye. "Oh, we *are* kin. You have all my family's finest qualities. Stubbornness, a fine intellect, bull-headedness, an appreciation for facts…and did I mention bull-headedness?"

Faye proved his point by saying, "Well it's *not* proof."

"No. It's not. But short of a birth certificate, which we're never going to get, or a letter from Lamarr Longchamp that says, 'I've fathered a bastard child with my wife's chambermaid,' then we'll have to make do with this. All the evidence says that Lamarr freed his out-of-wedlock son, educated him, gave him land, and left him a generous inheritance. Welcome to the family, Cousin."

He raised his coffee mug, and everybody followed suit, though Dauphine was a little slow, because she'd been fumbling in her apron pocket. Faye sure hoped the mambo wasn't planning to throw coffin nails at the brand-new kinfolk.

"So what's going to happen to Matt and Charles and Leila?"

Bobby said it as if he wanted to know, but also as if he were thrashing around for a topic that would spark a conversation with the pretty detective beside him.

Jodi came through for him. "Matt's case is straightforward. He confessed to murder last night in front of Faye and Joe and Dauphine. He came pretty damn close to confessing to Nina's attack. He also confessed to giving Charles money so that his parents would be rescued quickly. I'll have to say that I don't know how the law will deal with him there. Or Charles and Leila."

Louie had brought *beignets* again, so there was powdered sugar everywhere. Jodi licked some off her fingers and kept talking.

"Those two scumbuckets abused their responsibility and profited from it, but you can't necessarily call it theft when somebody hands you a barrel of money because they want you to do something for them. It's corruption, from an ethical standpoint, just as surely as it is when a government purchasing agent takes a bribe. But they weren't working for the government. They weren't working for anyone at all. They were volunteers. We've got people looking at the legal niceties, but there's one thing that's unquestionable."

"What?" Bobby asked.

Louie and Dauphine asked it, too, but Jodi was looking at Bobby when she answered the question.

"Charles and Leila committed a completely heinous crime. I don't care what the law says, when we finally figure out what that is. The details of what they did *will* get out to the media, starting with that ambitious little TV reporter that Nina startled so badly. Know why?"

"Why?" Faye said, already knowing the answer.

"Because I'll make sure she finds out. I'll make sure she reports every last creepy, slimy, icky detail. I'll make sure Charles and

Leila never look at a face in this town without being aware that the person behind that face knows what they did. Maybe they'll go to jail, or maybe they'll just have to leave town, but they'll pay. Trust me. They'll pay."

The glance that passed between Jodi and Bobby said that they both found jail and exile from New Orleans to be roughly equivalent. Faye felt the same way about Joyeuse. No other place would ever be home.

She hoped Charles' and Leila's punishment began with exile and mounted steadily higher. It couldn't be a fun thing to live in a Louisiana prison with people who knew that you sold life and death to Katrina victims. Faye hoped they both got prison terms, and that they both enjoyed them as much as they deserved.

Chapter Thirty-three

Faye scraped the leftover scrambled eggs off her plate and into the kitchen trash. They had been light and fluffy, and the bacon going into the trashcan with them was just crisp enough. Or it would have been if she'd ever gotten around to eating it. The quality of the food was evidence that Joe, not Faye, had been the one who cooked breakfast.

"Joe?"

"What, Faye?"

His voice was as strong as the Mississippi River and as steadfast. Like the river, he changed direction at times, but there was never any doubt that he would keep going.

Faye focused her fearsome powers of concentration on washing the bacon grease off her plate, so that she didn't have to look directly at him. Looking straight at Joe always scrambled her thoughts.

"I want to go home to Joyeuse. Today."

Joe took the wet plate from her hand and started wiping it hard enough to dull the glazed finish. He, too, seemed to find that the task at hand required his complete attention.

"That's a powerful long drive for somebody who needs to be at work bright and early tomorrow morning."

"Within the past week, somebody's tried to murder my entire team—Nina, Dauphine, and me. As it is, Nina's doctors think she's going to be as good as new. Unfortunately, I'm going to be short an assistant until then, though it'll certainly help if you agree to take the job temporarily. Considering all that, I think my employer will understand if the report is a few days late."

Joe knew Faye. Faye knew he did. She could see him reading her like a book—an infuriating and inexplicably illogical book with a serpentine plot that took too long to get where it was going. But she was a book that he just couldn't put down. He kept rubbing the glaze off the plate in his hand, because he knew she wasn't finished with whatever it was that she was trying to say. So she kept talking, swishing a dishrag around inside a coffee cup with unnecessary vigor.

"Besides—" The cup in her hand trembled, but just a bit. "My boss should be extra understanding in this case. I've never heard yet of an employer that didn't cut a girl some slack when she got married."

The cup trembled a little harder in her hand, but she plunged ahead. "New Orleans would make the most romantic honeymoon spot I can imagine. I have some consulting money burning a hole in my pocket. We could get married at Joyeuse, then come back here and stay in a hotel where they'll treat us like royalty. We can eat in restaurants so old they're haunted by dead chefs. And we can drink lots of champagne that has spent lots of time in a cave in France. What do you say?"

Now it was Joe whose dishcloth had suddenly become fascinating. He finally looked her in the eyes and asked, "You're not gonna make me wait till Christmas? Or Halloween? Or for some stupid holiday like Columbus Day?"

Faye seemed to have forgotten how to talk, so she just shook her head.

"When, Faye?"

Faye finally found her voice.

"Tomorrow. At home. At Joyeuse."

Author's Note: All of the characters and situations in *Floodgates* are fictional. Any resemblance to real people is completely unintentional. In particular, the motive for Shelly's murder and the despicable things done by Charles, Leila, and Matt are totally imaginary crimes dreamed up by a mystery writer.

Guide for the Incurably Curious: Teachers, Students, and People Who Just Plain Like to Read

I've always included Authors' Notes in my books, to answer questions like, "Where, exactly, is Joyeuse?" and "Are the Sujosa real?" The answer to both those questions is that they only exist in my imagination. Still, a lot of what I write is based on fact. I think that's an important way to approach stories about an archaeologist. I believe it's perfectly valid for me to make up stories about Faye, because she's quite real to me but, in the end, she's a fictional character. Still, when she delves into the past, I feel a responsibility to make that past real, or at least plausible. I enjoy taking the opportunity at the end of my books to talk to you about where some of those lines between fact and fancy lie.

Since my books are being read in classrooms and in book groups, I think of my "Guides for the Incurably Curious" as opportunities for me to participate in those discussions. I visit many classrooms and book groups over the course of a year, and these are the kinds of questions people like to ask. If you or your class or your book group would like to chat further, contact me at maryannaevans@yahoo.com. I answer all my e-mail, when humanly possible, and I'd love to hear your responses to some of these questions.

1. What did you think of the New Orleans setting for this book? Do you think Faye's response to this unique and historic city was right for her character?

I grew up a hundred miles from New Orleans and, as a child, I visited relatives in the city occasionally. While in college, I spent a summer working offshore. This meant that I drove to New Orleans once a week, on my way out to the natural gas platform where I worked. Since then, I've visited for reasons as varied as business trips, a child's college visit to Tulane, and plain old tourism. Simply put, I love the place. I love the food. I love the ancient look of the *Vieux Carré*. I love the food. I love the locals with their infectious zest for life and their improbable accents. I love the music. Did I mention that I love the food?

When I proposed this book, my editor was skeptical, saying that New Orleans had already "been done." I made my plea, pointing out that I have a personal history in the area. I told her that the destruction left by Katrina would make New Orleans a unique place to do archaeology because Faye would be digging through a physical layer of history left behind by the floods. This layer was history, just as surely as the layer left behind by Andrew Jackson's Battle of New Orleans was history, but the Katrina debris is only a few years old. I think that's interesting. And then I told her that I knew New Orleans had "been done," but that I didn't think it had been done by a novelist who was also an engineer and who might just have something to say about the levee failures. She saw my point, and you hold the resulting book in your hands.

And then there's the question of Faye. I might love New Orleans, but how would *she* feel about it? Well, Faye's not me, but she shares my passion for American history. New Orleans is American history all rolled up in a single package. I knew she'd be fascinated with the place, and I did my best to communicate that. You'll have to be the judge of how well I did.

I enjoyed a memorable trip to New Orleans while preparing for this book. I was saddened to see that the cleanup there was still not complete, but I found that the city's beauty and convivial spirit were undimmed. If you have travel dollars in your family budget, I urge you to spend them there. It would be a very pleasant way to help rebuild a city that is truly an American original.

2. Did you enjoy reading the thoughts of Colonel James McGonahan and Chloe Scott, as presented by Louie Godtschalk?

I love writing the parts of my books that give a sense of history as seen through the eyes of characters from the past. I get to speak in the voices of people who couldn't possibly be part of Faye's stories any other way, and this keeps the work fresh for me.

Colonel James McGonahan is one of my favorite historical characters. When I conceived of this book, I knew that I wanted to highlight engineers in some way. I'm an engineer by training, with a bachelor's in engineering physics, a master's in chemical engineering, a license as a Professional Engineer, and a number of years of experience as an environmental engineer. When people ask me why I write about an archaeologist, I give them an answer that is only half-joking: "Who wants to read about an engineer?" My profession has a stodgy, geeky reputation that's not entirely undeserved. But popular opinion forgets one thing about engineers: we have an insatiable need to know how things work. My own philosophy has always been that interested people are interesting people. Thus, engineers tend to be especially interesting people. Writing Colonel McGonahan's memoirs gave me a chance to show you how fascinating we can be.

Chloe Scott gave me a chance to "be" a modern working engineer, something I actually know a bit about. I wanted very much to deal with the levee failures in this book, and I also wanted very much to avoid blaming any one person or agency for the catastrophe. The flood protection system for New Orleans began when the city was first designed, and it has been evolving for nearly 300 years now. Human error, institutional problems, political maneuvering—there are any number of possible contributing factors for the disaster after Katrina. Some of those possible reasons have been mentioned by characters in this book. I read extensively on the subject but personally do not feel at all able to pinpoint blame, nor do I want to. Chloe's resolve to do the best she could with the resources at hand presents an engineer's approach to life, so I have let her tell us what that approach means to her.

3. How did you respond to the feelings of those characters who survived Hurricane Katrina? Did they ring true?

I wrote the scenes depicting the feelings of Katrina survivors by trying to imagine myself in their shoes. That's how I write all my characters, actually. I could easily imagine myself feeling Nina's outrage and Matt's shocked withdrawal and Bobby's horror. Most of all, I tried to communicate a feeling that I think is common to survivors of a traumatic event: the feeling that it's never over. People do move on, some more successfully than others. But the mental image of disaster lurks in their brains, ready to be triggered by the sound of a high wind or by news of a tropical depression forming off the coast of Africa. You can learn to live with those fears, but I don't think they ever really go away. I kept that image of permanent disruption in mind when I crafted my characters.

4. How did you respond to the news that Bobby Longchamp was a distant relative of Faye's?

I explored Faye's mother's family fairly thoroughly in the earlier books, but have never done anything with her father's people. People often ask me how to pronounce her name, and I always say that Faye's family has been in the Americas for centuries and she's got a southern accent as thick as mine. She pronounces it like an American: LAWNG-champ.

When I wrote the scene introducing Bobby, I hadn't yet given him a last name. I knew he came from New Orleans aristocracy. When it came time to name him, it struck me that *this* was a man who would pronounce Longchamp like a Frenchman: LAWN-shaw. (Or something like that.) I decided that Faye didn't need to be alone in the world with no kin, so I gave her Cousin Bobby.

Coincidentally, I also just met a very distant cousin—fifth cousin, once removed—through the wonders of the internet. It has been fun getting to know each other and discovering family traits that seem unexpectedly strong after an interval of six generations. I enjoyed giving Faye that same experience.

5. **Did you think Faye's pre-wedding jitters felt true to her character? How did you feel about Joe's response to her behavior?**

Faye's relationships with men have always been colored by the absence of men in her home while she was a child and the abandonment many women in her family suffered. Her love interest in *Artifacts* was years older than she was, a literal father figure. Two possible relationships in *Relics* failed over issues of trust. She perceived that the man she was dating was living a lie, and a man she might have dated rejected her because he disagreed with her on an important ethical issue. Beginning in *Effigies* and ending in *Findings*, she is involved with a man who is her age and thus not a father figure but who is powerful and possibly controlling. She has had important platonic friendships—Sheriff Mike, Douglass, and possibly Wally—with much older men who may also have filled the hole in her life left by her father. And her world was rocked in *Findings* when two of these men were murdered.

Given this history, is it any surprise that she is terrified to think Joe might leave her?

Joe understands Faye, and he loves her. He is the least confrontational person imaginable, but he is not a doormat. This is not a situation he could let continue forever. I'm very glad that Faye figured out her feelings before Joe had to sit her down and explain things to her. ☺

To receive a free catalog of Poisoned Pen Press titles, please contact us in one of the following ways:

Phone: 1-800-421-3976
Facsimile: 1-480-949-1707
Email: info@poisonedpenpress.com
Website: www.poisonedpenpress.com

Poisoned Pen Press
6962 E. First Ave. Ste. 103
Scottsdale, AZ 85251

9 781590 587805